Mother's Day, Muffins, and Murder

THE ELLIE AVERY MYSTERIES*
by Sara Rosett

MOVING IS MURDER

STAYING HOME IS A KILLER

GETTING AWAY IS DEADLY

MAGNOLIAS, MOONLIGHT, AND MURDER

MINT JULEPS, MAYHEM, AND MURDER

MIMOSAS, MISCHIEF, AND MURDER

MISTLETOE, MERRIMENT, AND MURDER

MILKSHAKES, MERMAIDS, AND MURDER

MARRIAGE, MONSTERS-IN-LAW, AND MURDER

*Available from Kensington Publishing Corp.

Mother's Day, Muffins, and Murder

Sara Rosett

KENSINGTON BOOKS
http://www.kensingtonbooks.com

KENSINGTON BOOKS are published by

Kensington Publishing Corp.
119 West 40th Street
New York, NY 10018

All Kensington titles, imprints, and distributed lines are available at special quantity discounts for bulk purchases for sales promotion, premiums, fund-raising, educational, or institutional use. Special book excerpts or customized printings can also be created to fit specific needs. For details, write or phone the office of the Kensington Special Sales Manager: Attn. Special Sales Department. Kensington Publishing Corp., 119 West 40th Street, New York, NY 10018. Phone: 1-800-221-2647.

Library of Congress Card Catalogue Number: 2016955143

Kensington and the K logo Reg. U.S. Pat. & TM Off.

ISBN-13: 978-1-61773-150-1
ISBN-10: 1-61773-150-1
First Kensington Hardcover Edition: April 2017

eISBN-13: 978-1-61773-152-5
eISBN-10: 1-61773-152-8
First Kensington Electronic Edition: April 2017

10 9 8 7 6 5 4 3 2 1

Printed in the United States of America

To
Mom

Chapter One

"How many more days of school are left?" Livvy asked.

"I'm not sure." I waited until Nathan climbed out of the minivan after Livvy, then picked up the plastic container of blueberry muffins, as well as paper plates and napkins, and clicked the button on the key fob to lock the minivan. "Let's see—it's the second week of May, so you probably have around fifteen days or so left."

We turned toward the low, flat-roofed brick elementary school building. Despite it being thirty minutes before the first bell of the day, the school parking lot was packed, and I'd had to park at the farthest point away from the school, on the grass near the fence that enclosed the school grounds. The sun was barely over the tops of the tall pines that ringed the outer edge of the back of the school's property, but the air was already dense and muggy. Spring was a fleeting season in middle Georgia. Ninety-degree days had been our norm for several weeks, and today would be just the same, sunny and humid.

I'd parked beside an old Subaru. The hatchback was

open and a small, gray-headed woman was pulling something out of the back of the car. "Twelve," she said as we came even with her. "Twelve days left in the school year, not counting today—for students, that is. Teachers have seventeen."

"Mrs. Harris," Livvy said with delight as she moved to give the woman a hug. I smiled, glad to see that despite the grown-up veneer Livvy had acquired over the last year or so—she was a big fifth-grader now—she was still happy to see her former first-grade teaching assistant.

Mrs. Harris pulled Livvy in for a tight hug against her flat chest. I wasn't sure how old Mrs. Harris was. Wrinkles scored her face, and she'd tamed her iron-colored hair, which was wiry with white strands, into a flat bowl cut that just brushed her eyebrows, earlobes, and the back of her neck, a few inches above her collar. With her inquisitive dark eyes and delicate frame, she reminded me of a sparrow. She had a way of nudging the students toward the right answer with her encouraging smile and expressive face, something I'd seen firsthand when I'd volunteered in the classroom, first with Livvy and then with Nathan.

The first-grade teachers might rotate in and out, but Mrs. Harris was a steady, unchanging presence in the first-grade hallway. She worked with Mrs. Dunst, who had been Nathan's first-grade teacher last year.

Nathan played it a bit cooler, but he gave her his full attention when Mrs. Harris looked toward him and asked, "So how is your year going, Nathan? Isn't that nice Mr. Spagnatilli your teacher this year for second grade?"

Nathan nodded. "Yes, Mr. S. That's what we call him. He's great."

I exchanged a glance with Mrs. Harris. "High praise, indeed," she said, and I agreed.

"He likes science, and he has a snake," Nathan said. "In the classroom."

Livvy rolled her eyes. "It's in a tank."

"So I've heard," Mrs. Harris said. "And fish, too."

Nathan's head bobbed again. "Yep. And a full-size skeleton, so we can learn about bones and everything. He's cool. He let us decorate Mr. Metacarpal—that's the skeleton—for Halloween."

"Excellent," Mrs. Harris said. "Now, I wonder if you could help me?" she asked, and I recognized the inquisitive tone she used in the classroom. She managed to convey that Livvy and Nathan helping her would be both a privilege and an honor. I'd seen her in action when the kids had been in first grade, and she always had kids straining, their arms raised high in the air, in hopes that they would be the lucky one she singled out to help her.

Both kids instantly said yes, and she turned to the open hatchback. "I have quite a load of muffins in here, and I have to get them to the first-grade classrooms."

Livvy had already shifted a plastic tub into her arms. Nathan said, "I can take two. No, three."

Mrs. Harris removed the top tub, which was teetering dangerously, from Nathan's arms. "Two is more than enough, Nathan. Thank you. Just drop them in the classroom, and go to the cafeteria."

The classrooms didn't open until eight o'clock, and students who arrived between seven-fifty and eight o'clock went directly to the cafeteria to wait for the bell that signaled they could go to their classrooms. The kids hurried away at their quick pace, while I waited for Mrs. Harris. She picked up the last tub of muffins, closed the hatchback, then fell into step with me.

"So you're the designated muffin person today?" I asked.

"Oh, yes. I always think it's a bit sad to ask the mothers to bake and bring muffins for their own celebration," she said with a birdlike tilt of her head toward the plastic container I carried. Today, as the sign in front of the school proclaimed, was WEDNESDAY—5/10—MUFFINS WITH MOM DAY, the school's nod to Mother's Day. The sign also listed the next end-of-year activity, Field Day, which was scheduled for Thursday and Friday. I had pretty much cleared my calendar for the rest of this week because I knew I would be at the school for Field Day, and next week was Teacher Appreciation Week, which I had agreed to coordinate.

"After all," Mrs. Harris continued, "we don't ask the fathers to bring donuts for Donuts with Dad Day."

"Funny how it always works out that way, isn't it?" I missed the days of having my kids in Mrs. Harris's classroom. She was as much about looking after the parents as she was about caring for the kids. I was now a seasoned "room mom," and looking back, I could see that Mrs. Harris had done a lot, and she didn't focus only on the kids. She'd also helped ease the parents through the transition to sending their kids to class each day.

A car pulled into the lot, and we both shifted to the left, as far as we could get from the blue Ford Fiesta. It whipped through the parking lot, bumped off the edge of the asphalt, and surged onto the grass between the two wavy rows of cars that had parked rather haphazardly in an open area, the elementary school's makeshift overflow lot. A tight turn slewed the car into a slot barely wide enough for it, between two hulking SUVs. The door opened a crack, and a blond head popped out. The woman worked her way out of the car, contorting herself in the narrow space, reminding me of those nature shows where you see a butterfly fighting its way out of a chrysalis.

She wrestled a huge tote bag out of the car behind her, then emerged from between the two cars and smoothed her Peter Pan shirt collar. "Hello, Mrs. Harris," she said as she caught sight of us.

"Ms. McCormick," Mrs. Harris said with a nod. I slid my gaze toward Mrs. Harris. There was something in her tone, a reservation, that hadn't been there moments before.

Ms. McCormick was all breathless smiles. "Gorgeous day, isn't it?" Her eyes were startling blue, so much so that I wondered if they were those fake contact lenses that you can get to change your eye color. Dark lashes fringed her vibrant eyes, and a bright shade of red lipstick highlighted her full lips. "Hectic morning. I'm running late." She slung a tote bag over her shoulder. "Have to dash." She motored away, her heels sinking into the grass, making her work even harder to cover the ground to the parking lot.

"She's the new teacher?" I asked. I knew one of the fifth-grade math teachers had moved in January, and Ms. McCormick was the new math teacher. Mid-year moves weren't that unusual in North Dawkins since it was a community that surrounded an Air Force base, which was where my husband, Mitch, worked.

Livvy had Ms. McCormick for one class period each day and had mentioned her. I now understood why she said Ms. McCormick was like a Disney princess. My part-time organizing business had taken up a lot of my time lately, and I hadn't been at the school volunteering as much during the last few months, so I hadn't met Ms. McCormick yet. I had asked my friend Abby, who was a teacher at the school and a fellow military spouse, if she'd met Ms. McCormick, and Abby had described her as a big-eyed beauty with a perky disposition. The profusion of happy faces and exclamation notes on homework pages suddenly made more sense, as did all the smiley-face emoticons in my email updates from Livvy's math teacher.

"Yes. She's been with us since Christmas break." Mrs. Harris's head was tilted back, her eyes narrowed thoughtfully as she watched the progress of Ms. McCormick across the asphalt to the school. "It's just not natural, you know," she muttered under her breath.

"What?" I asked.

"That buoyant disposition, not when you're in the public education system, anyway. I'm waiting for her to crack. It worries me." She raised her eyebrows and glanced over at me, seeming to realize that she'd spoken her thoughts aloud. "Of course, she seems to be an excellent teacher, and I shouldn't have—"

"Don't worry, Mrs. Harris," I said. "I won't say anything. But I know what you mean." I realized that Mrs. Harris had touched on the exact thing that had struck me. "I get her biweekly class update emails." The frequency of the emails surprised me. Most teachers only sent out the required quarterly grade report. "Her emails are very upbeat, rah-rah-type updates." I'd assumed that she was layering on the encouragement to motivate her students, but it did seem a little over the top.

"Yes," Mrs. Harris said. "Well, she is young. First teaching assignment, I believe."

We walked by the bus circle, then followed the sidewalk around the main parking area until we came to the school's wide, covered porch-like entry. I tugged open the heavy door for Mrs. Harris, then stepped inside behind her.

"Ellie," a voice thick with a Southern accent called, and I turned to see the woman who had been my arch-nemesis in the organizing world, Gabrielle Matheson, emerging from the school office into the lobby. I'd been the sole professional organizer in the small town of North Dawkins, Georgia, until newly divorced Gabrielle moved here and set up shop. After a rather rocky start, we'd become . . . well, not exactly friends. More like business associates with very different temperaments who managed to get along . . . most of the time. "I didn't know you'd be here today, honey."

To Gabrielle, everyone was "honey" or "sweetie." The men in her orbit ate it up. The women were less enthusiastic—at least that had been my observation. I would be the first person to admit that statement sounded catty, but it was true. Gabrielle was a gorgeous woman in her early forties—long black hair, beautiful green eyes, and high cheekbones coupled with a figure that curved in all the right places—it was easy to see why she was such a hit with the male portion of the population. She normally wore power suits with nipped-in waists and filmy shells with deep necklines, but today she was dressed down in a sleeveless green cotton tank and black skinny jeans.

I held up the plastic tub. "Muffins with Mom."

She looked toward the painted banner hanging across the wall that welcomed the moms to the school. "Oh, yes. That is so sweet, that you have time to come here and relax with your children."

So it was going to be one of those days. I fixed a smile on my face. "Yes, that is my favorite way to relax, supervising twenty-two eight-year-olds hyped up on sugar at eight in the morning."

She put her hand on my arm. "Oh, Ellie, you are so funny. I'd love to stay and chat, but I have to get these forms copied and distributed. It's the final stage of my decluttering plan for the classrooms. I'm implementing it personally in each school." She shrugged her shoulder slightly. "It's just so exciting and rewarding to see it all come together."

I wrinkled my nose at her. "I bet it is." The fact that Gabrielle had snagged the contract to help the school district reduce their paper consumption and increase efficiency was still a sore spot with me. She'd parlayed the initial job into several additional contracts that kept her very busy. I knew about the new contracts because she was always sure to give me an update whenever our paths crossed.

Take the high road, I mentally recited. It was a mantra that I tended to repeat when I was around Gabrielle. "I'll let you get to it," I said, and moved to the school's office to sign in and get my volunteer sticker. Student safety was always a concern, and anyone entering the school had to check in at the office, no matter how brief the visit.

Several moms were on their way out of the office, rectangular labels with their names and student associations stuck to their shirts. I put the muffins down on the tall counter that ran across the office, dividing it from the desks and the principal's enclosed office area in the back. As I typed my name into the search bar on the computer, I said hello to one of the "office ladies," as the kids called them. In the course of the last few years, I'd volunteered so much that I knew most of the women. "Is Marie out?" I asked, looking toward the first desk on the left, which didn't have Marie's usual pink cardigan draped over the rolling desk chair. There were also no papers or file folders stacked on the desk, only a couple of gnome figurines, a name plate that read MARIE ORMSBY, and one of those calendars made of two block letters that have different digits cut on each side and can be rotated to display the correct date. I'd seen them everywhere around the school. All the teachers and staff had one because Mrs. Kirk had given them out at the beginning of the year at the first staff meeting.

"No." Peg Watson shook her head, but didn't turn from stuffing pale blue envelopes into the wall of cubbyholes, the teachers' mailboxes. "She's on vacation this week. Jekyll Island."

"Oh, we went to one of the barrier islands last year," I said. "For a wedding. It was . . . well, it turned out to be quite an event."

"Hmm . . ." murmured Peg, but she didn't turn or look my way, so I didn't say anything else. I'd never heard Peg say more than five words anytime I'd been in. The most I saw of her was the top of her dark brown hair because she usually had her head bent over some task at her desk and let the other ladies in the office do all the chatting with the moms who came to check in for volunteer work. I thought she was in her thirties, but I wasn't sure because I'd never really gotten a good look at her.

"So Marie was able to work in one last vacation before her retirement? That's nice," I said.

"Yes." Peg picked up a stack of orange interoffice envelopes and moved back to the first cubbyhole.

The computer designated for volunteer check-in was an old model, and I had to wait while it processed my entry. Without Marie there to chat with, the office seemed very quiet except for the snick of paper going into the cubbies and the distant hum of the air conditioner unit outside the window. The small printer beside the computer finally spit out my name tag, sounding extremely loud in the small room. At the back of the room, the office for the principal, Mrs. Kirk, was empty. I knew she was outside, keeping an eye on the arrival of students, as she did every morning.

I'd once asked Marie if I'd done something to offend Peg—you never want to tick off the office ladies—but Marie had waved her hand and said, "Oh, she's just shy. Don't give it a second thought."

Marie was Peg's opposite, a sweet, cheerful, and chatty motherly woman with determinedly blond hair fluffing out around her face. She had been at the school since it opened its doors in 1985, and she was retiring at the end of this school year. I'd gotten to know her quite well this year because I had helped coordinate the gift wrap fundraising sale before Christmas.

A couple of moms on the PTA had argued that we needed to do another fundraiser before the school year ended, but that idea had gone down in flames at the last PTA meeting. Marie had been very interested in whether or not the idea of another fundraiser would go forward. She was the person who handled all the details for the PTA, placing orders, making deposits, following up on deliveries. A second round of fundraising would mean a lot of work for her.

I should let her know she was off the hook. "I need to leave a message for Marie," I said as another mom entered the office and headed for the check-in computer.

Peg tilted her head toward the end of the counter. "There's a sticky note and pen."

I jotted a quick note to Marie with the news that the idea for another fundraiser was a no-go, then pushed through the swinging half door at the end of the counter. "I'll leave it on her desk," I said as I stuck it on the one and zero of her block calendar. She'd be sure to see it there. I wasn't too confident that, if I left it with Peg, it would actually reach Marie.

Kids and moms were flowing into the lobby as I left the office to hurry down the hallway to Nathan's room. His teacher, Mr. Spagnatilli, and I quickly set up the muffins, paper plates, and napkins as well as the cartons of juice that he'd brought before the first bell rang, signaling that kids could go to their classrooms. The Muffins with Mom event took place during the twenty-minute window when the kids could arrive and go directly to their classrooms.

Nathan arrived, and he and I ate muffins, with me squeezed into a little chair beside his desk. "We're making something for our moms this week," Nathan informed me as we munched on our blueberry muffins.

"Interesting. Should I ask what it is?"

"No." He shook his head, his expression somber. "Don't ask, because I can't tell."

"Okay. I won't, but I'm looking forward to seeing it . . . whatever it is." I brushed the crumbs from my lap. "All right, buddy, I have to scoot over to Livvy's room and have a muffin with her before the last bell. I'll see you in the pickup line this afternoon."

The school was set up with several hallways branching off the central area of the school, which contained the school office, cafeteria, library, and nurse's office. As I moved through the central lobby area, I passed several moms who, like me, were packing in multiple stops during the short morning so that they could have muffins with all of their kids. Considering the muffins that the kids and I had eaten at home to "test" the recipe, plus the ones I would have this morning, I was glad they were mini-muffins; otherwise, I would have needed to go to the gym next instead of to the organizing appointment that was on my schedule.

I dropped into Livvy's classroom, which had a completely different atmosphere from Nathan's room. The bulletin boards were still covered with decorations and informative charts about reading tips and common spelling mistakes, and the desks were only slightly bigger, but there was a more grown-up ambiance. There were less crafts and more paperwork in these classrooms. The oh-so-sophisticated fifth-graders changed classes for every subject, so their backpacks hung on the back of their chairs. A few students were trying to send texts discreetly, their phones hidden in their laps under their desks. The cell phone thing was a sore spot with Livvy. She wanted one, and we'd decided that there was no need for her to have one until middle school, which was only next year, a fact that amazed me. Where had the grade-school years gone? I pushed that thought away and focused on chatting with Livvy while eating my cranberry muffin. I asked Livvy what book she'd picked up at the library.

"*The Mysterious Benedict Society.* I've only read the first few pages, and I think it's going to be good."

"Wonderful." Livvy was happiest when she had a good book. The trouble was keeping her in books. I recently introduced her to Nancy Drew and Trixie Belden. She'd run through all those books in a few weeks. "Oh, there's the eight-twenty warning bell," I said. I had five minutes to help clean up in Nathan's classroom and get off campus before the school day officially began with announcements immediately after the eight-twenty-five bell. I gave Livvy a quick one-armed hug. She glanced around, obviously hoping not too many of her friends had seen the display of affection, but I'd been fast.

I hurried back through the hallways, threading through moms and kids doing a good imitation of race-walking as they scurried to their classrooms and tried to beat the last bell. In Nathan's classroom, I brushed the crumbs into the empty plastic tub, swept up the extra plates and cups, and dumped the empty juice boxes in the trash before waving to Nathan and hurrying down the hallway to the lobby. I didn't want to get stuck listening to the morning announcements and the pledge of allegiance. It wasn't that I wasn't patriotic—Mitch was in the military, after all. Couldn't get much more patriotic than that. But the timing to get to my organizing appointment was tight, and the announcements often ran long, especially on a day like today when parents were in the building.

I was scooting along, making great time, when Gabrielle backed out of a doorway and collided with me, sending the plastic container spinning off across the white tile floor.

"Gabrielle, what on earth—" I broke off as I looked up from retrieving the plastic tub. Her face was a washed-out, pale color, the same tone as the shiny industrial tiles that lined the floor. "What's wrong?"

"There's somebody in there. A body." She pointed at the storage closet door.

"What? No, you must be mistaken." It was such a bizarre thing to say that I would have thought she was joking, but her color wasn't good and, except for the quick glance she'd sent me when we banged into each other, her eyes were wide and fixed on the door.

I reached for the handle, thinking that it must be a bundle of clothes leftover from some event, but the door wouldn't budge. The slim bar handle twisted down, but when I pulled, the door didn't open. "It's locked." I looked back at Gabrielle. "Do you have a key?" With all the organizing she'd been doing, it wouldn't be impossible that she'd have a key to one of the storage closets around the school.

"No." She shook her head, her ponytail slapping her shoulders. "It wasn't completely closed before. There was about an inch gap when I went in. The lights were off, and when I flicked them on . . . I saw her."

"Her?" That was pretty specific. "You're sure it was a woman?"

Gabrielle's head bobbed. "Yes. It was a woman." Gabrielle swallowed. "I could tell from the hand—long, narrow fingers and a ring with a big oval stone. It's definitely a woman."

"That's all you saw? A hand?" I asked.

"Yes, sticking up out of a trash can." She shifted her gaze from the door to my face. "I know what I saw."

I looked up and down the hallway, but it was the final moments before the tardy bell, and the hall was deserted.

"Come on, let's go to the office." Gabrielle didn't move. I wrapped an arm around her shoulders and propelled her in the direction of the lobby. "They'll have a key. I bet it was something else. . . ."

She stopped walking. "No. Ellie, it was a body. There is a woman in there, and she's dead; I know it. The skin was so white, it has to be . . ." She shivered and looked like she might be sick.

Before I could say anything, the tardy bell rang, and then the public address system crackled. Gabrielle started as if someone had given her an electric shock. Mrs. Kirk's voice came through the speakers, which were positioned in each of the classrooms as well as the hallways.

"Welcome, mothers, to Muffins with Mom Day. We're so happy you could join us this morning. We know you do so much to help your kids succeed, and we wanted to take a little time today to honor you. Students, let's give a round of applause for your fantastic moms."

Mrs. Kirk paused, and little bursts of clapping sounded from the classrooms on either side of the hallway as Gabrielle and I walked on toward the lobby.

Mrs. Kirk continued, "Moms, thank you for coming today. We're glad you could start your day with us, but after announcements, students must get to work, so all parents must leave campus after announcements. Today's lunch menu is a crispy taco, salad, milk, and a pudding cup. Teachers, don't forget—"

A high-pitched buzzing sound that hurt my ears cut through Mrs. Kirk's words. Gabrielle and I paused and looked at each other.

"That's not the fire alarm, is it?" I asked.

Gabrielle nodded. "No. They had a drill when I was here last week. Surely, they wouldn't have another drill so soon."

"And not in the middle of announcements," I said.

Mrs. Kirk's voice resumed, carrying on through the continued siren-like blasts. "Students, teachers, and parents, please exit the building in an orderly fashion."

Up and down the hall, teachers emerged from their classrooms, the students following in undulating lines as they marched down the hallway. Gabrielle and I started moving again. When we got to the lobby, I glanced in the office, but it was empty. Mrs. Kirk stood at the doors, watching the children file by and shushing any talking students into silence. Peg stood at Mrs. Kirk's side, a clipboard and bullhorn tucked into the crook of her elbow.

I looked toward Gabrielle, but she was still pale and shaken, her gaze darting around the entrance. Where was the take-charge dynamo who was always stampeding forward, snapping up organizing clients and jobs? I steered Gabrielle toward Peg and the principal.

I had expected Gabrielle to tell Mrs. Kirk what she'd seen, but Gabrielle looked at me with her wide eyes, so I said, "Mrs. Kirk, Gabrielle—"

Mrs. Kirk held up a hand, palm out. "Ladies, this is not the time. We must make sure all students and staff are out of the building. Please take your place in line over there." Mrs. Kirk was a sturdy woman in her fifties who liked to joke that she was tougher than Captain Kirk, a comment that went right over the heads of most of her students, but today she was all business.

I exchanged a look with Gabrielle, then glanced at the lines of kids still filing out of the school. Mrs. Kirk was right. The first priority had to be making sure the kids were safely out of the school, in case there was a fire. And any mention of . . . something . . . possibly a body, might be picked up on by the kids, who somehow always seemed to hear the very things we didn't want them to hear.

Mrs. Kirk raised her eyebrows at Gabrielle and me. At her elbow, Peg sent us a disapproving look.

"Of course, we'll wait," I said. "But it is very urgent that we speak to you as soon as possible. Very urgent," I repeated.

Mrs. Kirk's eyebrows came down in a frown as her gaze went from me to Gabrielle. She lingered, looking over Gabrielle for a moment. "Mrs. Matheson, do you need anything? To sit down?"

Gabrielle blinked, then seemed to pull herself together. "No. No, I'm . . . okay, I guess."

Mrs. Kirk gave a slow nod. "All right. I'll find you as soon as I can. Wait for me there, by the line of kindergartners."

"Right." We moved off through the line of benches that edged the circular car pickup lanes to wait with the smallest kids.

I turned to Gabrielle and said in a low voice, "Are you sure what you saw was a hand? Could it have been . . . I don't know . . . maybe a glove—a plastic glove—or something like that?"

My doubting tone shook Gabrielle out of her daze. "No," she said in a loud, adamant whisper. "It was a hand. I'm positive."

One of the kindergarten teachers frowned at us and made a zipping-her-lips motion. I mouthed, *Sorry,* and didn't say anything else.

We waited there, Gabrielle and I, until the last student had filed out. Occasional whispers, which were quickly silenced, floated on the morning air between pulses of the fire alarm. The wail of a fire engine joined the sound of the alarm, and less than a minute later, a fire truck lumbered up into the car circle pickup lane and came to a halt at the front doors of the school.

The kids went quiet for a moment—obviously this wasn't normal fire drill procedure—then there was a fresh burst of talking, which the teachers quickly squashed. The fire-fighters swung down from their truck, conferred with Mrs. Kirk, then entered the building.

We waited in the growing warmth of the sun. Eventually, the pulsing fire alarm stopped, and the firefighters emerged from the building and spoke to Mrs. Kirk again. She took the bullhorn from Peg and announced, "Thank you, students and parents, for following directions so well this morning. You may return to your classrooms." The teachers led their charges back into the school. Now, the kids were chattering and pointing as the fire truck pulled away.

Mrs. Kirk watched the first classes return to the build-ing, then came over to us. "Now, what can I help you with?"

Gabrielle shot a look at me out of the corner of her eye, then licked her lips. "There's a body in the storage closet in the blue hallway." The hallways were color-coded to help the kids navigate them, which came in handy, espe-cially during the first weeks of the school year. The first-and second-grade classrooms were in the blue hallway.

Mrs. Kirk's gaze had been divided between us and the children filing back into the school, but at Gabrielle's words, her attention snapped to her. "A body?"

"Yes," Gabrielle said firmly. "I know it sounds crazy, but I know what I saw."

"You saw this . . . when?"

"Right before the fire alarm went off. The door wasn't closed. I went in, turned on the light, and saw . . . her."

Mrs. Kirk looked to me. "You saw it, too?"

"No, the door closed and locked when Gabrielle came out."

Mrs. Kirk's gaze shifted from Gabrielle to me for a moment. Then she said, "Very well, come into the office while we check it out."

We followed her into the office, where she motioned for us to have a seat on the bench that ran along the wall opposite the tall counter, saying she would check the storage closet herself. "Best if you wait here. I don't want to draw too much attention to . . . this situation until we know what is going on, and having several parents in the hallway will do that."

I knew it was silly, but as I sat down on the smooth wood, I couldn't help but feel that I was back in grade school and had been called to the principal's office for some infraction.

Peg went behind the counter, stowed the bullhorn in a cabinet at the back of the room in the little nook that contained a bar sink and a coffee machine, then sat down at her desk without a look in our direction.

It was probably less than a minute before Mrs. Kirk returned, a concerned look on her face. She sat down beside Gabrielle on the bench. "Mrs. Matheson, there is nothing in the storage closet except cleaning supplies and extra paper."

Chapter Two

Gabrielle's spine straightened. "What are you talking about? Of course, there's a body there. I saw it." She surged up from the bench and strode out the door.

Mrs. Kirk shot an exasperated look at me, then hurried after her. After a beat, I hopped up and strode down the hallway, too, stepping through the last group of the moms who had walked their kids back to class and were now leaving the campus.

Gabrielle was tugging at the storage room door as Mrs. Kirk arrived with me on her heels. Mrs. Kirk had a set of keys in her hand. "Here, let me show you."

Gabrielle stepped back, her arms crossed and a determined look on her face. "I don't know how you could have overlooked it."

The shell-shocked look had worn off, and in a strange way, I was glad to see the old assertive—or perhaps aggressive was a better word—Gabrielle that I knew.

With a jangle of the keys, Mrs. Kirk unlocked the door and pulled it open.

"It's right there—"

Gabrielle stared inside the storage room for a second, then marched into the tiny room, flicking on the lights. "It's impossible. It's got to be here." She turned in a circle, her gaze raking every inch of the small closet, but there was nowhere for a body to be hidden.

The small square of space contained two sets of metal shelves, which were filled with cleaning supplies and paper products. Two tables with the legs folded leaned against the far wall and kid-sized chairs were stacked next to them.

Mrs. Kirk gazed at Gabrielle, a concerned look on her face. "It must have been a shadow or a trick of the light . . . or something." She half stepped into the closet and put a hand on Gabrielle's shoulder. "Let me make you a cup of coffee," Mrs. Kirk said as she drew Gabrielle out of the closet.

"I know what I saw." Gabrielle allowed herself to be maneuvered out of the closet, but shrugged her shoulder so that Mrs. Kirk's hand dropped away.

"Was the light on when you looked inside the closet?" I asked. If Gabrielle had only opened the door an inch and it had been dark in the room . . .

A boy I recognized from Nathan's class came down the hallway, carrying a piece of paper. His steps slowed as he reached us.

"No," Gabrielle snapped. "The light was off, but I could see the arm sticking up out of the trash can just fine. It *had* to be a body. It couldn't be anything else."

Mrs. Kirk smiled at the boy. "Hurry along, Ned. No dawdling." He picked up his pace, but snuck several glances at us over his shoulder.

Mrs. Kirk turned off the light. I'd been holding the closet door open, looking at every inch of the room, hoping to see something odd—a dropped rubber glove or piece of cloth that might have resembled a hand in a poorly lit space, but that didn't seem to be a possibility. Not even a bit of dust or scrap of paper marred the spick-and-span floor. I released the door and it sighed on its pneumatic hinge as it closed slowly.

"Wait." Gabrielle stuck out a hand, halting the door. "Where is the trash can?"

"I'm not following," Mrs. Kirk said.

"The trash can," Gabrielle said, her voice triumphant. "It was one of those big ones—you know, the thirty-gallon ones on wheels, like the kind in the cafeteria. It was right here by the door. Where is the trash can now?"

Mrs. Kirk blinked a few times. "Klea probably moved it to the cafeteria," she said gently, referring to the one of the school's janitors. With her cap of curly dark hair and a quick smile, Klea was a familiar sight around the school. I'd met her a few years ago when I'd helped with the annual book sale, which had been held in the library. Setup had involved rearranging furniture to make room for the book displays. Klea had helped me pack away the unneeded tables and chairs from the library and found space to store them at the back of the stage, which filled one side of the cafeteria. (For plays and events, the cafeteria could be turned into a makeshift auditorium.) Klea and I, along with a few other moms, had lugged tables and chairs up the stairs to the stage for a couple of hours. She could have left the moving of everything to us, but she'd pitched in and helped. I'd also met with Klea two weeks ago for an organizing consultation. I made a mental note to check in with her today and see if she'd made a decision about whether or not to hire me.

Gabrielle looked mulish. "I know what I saw. It was here."

"I'm sure you *thought* you saw something," Mrs. Kirk

said in a soothing tone, one that I'd heard her use with especially upset kindergarteners during the first week of a
new school year. "But whatever you saw, it's not there
now. Let's go back to the office. We can talk there." Mrs.
Kirk motioned for Gabrielle to release the door.

Gabrielle didn't look happy, but she let the door close
and followed Mrs. Kirk back to the office. I fell into step
beside Gabrielle, consulting my phone as I walked. I still
had time to get to my appointment if I left now. Gabrielle
must have been imagining things. I'd learned that she was a
bit prone to exaggeration. She must have seen a shadow . . .
or something . . . and jumped to the conclusion that it was a
body.

Mrs. Kirk went into the main office, and Gabrielle was
about to follow Mrs. Kirk into her separate office at the
back of the room when she noticed that I'd peeled off from
their little group. I swiveled the mouse and waited for the
screen to come up so I could check out, another require-
ment for all visitors to the school campus.

"Ellie, what are you doing?" Gabrielle saw the checkout
screen load, and she widened her eyes. "You can't leave
now. We have to figure out what happened."

"Gabrielle, I have an appointment with a client in twenty
minutes." Gabrielle was a businesswoman and I figured
she—of all people—would understand that I needed to
leave. She shot a quick glance over her shoulder to make
sure Mrs. Kirk was inside her separate office, then turned
back to me and whispered, "You heard Mrs. Kirk. She
doesn't believe me. She spoke to me like I was a pre-K kid
who'd had a bad dream during naptime. I can't have her
thinking I'm . . . losing it. I need to stay in good standing
with the school district. You know how much bad word of
mouth can hurt an organizer."

I sighed. She was worried. I could see it in her strained

expression. And I'd learned a while back that even though Gabrielle presented a tough and confident exterior to the world, she had issues—and some of them had been financial issues. As much as I would have liked to have landed the organizing contract with the school, I knew she needed it and I wouldn't want to see her in a precarious financial position.

"And there's your kids," Gabrielle continued. "They go to school here. Don't you want to make sure everything is really okay?" she asked, sensing that I was wavering.

"Of course I want to make sure they're safe, but like Mrs. Kirk said, there's nothing in the storage closet."

"You saw me seconds after I looked in there. Did I look like someone who'd imagined . . . a body?" She lowered her voice as she said the last two words and looked out of the corner of her eye at Peg. She had been sitting motionless at her desk on the other side of the counter, but suddenly became very busy, quickly unwinding the string that held an interoffice envelope closed.

"No, you didn't." Gabrielle had looked truly shaken to the core.

I picked up my phone and called my client, asking if I could reschedule. I could tell from her voice that she wasn't thrilled with the idea, but she did agree that we could reschedule for next week.

I ended the call and followed Gabrielle into Mrs. Kirk's office. She had an insulated carafe on a credenza and handed us each a cup of coffee, then waved us into chairs across from her desk before closing the door on Peg's curious gaze.

"We should call the police," Gabrielle said.

Mrs. Kirk sat down behind her desk and sipped her own coffee before saying, "I know you've been putting in quite a few hours on the organizing project, Mrs. Matheson. You could probably use a break. I think you should take the rest of the day off."

Gabrielle shook her head and looked briefly at me in amazement before turning back to Mrs. Kirk. "I don't need time off. We need—"

"To find that body," Mrs. Kirk said. "Yes, I understand that's your concern. But what would you suggest we tell the police? You saw for yourself that there is nothing for them to investigate in the storage closet."

"Well, then it must have been moved."

"Where?" Mrs. Kirk set her coffee down. "Where could it have been moved that it wouldn't have been noticed? I did think there might be some sort of prank going on when I went to look in the storage room after you told me what you thought you saw. When it was empty, I checked the bathrooms on this hallway as well as the other storage closet in the next hallway. As you know, that is the only other storage closet we have. There was nothing out of place. Every classroom we have is in use, and the cafeteria as well as the library and the gym are open and staffed at this time of day. There are very few quiet, disused places here. If there were a body on this campus, I assure you, Mrs. Matheson, we would have heard about it by now."

I took a small sip of my coffee. It wasn't my favorite drink, but I didn't want to be impolite. I thought that while Mrs. Kirk was mostly right, there were a few places that weren't always bustling, like the gloomy backstage area. And each classroom had storage closets, but I didn't suppose we could go from room to room and search without alarming the students. Mrs. Kirk didn't look like she'd allow it.

Gabrielle seemed to be winding up to continue arguing her point, but Mrs. Kirk looked immovable. I put my coffee cup down on the edge of the desk and said, "Perhaps we could check and make sure all the teachers and staff are accounted for?" I looked at Gabrielle. "You thought it— the body—was an adult, right? You said it was a woman, didn't you?"

Gabrielle nodded, her gaze fixed absently on the desk. "Yes. It was definitely a woman. I just—knew." She suddenly looked up. "There was a ring on one of the fingers. Not a wedding band. It was silver with a large dark stone. Maybe it was green. I'm not sure. But it was feminine. The stone was a big oval, maybe half an inch long. A man wouldn't wear something like that. And the arm was thin and didn't have any hair on it."

"You couldn't see a sleeve?"

"No."

"So." I looked toward Mrs. Kirk. "Would it be possible for you to check and make sure everyone is accounted for— all the teachers and staff? That would make Gabrielle feel better, right?"

Gabrielle looked as if she was about to argue, but I kicked her foot, and she nodded after a second.

Mrs. Kirk seemed to be suppressing a sigh, but then she said, "Yes. We can do that." She stood and walked around her desk. As she opened the door and spoke to Peg, Gabrielle leaned toward me and said in a whisper, "That's a start, but you know as well as I do that there are places in this building where someone could stash a body."

"Let's make sure everyone is accounted for first," I said in an undertone.

Mrs. Kirk returned to the office. "Peg says that we have only one substitute today. Mrs. Patel is out." Mrs. Kirk sat down and brought up a file on her computer, then dialed a phone number. After a few seconds, she said, "Mrs. Patel, this is Mrs. Kirk. Sorry to bother you today. We've had a bit of a mix-up here in the office and I just needed to speak with you to confirm that you're out today. . . . Yes, the substitute is here and everything is fine. . . . Okay. We will see you tomorrow."

Mrs. Kirk hung up the phone. "She's traveling to her son's graduation ceremony in Florida."

"What about the staff?" Gabrielle said quickly, as she glanced over her shoulder to the empty desk in the office. "What about . . . Mary, isn't it? Where is she?"

"It's Marie," Mrs. Kirk said. "She's on vacation." She didn't bother to disguise her sigh this time. "I'd rather not bother her, but I can see that you're quite determined to track down everyone." She consulted her computer again and dialed another number.

"Marie. It's Mrs. Kirk," she said, shooting a rather disapproving glance at Gabrielle. "Sorry to bother you, but I needed to check on when you'll be back in the office. . . . Monday? Excellent. That's what I thought, but I didn't have a note of it here. How is your vacation? Oh, that's a pity. I hope it clears up for you soon. . . . All right. See you next week."

Mrs. Kirk replaced the phone. "She's on Jekyll Island, waiting out a thunderstorm."

Peg appeared in the doorway. "If you're checking on the staff as well as the teachers, everyone is here, except for Klea. I just got a text from her saying she didn't feel well and was going home. Vaughn said he can cover for her for the rest of the day."

Mrs. Kirk shook her head impatiently. "Put it in the system, then. Klea never has liked using the computerized personnel system."

As Peg stepped away from the door, Gabrielle said, "And what about the moms who were here today? How can you be sure that they're all . . . okay?"

Mrs. Kirk tapped a few keys and studied her monitor.

"The only people who signed in this morning before the first bell who haven't signed out are you and Mrs. Avery. And before you say someone could have signed out another person . . ." She swiveled her chair and looked out the windows behind her desk, which overlooked the front of the school. "The overflow lot is almost empty. I see only two extra cars, which I suspect are yours and Mrs. Avery's. So I do believe we can rest assured that all visitors to the campus have left . . . except you and Mrs. Avery."

Mrs. Kirk linked her fingers together and placed them on her desk. "As you can see, everyone is accounted for. No need to worry. Now, Mrs. Matheson, I do think you should take a break."

Gabrielle stood up. "Oh, no. I couldn't possibly do that. I have too much to do. I know you think I'm imagining things, but I assure you I did see a body. I can't explain what happened to it, but I know what I saw." She gave a sharp nod of her head and left the office.

Mrs. Kirk leaned over her desk and said in a low voice, "She told me yesterday that she would finish today by noon. Can you keep an eye on her for a bit this morning?"

"As it works out, my schedule is clear, so yes."

I caught up with Gabrielle in the lobby. "What are you going to do?" I asked.

She crossed to the little nook where the janitors had their office. "Look around."

"What about implementing your de-cluttering plan?"

"That will have to wait." She tapped on the door, then opened it. The little office was empty. A messy desk filled one side of the room and a short section of lockers covered the wall opposite the desk. A few scruffy plastic chairs and a small, round table with some books and papers filled the remaining space in the center of the room. "Nothing here. Let's check the workroom next."

I didn't argue with her or try to talk her out of her search. I knew her well enough to know that nothing short of an act of God—something like a hurricane or tornado—would slow her down. And I did want to be completely confident that everything was okay at the school.

The workroom contained two copy machines, a set of cubbyholes stocked with papers in a rainbow of shades, and a long table with staplers, pens, and sticky notepads ranging over it. I had spent many hours in this room copying and collating for various teachers. It didn't take long to confirm the room was empty. Next door, the teachers' lounge with its scattering of tables and chairs was also deserted.

We entered the cafeteria, which was already filled with the smell of ground beef and spices. The long rows of tables were empty and no one popped out of the kitchen to ask us what we were doing as we made our way up the stairs at the side of the stage. The red curtains were open, but the main lights weren't on. "There's a switch over here," I said, and found the panel on the wall. I flicked on a few. Gabrielle took stage right, and I took stage left. There was nothing but stacks of extra chairs on my side. We met in the middle of the area behind the back curtain and poked around, checking behind the scenery leftover from the first-grade play, a couple of trees painted on plywood, and a five-foot-high house that looked like so many of Livvy and Nathan's simple line drawings that they'd made when they were in pre-school.

"Nothing here," I said.

"I know." Gabrielle's hands were on her hips. She surveyed the area once more. "On to the gym."

"Mrs. Morrison isn't going to let us look in the storage room in the gym," I said.

"She will if I tell her I need to see them for my organizing project," Gabrielle said.

And Mrs. Morrison did. In fact, she handed over her keys and said, "I have to get out on the field. It's a tee ball day," before disappearing out the open double doors.

As Gabrielle took the keys, she must have caught the disapproving expression on my face.

"It's not a total lie," Gabrielle said as she unlocked the door. "I am working on another proposal for the school district and need to do a survey of a typical school. This is a typical school. I hadn't planned to do the survey today, but I can do it now instead of next week."

Gabrielle threw open the doors to the gym's storage room. A quick circuit of the room revealed nothing more than rolling racks of basketballs, portable netted goals for soccer, miniature orange cones, Hula-Hoops, and vests for playing capture the flag. It was the same situation in the library, except the librarian, Mrs. Roberts, unlocked the door to the storage room herself and watched us as we surveyed boxes, rolled-up posters, and a few dusty stacks of books with damaged spines or wavy, water-damaged pages. "Perhaps you'd like a notepad?" she asked, a thread of suspicion in her voice.

Gabrielle smiled brightly at her as she said, "I use my phone," and proceeded to take pictures of the room.

As we left the library, Gabrielle caught sight of the school's other janitor in the hallway. "Vaughn, could you unlock the records room for us? I just need to take a quick peek. It's for more organizing stuff."

Vaughn didn't seem to think the request was odd. In his fifties, he was a big, broad-shouldered man, pudgy around the middle, with thinning gray hair. We followed his lumbering stride down the hall to the main lobby, where the door to the records room was located, adjacent to the door to the main office. His hefty key ring tinkled like jingle bells as he spun it in the lock. He opened the door and stepped back, then waited for us to have a look around.

The fluorescent lights flickered on, illuminating four rows of filing cabinets. Gabrielle snapped a few photos. We both walked the aisles, then exited the room.

"Thank you, Vaughn. That was very helpful," Gabrielle said. Vaughn shrugged a shoulder as he relocked the door, then clipped the key ring to a belt loop and ambled away. He wasn't nearly as personable as Klea, I thought, glad that she had been the one to help with the book sale setup.

Gabrielle eyed a classroom door. "If only we could get into the classrooms . . ."

"No, Gabrielle," I said, using the firm tone that I took with the kids when I absolutely wouldn't let them do something. "That is where I draw the line. We've looked everywhere we can. There is no way Mrs. Kirk would approve of you going from classroom to classroom."

Gabrielle scowled at me.

"You do want to keep your organizing contact with the school, right?" I asked. "Disturbing every classroom would really tick off Mrs. Kirk, I can promise you that."

She sighed. "I know. You're right. But what if some poor teacher opens her storage closet door and a body tumbles out? Think of the trauma to the kids. It would be awful."

"It would be terrible, but I think you've got to let it go. Since nothing has happened so far, I think we can probably assume . . . it . . . the body . . . whatever it was . . . wasn't moved to a classroom." I tried to keep the doubt out of my voice, but she zeroed in on it.

"I know you're thinking that I hallucinated or something, and you've been humoring me, but I didn't imagine it."

"Okay, let's say it was a body, and it was moved," I said. "Why would someone move it to a classroom? It would probably be discovered very quickly, if that were the case. I think the areas we've just searched, the out-of-the-way places, would be a much more likely place to leave a body, and we didn't find anything."

"I know." She closed her eyes for a second, then snapped them open. "Okay. Have it your way. We'll stop. But if some poor kid is scarred for life, it's your fault. I guess I better try and do some actual work, although I have no idea how I'll be able to concentrate. You're so lucky that you're just a part-time organizer. At least all you've got to worry about is end-of-year parties and Teacher Appreciation Week."

I gritted my teeth and went to the office to sign out.

I negotiated through the car circle's double one-way pickup lines at the school that afternoon, stopping even with the front doors of the school when it was finally my turn. As Mrs. Kirk slid open the van's door, the walkie-talkie she held in her hand crackled with static, then a voice stated that bus number twelve was departing.

Afternoon pickup at the elementary school was as practiced and as tightly timed as a symphony performance. Parents swooped in through the parking lot, bypassing the turn for the rows of parked cars that filled the back half of the lot. Instead, they followed carefully marked-out yellow lines, which separated us into two lanes that curved up to the front of the school and then continued on to the exit on the other side of the lot.

The car circle was a loop that, in theory, should move smoothly and let cars flow through with a brief pause to pick up their students. In reality, the double lines moved in fits and starts. Drop-off or pickup time meant gridlock for the streets surrounding the school as the car circle line backed up and clogged the roads. Kids waited on benches in areas designated according to their grade, and the teachers and staff sorted the kids into appropriate cars, relaying names of students along the walkie-talkie network as their turn arrived. Like a conductor, Mrs. Kirk supervised it all, directing all the various players so that the line moved fairly smoothly—most of the time.

To Livvy and Nathan's great disappointment, we lived too close to the school to be included on the bus route. I'd told them they would have to wait until they were in middle school to enjoy riding the bus. I wasn't looking forward to Livvy riding the bus to school next year—as a friend said to me once, all the bad stuff seemed to happen on the bus—but I thought it would probably be one of those things that appeared to be great at a distance, when they were impossible, but quickly lost their luster with day-to-day familiarity. But that was still several months away, and although I was really good at worrying about things in the future, I put those worries away and concentrated on the here and now.

Gabrielle's worry about the body turning up in a classroom must not have been realized because all was normal. Otherwise, I doubted the car line would move smoothly and that the kids would be as relaxed as they were. Shrieks and laughter and chatter flowed in through the open door as Livvy and Nathan climbed in.

As Nathan settled into his booster seat, he asked, "Mom, is it true that there was a zombie in the storage closet?"

Okay, so not everything was completely normal . . .

"And so now a kid in Nathan's class told everyone that he saw a zombie in the closet," I said into the phone later that night.

"So I bet that made bedtime fun." Mitch's voice came over the line faintly. Usually the connection was good no matter where he was in the world, but this time he really did sound like he was on the other side of the ocean, which he was. His job as an Air Force pilot had taken him to Europe, where he was participating in exercises that would last for the next two weeks. It was the middle of the night where he was, but he'd just finished a night sortie and had called after he landed. We worked in our phone calls whenever we could because the time zone difference made it a challenge to connect.

I had been walking around the living room, picking up action figures and books with one hand while we talked. "Yes. Livvy said the zombie thing was 'moronic.'" Livvy had taken to dropping words she'd learned while reading into conversation, which I thought was great. I was glad her vocabulary was growing, but Nathan had thought she'd accused him of being a moron, which had resulted in an argument.

"That's my little word geek," Mitch said after I related the story. Then his voice turned serious. "But do you think Gabrielle really saw a body?"

I put the books and action figures on the coffee table and curled up on the couch, tucking my feet under me. "I don't know. She was certainly frightened when she backed out of the closet, but there was nothing there when we checked later. And I mean literally nothing. Not even a scrap of paper or a bit of dust. And Mrs. Kirk checked on all the teachers and staff. Everyone was accounted for."

"But the school was full of parents—moms—right?"

"Yes, but Mrs. Kirk checked the sign-in system and everyone had signed out again, and there weren't any stray cars left in the parking lot." I picked up one of the action figures and propped it up on the arm of the couch. "And Gabrielle and I looked everywhere we could think of around the school, except in every classroom. Gabrielle wanted to check the storage closets in each room, but I knew Mrs. Kirk wouldn't stand for that." I sighed. "I don't know what Gabrielle saw."

"Probably nothing," Mitch said. "She probably imagined the whole thing."

I didn't really agree with him. Gabrielle was about the least imaginative person I knew, but I knew Mitch was trying to help me not worry. And with him thousands of miles away, I didn't want him to be anxious about us, so I said, "Maybe." I knew being stranded in a foreign country was no fun for him when things went wrong. Of course, we were usually talking about fairly minor things, like leaky pipes or the washing machine suddenly not working.

But he must have had reservations as well because he said, "Ellie, be careful, okay?"

I heard a noise from down the hall and uncurled my legs. "I will. Zombies or no zombies, I'll watch out. I think Nathan's up. I've got to go."

"Okay, put the little man on," Mitch said.

Nathan's head appeared around the corner.

"Oh good, you're up," I said, and Nathan looked surprised. "Dad wants to talk to you."

I held out the phone and listened to Nathan say, "Okay" about seven times. He hung up and said, "Dad says not to worry, that zombies don't really exist. They're just made up."

"Good. That's good," I said, and didn't add that I'd told him the same thing at least twenty times tonight. "Let's go back to bed." I escorted him back to his room, tucked him into bed, read him a *Nate the Great* book, and didn't hear a peep out of him the rest of the night.

Organizing Tips for PTA Moms

Routines to keep school year running smoothly

Use a wall calendar to keep track of doctor and dentist appointments, music lessons, sports practices, and school events.

Try to schedule activities into blocks to save time. Can you coordinate music lessons for one child with the orthodontist appointment for another child? Try and plan evening activities so that they fall on a few nights of the week, giving you some "at home" nights each week.

Do as much the night before as possible. Pack lunches, lay out clothes, and prep backpacks with homework.

Chapter Three

"Sunscreen, bug spray, water, snack bars, camera, and water bottle," I said as I checked my tote bag. I removed my folding chair from the back of the van and closed the hatch. "I think I'm ready for Field Day."

Abby, standing next to me by her car, said, "You forgot a hat," and handed me a baseball cap, then squinted up at the clear blue sky. "I think we'll need it." Field Day was scheduled for the coolest time of the day, first thing in the morning, but the air already had a steamy quality, and I knew that by the time we left in a few hours, we'd both be drenched in sweat.

"At least you get to wear blue tomorrow." Abby repositioned her orange cap, which matched the orange T-shirt she wore. Abby taught third grade at the school, but she'd taken today off so she could spend all of Field Day cheering on her son, Charlie. Otherwise she'd have had to spend the whole time on another part of the field with her class and missed the seeing Charlie participate in any of the events. There were a couple of other teachers who were also moms, and they were covering for each other during Field Day.

Each grade wore a different color for Field Day. Nathan and Charlie were the orange group. Tomorrow, the older grades would have their Field Day, and Livvy was in the blue group. To encourage school spirit—and raise funds for the school—the parents also ordered matching shirts, which meant that I had an orange, as well as a baby-blue, Field Day T-shirt.

We joined the throng of parents making their way into the school. We stopped off at the office and signed in; then, with our name-tag stickers on our T-shirts, we headed through to the back of the lobby and out the doors that led outside. We crossed the blacktop marked out with lines for a basket-ball court and joined the mass of kids and parents on the wide open stretch of grass directly behind the school that was known as the back field. A thick belt of tall pines lined the right-hand side of the back field, extending from the school to the far end of the property. The open, grassy area beside the wooded area wrapped around to the front of the school, and that area was called the side field, even though there was no clear separation between the fields. A chain-link fence enclosed the side and back fields, but not the woods.

Unlike so many of the newer neighborhoods that had popped up around North Dawkins before the housing bubble popped, the school was located in an older neigh-borhood. Small Craftsman-style homes from the twenties, thirties, and forties ringed the school, and I could see some parents departing from them and making their way along the chain-link fence to the school's main doors.

A few parents slipped in through the woods, which were strictly off-limits to the kids during recess, but I didn't blame the parents for taking the shortcut. Mrs. Harris was there in her yellow first-grade shirt and wide-brimmed straw hat, fluttering around the parents who emerged from the trail that cut through the woods, welcoming them to Field Day, and then shifting them toward the school building, reminding them to check in at the office before staking out a spot on the sidelines. The shade under the tall pines looked cool and inviting, and I thought longingly of the little trail that ran in a rough diagonal line through the trees and came out on the far side of them, at the street that ran along that side of the school. I knew many kids who lived on that side of the school took the tree-lined path home, a route that cut their walk in half. I'd taken a turn on it myself a few times.

I wasn't big on running or aerobics, so I tried to walk as much as I could. That usually meant walking in our neighborhood after dinner, when the sun had dropped below the treetops and the air was a bit cooler, but I also tried to add walks in during the day when I could. Sometimes I finished up my volunteer work at the school and had a little time to burn before dismissal. If the weather wasn't too sweltering, I'd check out at the office, go through the woods, and then walk through the surrounding neighborhood streets, working my way around to the parking lot, making a loop, and getting in some steps before waiting in the car line.

"Here's second grade," Abby said, staking out a spot beside a fresh chalk line. I turned my back on the woods and unfolded my chair, got my camera ready, and settled in to wait for the first event. It was a carnival-like atmosphere, with the kids and parents in their brightly colored shirts and the happy chatter of several hundred kids.

Abby and I were scheduled to man the refreshment booth, a table under a blue shade canopy stocked with bottled water and juice bags, during the second hour, so we were free to be spectators during the first round of events.

The classes in each grade competed against each other, and I spotted Nathan in line behind Mr. Spagnatilli. Nathan was talking to Charlie, who was in line beside him in another line for another classroom. The word "upset" didn't begin to describe how he and Charlie had felt when they had been assigned to different teachers this year, but although the beginning of the year had been rough, it had worked out to be a good thing. Nathan now had a few more friends, and I thought Charlie did as well.

The bullhorn screeched, and we all cringed. Then Mrs. Kirk's magnified, yet hollow, voice said, "Welcome to Field Day, students and parents." She usually wore suits, but today she had on a T-shirt, jeans, and tennis shoes.

A high-pitched shout of excitement went up from the student sections, which were spaced around the schoolyard. The parents clapped, and a few of them, including Abby, whooped. Mrs. Kirk gave detailed instructions that I'm sure most of the kids totally missed, but the teachers knew what to do and got their classes lined up for the first event, the three-legged relay race.

Nathan and his partner, a girl with her blond hair in dog ears, both looked embarrassed—until Mrs. Morrison, the P.E. teacher, took over the bullhorn and raised a starting pistol high over her head as she announced the first event.

Silence fell over the field like a blanket, muffling all sounds except for the distant bark of a dog. Mrs. Morrison's voice came through the bullhorn. "Three—two—one." When the report of the blank echoed over the field, the students and parents came to life, shouting and cheering. I managed to get some photos of Nathan and his partner, who both suddenly became so focused on making it from one end of their narrow lane to the other and back to the starting point that they forgot to be embarrassed. They loped back and touched the next group of kids, then collapsed, giggling, on the grass.

Nathan's class came in second, and the results were reported to a group of teachers stationed near the blacktop, who kept track of the outcome of each event. At the end of the day, each kid would go home with a collection of different-colored ribbons for the place their class had finished in the different events.

The next event was the egg race, and instead of focusing on speed, the kids were now carefully treading with a heel-to-toe stride as they balanced an egg on a spoon. Next up was the bottle-fill race, which took forever as the kids carried a single cup of water to a huge bottle at the far end of the their lane. Charlie's class won that event, and he grinned happily at Abby as the kids high-fived each other. The second-graders went off for a break and ate Popsicles under several shade canopies while Abby and I went to man the refreshment booth, where we handed out water bottles dripping with condensation to students and parents; then we went back for the second half of Field Day, which included sack races, the fifty-yard-dash relay, and the Frisbee toss.

By the time we got to the last event, the Frisbee toss, the sun was high in the sky and the back of my shirt was plastered to my shoulder blades. The kids' faces shone with sweat, but most of them were grinning and looking forward to the promised treat of ice cream bars for dessert after lunch in the cafeteria. I knew that the rest of the day would pretty much be a write-off in the classroom, with lots of educational videos being shown. Nathan had already had his turn at the Frisbee throw, and I was lounging back in the chair, fanning myself with the brim of my hat, when one of the boys in Mrs. Dunst's line put all he had into throwing the Frisbee, but his aim was way off. The

Frisbee went sailing over the line of spectators and into the woods.

Under her sun visor, Mrs. Dunst, who was seven months pregnant, looked exhausted. "I'll get it," I said, and hopped up.

I walked along the hard-packed dirt path that ran along the edge of the woods, then followed it as it turned into the shadow of the trees. The red Frisbee rested a few feet away on a layer of dead leaves and pine needles that lined the path. A woman holding a large ice chest was farther along the trail, deeper in the woods, and stood with her back to me, looking into the trees.

I tossed the Frisbee back toward Mrs. Dunst. My aim was terrible, too, and it went wide, but Mr. Spagnatilli caught it and handed it off.

I started back toward the schoolyard, but glanced back at the woman. She hadn't moved and still stood motionless, her gaze fixed on something off the path. It looked like Karen Hopkins, one of the other moms from Charlie's class. Her white-blond hair, cut in an inverted bob, was easy to recognize. "Hey, Karen, are you okay?" I called.

She turned slowly toward me and blinked. She didn't seem to recognize me.

"It's Ellie. Nathan's mom," I said, but there was something in her face that made me hurry down the path to her. "What's wrong?"

She carefully set down the ice chest as if it were made of delicate crystal. "Get Mrs. Kirk," she said in an unsteady voice. "There's a body over there."

She pointed through the trees, and I saw it immediately, a trash can turned on its side, half hidden by several pine branches. At the same time, I noticed a low hum as flies buzzed around the trash can. An unmistakably human form, a woman's head and shoulders, had tumbled partially out of the can. She was turned away from us, but her short dark hair was visible through the screen of pine branches and needles that covered her. I felt sick as my gaze traveled over what I could see of the figure. One arm extended out from the body, and rested in a pile of fallen leaves. I saw a silver ring with a large oval stone on one of the slender fingers.

Chapter Four

Karen spoke and I jumped as she said, "You can see the trail it left." She motioned at the ground near our feet, tracing the four lines of compressed dirt, leaves, and pine needles that branched off from the main path.

"I was going to run the ice chest home," Karen said in her shaky voice. "I didn't want to lug it all the way through the school and around the fence. It's so much faster this way. I live on Chestnut, right over there. This way is faster, but then I saw the gray color—the trash can. The light hit it just right, and it caught my eye." She swallowed and looked away from the trash can and the figure in the woods. "I wonder how long . . . it . . . has been there? Do you think it was there this morning when I walked over?" she asked, her voice cracking.

"I don't know," I said, but the low drone of the flies made me think it probably had been. "You're right. We do need to get Mrs. Kirk." I glanced over my shoulder. The kids must have finished the last event. Through the trees, I could see the kids returning to the school in orderly lines with parents and teachers streaming along beside them. A few teachers remained on the rapidly clearing field, picking up equipment.

"You go," Karen said. "I'll wait here." She glanced at the trash can, then quickly looked away again. "I'll sit down here and wait." She plopped onto the ice chest.

"Are you okay?"

"Yes." She ran a hand over her forehead. "I don't think I could walk if I wanted to. One of us has to stay here to make sure none of the kids come by. . . . Some of the early release students go home this way."

"Of course." I'd forgotten about the half-day kindergarten students. They would be dismissed now that Field Day was over. I shivered, thinking that at least it had been an adult, not a student, who had discovered the body. "I'll be as quick as I can."

Karen nodded, and I trotted away. It didn't take long to cover the short distance under the trees. I emerged from the woods and surveyed the almost empty field. Abby waved to me. She'd collapsed both our chairs and had packed up all our extraneous stuff. "What happened to you?"

"I'll tell you in a minute," I called as I spotted Mrs. Kirk at the refreshment station. She and Ms. McCormick were stacking unused water bottles on a cart. I hurried in their direction, and reached the table just as Ms. McCormick left, pushing the full cart over the bumpy grass.

"There's been a death, in the woods," I said.

Mrs. Kirk had gripped the edge of the table to tilt it on its side and fold in the legs, but she stopped, arms braced on the tabletop. "What?"

Ms. McCormick stopped wheeling the cart away and turned back to us.

I motioned toward the school building. "You've got to stop the parents who are leaving," I said to Mrs. Kirk. "The police will want to talk to them."

"So it's an accident?" Her face was concerned and a little frightened.

"No. It's . . . well . . . you better see for yourself."

She nodded and walked swiftly across the grass with me. "It's along the trail." We turned into the shadow of the tall pines, and I shuddered. The buzzing of the flies seemed louder, but maybe I was just aware of it now.

Mrs. Kirk hurried along the trail and stopped beside Karen, who was still sitting on the ice chest, her face pale and scared. "Mrs. Hopkins—" Mrs. Kirk began, her voice concerned, but then her gaze was drawn to the trash can a few feet away as Karen pointed at it.

Mrs. Kirk darted through the trees, circling around so that she could see the face. She stopped abruptly, sucked in a breath, and put her hand to her mouth. "That's Klea," she said in a high-pitched, breathless tone that I'd never heard her use. Her voice was tinged with surprise and disbelief.

"Not Klea," I said, thinking of the way she always smiled at me in the hall. And when I'd entered her jumbled house for a consultation, she'd shrugged and laughingly said, "It's a mess, I know, but I have the excuse that I just moved." Of course, anyone dying out here alone in the woods was awful, but to think it was someone I knew and had chatted with at the school and even met in their home . . .

"I'm surprised it's not Peg," muttered a voice behind me. Startled, I jerked around. I hadn't realized anyone else had followed us into the woods, but Ms. McCormick stood beside me, her face almost perplexed, and behind her, Abby was just making her way up the path.

Ms. McCormick saw my sharp look and waved a hand. "Sorry. I didn't mean to scare you. It's the hair. . . . They both have short brown hair." I heard the wail of a siren in the distance.

Abby reached Ms. McCormick's side and halted as she took in the scene. "Oh, no," she whispered. "How awful. Is it . . . anyone we know?"

"Klea," I said, and because she looked puzzled, I added, "One of the school's janitors."

"Oh, Klea," Abby said as realization dawned. "I thought it might be a parent . . . you know, with so many visitors on campus." She looked toward the trash can and the crumpled body. "How terrible. But how did she get out here? What happened? I mean, it can't have been an accident or something like that. . . . Someone put her there. So that means . . . but why would someone kill a janitor?"

Abby had a tendency to chatter when she was upset or nervous. I sent her a warning glance. "We don't know anything yet."

"Mrs. Avery is correct," Mrs. Kirk said. She seemed to have braced herself and spoke in her normal tones as she walked back through the trees to the trail. "I suggest everyone return to the school. I will stay here until the police arrive." She removed a cell phone from her pocket, but Karen held up her phone.

"I already called," she said to Mrs. Kirk, then looked at me. "When you left to get Mrs. Kirk . . . I realized we should do that first. I'm a little muddled"—she gave a brief smile—"but I did think of that."

"Good. Then they are on the way—"

A siren had grown louder and seemed to be coming from the front of the school. "I wish we could have caught them and told them to come here instead of the main entrance to the school. It will upset the students." Mrs. Kirk unclipped a walkie-talkie from the waistband of her jeans. "Peg, send the police to the back field as discreetly as possible." Mrs. Kirk nodded at Ms. McCormick. "Go meet them at the back door and bring them here."

Ms. McCormick licked her lips and tucked a strand of blond hair behind her ear. "Couldn't someone else do that? I have to get those water bottles. . . ." She quailed under Mrs. Kirk's disapproving gaze. "Yes. All right," she said, and hurried down the trail.

"At this point, I think we should all wait here," Mrs. Kirk said. "Since the police are on the scene now, I'm sure they will want to speak to each of us."

The investigators did want to speak to us, but it took a long time to get around to it. It was actually the sheriff's office that responded to Karen's 911 call because the school was in an unincorporated area of Dawkins County. The uniformed deputy who arrived first took one look at the scene in the woods and called for a detective and the forensic team.

After the first deputy took our names and the bare facts about the discovery of the body, we were told to wait on the field. More police arrived and moved in and out of the woods; then plainclothes officers began to arrive. We were moved to the school office when a deputy began to unroll the crime scene tape to cordon off the woods. As we walked to the building, I saw Detective Dave Waraday striding across the field from the school to the woods. He didn't see me, and I was relieved.

There had been a little misunderstanding between Detective Waraday and me in the past. He'd thought I was an excellent suspect in a murder investigation. If he was assigned to this case, then I knew I would have to talk to him, but later was certainly fine with me.

Unfortunately, it was sooner rather than later. I sat on the hard wooden bench in the school office for only a few minutes before a deputy entered and asked me to come with him. He escorted me to one of the pre-K classrooms. The classroom must only be used in the morning, because there were no backpacks hanging on the hooks and the cubbyholes for lunch boxes and take-home folders were empty.

Detective Waraday sat at the teacher's desk, looking a little out of place surrounded by kids' artwork and posters illustrating the letters of the alphabet. He wore a black polo shirt embroidered with the words DAWKINS COUNTY SHERIFF'S DEPARTMENT. He stood when I entered, and his badge, which was clipped to the waistband of his khaki pants, caught the light as he moved.

He gestured for me to have a seat in a chair that had been pulled up across from the desk. Detective Waraday had one of those baby faces that made him look far younger than his actual years. As I sat down across from him in the folding chair, I noticed a couple of fine lines radiating out from the corners of his eyes, but that was the only thing that made him look slightly older. His short hair was still brown and thick and he was as trim as ever. I'd known him for several years, so I supposed he must be in his thirties by now, but he looked younger than that.

"So, Mrs. Avery," he said as he sat down. "Why don't you tell me why your phone number is in the victim's incoming call log?"

"Oh." I blinked. It wasn't the question I expected. I'd thought he'd want to know about this morning on the field, but I switched gears mentally. "I'd forgotten about that. I called her yesterday. I had an organizing consultation with her two weeks ago. I was following up to see if she wanted to hire me."

"So you called and left her a message?" Detective Waraday asked.

I relaxed my shoulders a bit. His tone wasn't accusing,

and he wasn't nearly as hostile as the last time we'd interacted.

"Yes. I didn't hear back."

"Because she was already dead by then," Detective Waraday muttered more to himself than to me as he made a note. "The organizing consultation," he said, giving the words a special emphasis. "What does that involve?"

"It depends on what the client is interested in. That's what the appointment is for, actually. Some people just want help with one specific thing, and other people wave a hand at their garage or a bedroom or a closet, and say, 'Take care of this.'"

"And what did Mrs. Burris want?"

"Mrs. Burris—? Oh, Klea, you mean. I think of her as Klea," I said, realizing that it was sort of odd that all the other adults at the school, the teachers and the parents, were addressed by their surnames, but not the janitors or the office staff. Now that I thought about it, it made me slightly uncomfortable. It was a bit patronizing. I gave myself a mental shake and focused on answering Detective Waraday's question. "She had moved to a smaller house— on Maple—right across from the school," I said. "She wanted some help downsizing. She had too much stuff."

"So it would have been a big job?"

"Yes, if she decided to hire me, but I hadn't heard back from her. That's why I called."

"And is that normal?" Detective Waraday looked up from his notepad. "For potential clients to not make a decision?"

"Oh, yes. All the time. I'd love it if all my consultations turned into actual jobs, but that doesn't happen. People decide they can do it themselves, or they don't want to pay my fee, or they put it off until later. Some people, I just never hear from again," I said with a shrug of one shoulder. "That's why I like to follow up at least once. If I haven't heard from someone after a week or two, I contact them once to see if they're interested. If they're not, I leave it at that."

"And how did Mrs. Burris seem when you met with her for the appointment?"

"Um . . . fine. She wasn't self-conscious about the state of her house. Some people are embarrassed about their clutter, but she wasn't."

"Did she seem worried or nervous?" Detective Waraday asked as he wrote.

"No."

"She didn't say anything to indicate she was frightened?"

I shook my head, then stopped. "There was one thing, but . . ." I shrugged. "It was probably nothing."

Detective Waraday looked up. "What is it, Mrs. Avery? Everything is important at this point."

"Okay. Right. Well, I asked her if the traffic bothered her—you know, from the school. It can get pretty hectic during drop-off and pickup times. Klea laughed and said train tracks could run right through her backyard, and she wouldn't care. Then she said, 'Anywhere away from Ace is peaceful, no matter how much traffic there is.' She didn't say anything else, and I didn't ask, but I assumed Ace was a relative."

I expected him to wave off the comment as unimportant, but he only nodded and made a note. Then he said, "Now tell me about today, finding the body."

"I think I better tell you about yesterday first." No one else from the little group who had found the body had been called for an interview, so I didn't think he would have heard the story from anyone else.

He raised his eyebrows. "Why?"

"Because Gabrielle Matheson—you remember her from . . . that other case a while back?"

"Yes, ma'am. I don't think anyone forgets Gabrielle Matheson after they meet her," he said with a hint of a smile.

"That's probably true. She's working here at the school as a consultant. Yesterday, she thought she saw a body in a storage closet."

Organizing Tips for PTA Moms

<u>Room Mom Tips</u>

Send a welcome message to the parents in the classroom, introducing yourself and highlighting the upcoming volunteer opportunities.

Contact parents early in the school year and set up a tentative event calendar for the whole year so that the events at the end of the year are covered.

Be specific when asking for volunteers. Outline the time commitment (a volunteer for carnival night will have a "one-hour shift manning the ring-toss booth") and clarify any additional requirements. A field trip chaperone may need to complete additional forms for background checks before being cleared to participate.

Ask about food allergies and plan accordingly.

Coordinate with the teacher for party planning, asking what has worked well in the past and what hasn't.

For Teacher Appreciation Week, make a list of the teacher's favorite foods and activities, which you can either share with other parents or use to coordinate for a classroom gift.

Give parents a variety of ways to help. Some parents can donate their time while others can provide a monetary donation for campaigns and events, while still other parents may be able to prep crafts or send snacks or supplies.

Chapter Five

Detective Waraday raised his eyebrows. "A body? As in a dead body?"

I nodded and described what had happened from the moment Gabrielle backed out of the closet to the informal search of the school that Gabrielle and I had conducted.

Detective Waraday put his pen down and rubbed his forehead for a moment, muttering something that I couldn't hear. He looked up. "You know, I promised myself I wouldn't make any comments about you being in the thick of another murder investigation, but I'm very tempted to break that promise. The law of averages . . ." He shrugged and seemed to be speechless for a moment, then finally said, "Statistically, you're a menace to the community. Wherever you go, dead bodies pop up."

"That's not true." I shifted in my seat. Well, it was sort of true. I had gotten involved in quite a few investigations, but it's not like I went looking for trouble. But trouble did seem to cross my path frequently. "I didn't find the body this time," I said a bit defensively.

"No, but you managed to be on hand at the scene of the crime—both times, in fact. You were there at the initial discovery and also later when the body was found in the woods." Detective Waraday again massaged his forehead, then dropped his hand and refocused on me. "And no one thought to call the police or the sheriff's office yesterday?"

"Gabrielle wanted to, but Mrs. Kirk talked her out of it. There wasn't a body in the storage closet or anywhere on campus after the fire drill, and no one was missing. All the teachers and staff were accounted for." I sat up straighter. "Oh, I just remembered, Peg said she got a text from Klea that morning that said Klea wasn't feeling well and had gone home. Gabrielle insisted Mrs. Kirk check on all the adults."

Detective Waraday nodded. "Yes, that text is in Mrs. Burris's phone."

"But then—that means Klea was fine after the fire drill?" I asked, perplexed. "Gabrielle saw the body *before* the fire drill. It was after the drill when Peg said she'd received a text from Klea that she was going home." I got that same sick feeling that I'd had earlier. "You don't think . . . there couldn't be two dead bodies, could there?"

"No," Detective Waraday said decisively. "I think that, after Mrs. Burris was killed, the murderer used Mrs. Burris's phone to send the text so no one would realize she was missing. Apparently, the victim kept the phone in her pocket, not in her locker with her other belongings, so it would have been on her body."

"Oh." I fell back against the chair, not liking the word "victim" and its ramifications. I didn't like how it depersonalized Klea. She had become a tag, a descriptor, but it also meant something else, something that scared me. "Then it *was* murder?"

Detective Waraday pressed his lips together and sighed. "I'm afraid so. She was strangled."

"Poor Klea. That's . . . awful," I said. "I keep saying that—that it's awful and terrible—but it doesn't do the situation justice." I noticed Detective Waraday looking at me very closely, and I had the feeling that he had told me how she died to watch my reaction to his words.

"There never are words for something like this," he said quietly. After a few seconds of silence, he picked up his pen and beat out a quick tap on the paper. "Getting back to yesterday, what did you do after you and Mrs. Matheson looked around the school?"

"I went to the Comm," I said. "That's the grocery store on base," I added, not sure how familiar Detective Waraday was with military jargon. The full name of the store was actually the Commissary, but Mitch and I always used the shorthand name of "the Comm" when we talked about it. "I was supposed to have an appointment with a client, but when I had to reschedule the appointment, I went to the store instead. I went directly there from the school." I reached for my phone. "I remember the checkout line I went through. It was Janelle. She's there all the time and it seems like I always get her line for some reason. She might remember I was in—the computers had a glitch and she couldn't get my paper towels to ring up and she had to call for a price check. Do you want her information?"

"No, that won't be necessary."

I put my phone away, realizing that if Detective Waraday wasn't concerned with my movements during the late morning, he—or the medical examiner or whoever had examined Klea's body this morning—must be pretty sure Klea had died before early afternoon. And Gabrielle was sure she had seen a dead body, and that had happened in the morning, before the announcements, which had occurred right after the eight-twenty-five bell.

Detective Waraday opened his mouth to ask another question, but stopped and said, "You're frowning, Mrs. Avery. Is something wrong?"

My thoughts coalesced, and I said slowly, "If Klea was killed Wednesday morning before the eight-twenty-five bell—which is when Gabrielle thought she saw something in the storage closet—why did no one notice Klea was missing during the fire drill? Don't they have procedures for that? It can't just be the kids that they keep track of. They have to account for the adults in the building too."

"There are procedures in place, but the procedures only work when people follow them. The janitors are supposed to exit the building and line up on the field with the cafeteria workers. Vaughn Lang, the other janitor on duty that morning, didn't see Klea, but he assumed she'd been caught on the other side of the school when the alarm sounded. He thought she had exited through the other doors and was in the group that lines up near the bus circle. He says that he was about to speak up, but then the firefighters came out of the building with the news that it was a false alarm. If the fire had been a real one, he says he would have said something, but he didn't want to get Mrs. Burris in trouble."

"Did anyone see her at all yesterday morning—alive, I mean? Maybe she didn't even come to the school. Maybe Gabrielle *didn't* see her body in the closet, after all. Maybe she just imagined it," I said, thinking that Gabrielle would be so upset if she could hear me. As terrible as it was that Klea was dead, the thought that it might not have happened on school grounds made me feel a little better. I didn't want to think that someone had committed a murder in the school where my kids spent so much of their days. "Klea lived right across the street, and I know she walked to work. I usually see—I mean, I usually saw her walking along the chain-link fence when I dropped the kids off in the morning."

"Mr. Lang had a short conversation with her yesterday morning at seven-thirty in the janitor's office."

"Well, if he's the only one who saw her . . ."

"He's not," Detective Waraday said quickly. "And her belongings—a purse and a sweater—were retrieved from her locker. I doubt she left them there overnight."

"No," I said with a sigh. Which meant the death *had* probably occurred on school property. I shivered. "No woman would go off and leave her purse."

Detective Waraday said, "Glad we agree about something. Now then, tell me about today. I understand you went into the woods during the Field Day event?"

"Yes, to get a Frisbee. I saw Karen standing beside the path. She was very still. I called out and asked if she was okay, and when she turned to look at me, I could tell from her expression that something was wrong."

He asked me questions, taking me through the morning, and jotted down my answers. Finally, he put his pen down. "Okay, Mrs. Avery. I think that's all we need for now, unless there is something else that you think is relevant?" he asked.

I searched his face for a trace of condescension, but he seemed to be completely serious. "Um, no, I can't think of anything else."

He nodded and stood, then walked with me through the miniature tables and chairs, which, while they were the perfect size for five-year-olds, made me feel like a giant.

Before we reached the classroom door, I stopped. "Detective Waraday, do you think the students here are in any . . .

well, I don't want to be alarmist, but do you think there's any danger? If Klea was killed in the school . . ." I paused, trying to think how to put things, but gave up trying to think of a diplomatic way to phrase my question. "I have two kids in school here. If there's any chance that they might be in danger, you would let Mrs. Kirk know, wouldn't you?" After the discovery of Klea's body, Mrs. Kirk had decided not to dismiss school. Aside from the chaos an unexpected early dismissal would cause, Mrs. Kirk had said she wanted to keep everything as normal as possible for the students.

I expected Detective Waraday to brush off my concern, but he looked at me with sympathy. "We don't know all the details yet, so I can't say anything with one hundred percent certainty, but I assure you that if I thought there was a threat to the students here, I would make sure they were all escorted home, if need be. No, early indications point to . . ." He pursed his lips and tilted his head. "Let's say off-campus issues in Klea's life will be our primary line of pursuit at this time. I had to ask you all the questions about yesterday and this morning to make sure I had the full picture."

"Right. Thank you for the information. That makes me feel a little better."

"I'd appreciate it if you kept the information about what Mrs. Matheson saw—or thinks she saw—in that storage closet quiet."

"I won't say anything else, but Mrs. Kirk knows about it as well as Peg. She works in the office, so if either of them mentioned it to someone, the story is already out."

He nodded, then said, "I understand that, but if you'd not talk about it with anyone else, that would be best."

"Of course."

He opened the door of the classroom, and his sheriff's deputy badge and shirt were quite a contrast to the brightly colored spring flowers that were taped to the door. He lifted his chin at a waiting deputy and said, "Escort Mrs. Avery back to the office. She's cleared to leave. I need to speak to Karen Hopkins."

The deputy and I walked side by side through the quiet hallways, his equipment belt jangling with each step. Voices of teachers and students floated out of classrooms as we walked by, which was a little jarring. It was odd to think that school was still going on a short distance from where Klea's body had been found, but as I'd found out a few years ago, Detective Waraday was a very thorough investigator, and if he felt that Klea's death wasn't related to the school, then there was no need to panic and pull the kids out before the school year ended.

I sincerely hoped Detective Waraday was right, but I knew that sometimes the initial line of inquiry didn't always pan out, and I resolved to be a little more active in my volunteering. I was already scheduled to be at the school quite a bit over the next few weeks for all the end-of-the-school-year activities. I might just have to expand those volunteer hours even more until Klea's murderer was caught.

Organizing Tips for PTA Moms

When to say no to volunteering:

- If a volunteer job makes you anxious.
- If you don't have the skills to accomplish what is asked of you.

- If your schedule is already full and you don't have the time.
- If you are in a season of life like new motherhood or caring for elderly relatives that consumes your time.
- Remember, you don't have to give a reason or excuse. Say that you can't take on the job and then don't let anyone guilt-trip you into changing your mind.

Chapter Six

I was worried about how the kids would react to the news about Klea's death, which I broke to them after school on the way to the special parent-teacher meeting that Mrs. Kirk had announced would take place immediately after dismissal. But while Livvy and Nathan seemed surprised by the news, they both displayed the typical resiliency of kids. When we got home after the meeting, Livvy said it was sad and sat still without saying anything else while she ate a clementine. Then she asked, "Will school be cancelled tomorrow?"

"No. Mrs. Kirk says everything will go on as scheduled."

Livvy nodded, slid off her chair, and reached down to pet Rex, our overly friendly Rottweiler. "I want to get the computer game Ms. McCormick has," she said.

I was used to abrupt topic shifts from the kids, so I said, "What's it about?" Livvy didn't spend a lot of time on the computer and I liked that she usually picked books over games, so I wasn't sure I wanted to encourage her to shift her priorities.

"It's called *Adventure-matics*. You know, like part adventure, part math. It's really cool. The first levels are easy, but then it gets harder and harder. Ms. McCormick lets us play it if we finish our classroom work early."

"I see." The school classrooms had all been outfitted with computers during the summer. Not every desk had a computer, but all the rooms now had a computer section.

"I finished the treasure hunt level today," she said.

The way she said it, I could tell it was an achievement.

"Good job. What was it about?"

"Well, it's kind of sneaky, actually. You land on this island, and you have to do all sorts of fractions to figure out the map and get across the island. The lagoon with the piranha was really tough. If you get it wrong, you fall into the lagoon and get eaten, but if you get it right you get more of the map. Then, when you get all the way across the island and work that last problem, it unlocks the treasure chest and then you can go on to the Jungle Trek. That's where I am."

"Sounds like something worth looking into. I'll check for it online."

"Oh, Ms. McCormick says it's not available yet, that she's got a special test version but she'll tell us when it's out."

Livvy went off to find her book. After a few seconds, Nathan, who was still sitting at the table twisting the rind of the clementine into different shapes, said, "So it really wasn't a zombie." He looked relieved, and I realized he was still thinking about the news about Klea. I guess a death was better than a zombie in his way of thinking.

Later that night, over a plate of cookies, Abby asked, "So what are you going to do?" She touched a white piece of paper on the counter beside a plate. "Do you believe this? That everything is okay?"

The note had gone home with all the kids and explained

that Klea's body had been discovered and that the sheriff's department was investigating. Detective Waraday, along with the school superintendent and counselors, had been there after dismissal to answer questions at the special Parent-Teacher Association meeting. Abby picked up a cookie. "They really didn't tell us anything at that meeting today."

"I know. It was vague," I said. Detective Waraday hadn't mentioned anything about primary lines of inquiry being off campus, so I kept that bit of news to myself, but I did wonder why he'd told me that earlier today. Had he again been watching for my reaction? Had he been trying to catch me out, or scare me? He had tried to use those tactics in the past, but I didn't think that was what was going on this time. The meeting at the school had been full of generalizations and reassurances: *working around the clock to find the culprit, stepped-up law enforcement presence at the school, no specific or credible links from the murder to the school—at this time.* "I'm sure they're doing everything they can, and if they do have any leads, they can't really announce them to the whole school."

Abby frowned. "Wow, you're cutting Detective Waraday a lot of slack—much more than you did before."

"I'm not a suspect—thank goodness—this time . . . just a concerned parent. At least that's how it felt today when he talked to me. A lot less threats and more sympathy. It was a nice change," I said.

"So I guess the question is—are you sending the kids to school tomorrow?" Abby glanced into the living room, where Livvy was sprawled in a chair with a book in her lap while Nathan and Charlie had practically every action figure they owned strewn around every flat surface in the room. Rex had uncurled himself from his cushion by the window and trotted through the room, knocking down the action figures and poking his nose over Nathan's and Charlie's shoulders to breathe heavily in their faces for a while before loping off to patrol the backyard for squirrels.

"I think so," I said slowly. "Mitch and I talked about it on the phone a little while this afternoon. The kids don't seem frightened or traumatized. And I'm sure there will be lots of law enforcement types on campus at least for a few days."

Abby dusted the cookie crumbs from her fingers and said, "It's not like we have a rigorous academic schedule for the next few weeks. I could keep Charlie home, and he wouldn't fall behind."

"But you have to be there," I said. "Or are you thinking of staying home as well?" Mrs. Kirk had made it clear that attendance for both students and staff, at least for the rest of the week, was optional.

Abby sighed. "I'd like to, but then I think of all my kids. I know at least some of them will be there tomorrow, and I hate to think of them having a substitute in case they're worried or scared." She sighed and pushed away from the counter. "No, I don't think we'll stay home. I'd feel better being there on campus."

I was glad Abby would be there tomorrow. I knew I couldn't actually spend every minute of the day in the school, so having her there sort of as my backup for Livvy and Nathan made me feel better. "I'll be there, too," I said, "for Field Day again."

"Right, the upper grades. I'd forgotten about that."

"And if I wasn't scheduled to be there tomorrow, I think I'd drop in and volunteer anyway."

I'd never seen so many volunteers the next morning. Apparently, I wasn't the only parent who liked the idea of being on campus. I think it must have been the best attended Field Day in the school's history. The back field was packed with parents. Apparently, the investigators had finished examining the school building, and were now concentrating only on the woods, which had been completely blocked off. Even the hard-packed dirt path that ran from the corner of the blacktop to the woods had been cordoned off with barricades.

It wasn't as hot today, and a thin screen of clouds coupled with a light breeze made the day feel pleasant. Even at the mid-point of the event, when I went to take my turn at the refreshment station, the weather was still nice. Since the day wasn't sweltering, I wasn't as busy handing out water bottles, and I watched the investigators moving around the trees beyond the crime scene tape. It looked as if they were methodically searching the whole wooded area.

Mrs. Kirk had opened Field Day that morning with a moment of silence for Klea, and except for the flutter of crime scene tape along the perimeter of the woods, once the event began, I thought that anyone strolling into the event would never know that a body had been discovered in the woods yesterday. Well, unless they listened to the conversations among the parents.

As I returned to the section of the field where Livvy's class was stationed, I dropped into my chair beside two moms who were deep in conversation.

". . . can't believe they're going on with Field Day as if nothing has happened. I mean, it's upsetting enough for the kids as it is, but to have to be out here—within sight of where it happened—it's just . . . I don't know . . . *not right*. And I told Mrs. Kirk exactly that, but she said she didn't agree—that the kids need the normalcy of routine and to cancel the second day of Field Day would only emphasize the tragedy in their minds. Can you believe that?"

The second mom rolled her eyes. "And if Field Day is going on, the kids are going to insist on going to school. Any other day and they'd gladly stay home, but not today."

The announcement of the next event drew my attention back to the field, and I spent the rest of the time snapping more pictures and cheering for Livvy and her class. They came in first in two events, one of them the fifty-yard relay, which the whole class was happy about since that event was the finale of Field Day for the upper grades. She was in a little huddle with two other friends as they walked back to the school for lunch, so instead of breaking up the group, I waved and shouted that she'd done a good job.

She smiled and waved back, then moved away with her friends as I packed up my chair. While I loved that she was a reader, it was good to see her interacting with her friends, too. I was in the lobby, making my way toward the office to sign out, when a hand gripped my elbow and a voice heavy with a Southern accent said, "Ellie, I can't believe you didn't call me yesterday. I *told* you there was a body in that closet."

A couple of parents moving around us shot disapproving glances our way. It seemed the parents were fine discussing Klea's death among themselves, but they didn't want it mentioned in front of the kids. "Hi, Gabrielle," I said, stepping out of the flow of parents and students streaming in the doors. "I did think about calling you, but it was too late by the time I was able to do it. I was kind of busy earlier in the day—being interviewed by the sheriff's department and then dealing with the kids."

She immediately looked contrite. "Oh, that's right. I wasn't thinking about your kids. How are they taking it? Are they scared?"

"No. They think it's very sad, but they're doing okay.

Mostly, I think because they didn't really know Klea. Did you know her at all?"

"Not really. Only to say hello to in the hall, that sort of thing. That detective—you know, the one who looks like he graduated from high school about two minutes ago? He came by my house yesterday afternoon. It was shocking to hear that they'd found Klea . . . like that, but at the same time I was half expecting it—not that it would be Klea, of course." She shook her head as she added, "Just someone." She gave a little shiver that made the silky material of her camp shirt shimmer. Her gaze traveled over the parents, students, and teachers coming inside the building through the double doors from the field; then she lowered her voice. "It's scary to think the murderer had to be someone here at the school."

"Why do you say that?" I wasn't surprised that she'd called it a murder, but that she was sure the murderer had come from the school. I'd watched last night's news, which had reported the discovery of the body in the field adjacent to the school. The news anchor had said the death was being treated as a homicide, so that was common knowledge. "I got the impression that the investigation wouldn't focus on the school."

Gabrielle's smooth forehead wrinkled into a frown as she scowled at me. "Not have something to do with the school? Of course it has something to do with the school. The body was discovered here."

"No, it wasn't. It was discovered in the woods."

"Well, I saw it here. So that means it was here, at least for a while. Then it was moved. And it was in a trash can from the school."

"How do you know that . . . for sure, I mean?" I'd thought the trash can in the woods had probably come from the school, but I hadn't looked closely at it. "Someone could have just taken a trash can off the grounds. There are usually two big trash cans on wheels by the back door on the blacktop. I know there were some on the field yesterday for the first day of Field Day."

"I asked—that's how I know." Gabrielle folded her arms. "Detective Waraday told me the trash can had the school's name on the side, and he had someone do an inventory. One trash can was missing. It *must* be someone associated with the school." She chewed on a corner of her lip for a moment. "It's a shame, really, that it happened on the morning of the muffins and mommy thing. It makes it so much more complicated . . . so many more people were here on campus. I printed off a list of everyone who checked in that morning from the sign-in system." As she spoke, she reached into a legal-size leather portfolio and removed several pages of paper.

"How did you do that?" I asked.

"I can run reports. It's all part of my organizing projects. I needed to know when the high-traffic times are for the office so I could help them streamline their routines. Of course, they can't afford to upgrade that check-in computer," she said in an aside. "If they could speed that up, it would help to reduce the line and get everyone out of there so much faster. But back to the point—I figured we could split the list. You check half, and I'll check half." She held out several printed pages.

"For what?"

"Alibis, of course. What else would we check?"

I blinked. There were so many objections . . . I didn't quite know where to start. "Gabrielle . . ." I said warningly.

"Oh, don't go all huffy on me. I remember how that detective treated you . . . last time," she said. She looked away and focused her gaze on the field outside the doors for a moment, and I realized she was regaining her composure.

The last time, when Detective Waraday and I had had that misunderstanding—when he'd suspected me of being a murderer—Gabrielle had been related to the victim. It was something she didn't like to talk about. She usually avoided the subject, and that was what she did now. She shifted her shoulders and looked back to me, then plowed on again, speaking quickly—well, as quickly as she could with her languid Southern accent. "That Detective Waraday made your life he—" She smiled at an inquisitive stare from one of the kindergarteners walking by on his way to the library, then cleared her throat. "He made your life very uncomfortable, all because you were the first person on the scene. That's *me* this time. Even though I didn't see her face, I *know* that was Klea's body in the storage closet. I can't risk a smidgen of rumor being associated with me. You know people won't call me if they think I had anything to do with Klea's death. No one is going to invite a suspected murderer into their home or business for an organizing consultation. My business would dry up faster than a puddle after a July rain shower."

"You do have a point," I said slowly. I knew she needed to keep the clients she had, but I wasn't about to start sleuthing. My conscience immediately prickled. I'd already promised myself I'd spend as much time at the school as I could, possibly poking around—to make sure everything was safe for my kids, of course—but that was totally different from teaming up with Gabrielle to look for a murderer. I'd been on a team with her before, and I wasn't looking to repeat that wild ride. "I don't think—"

"Oh, look, here's Vaughn." She nodded at the doors that opened onto the back field, where the janitor was carrying a table with the legs flattened against the tabletop. He paused to let a group of students go first, then maneuvered through the door. I switched my lawn chair to my other hand and caught one door to hold it open for him as Gabrielle tucked her portfolio under an arm and gripped one end of the table. "Vaughn, you are just the person I wanted to talk to," she said. As she helped him carry the table inside, she looked back at me and gave a jerk of her head.

I hitched my tote bag higher on my shoulder and walked behind them into the cafeteria, which today smelled like chicken nuggets. I didn't like following Gabrielle's directions, and I certainly wasn't signing on to be her sleuthing buddy, but I had wondered what Vaughn had to say about Klea's death. After all, he was her closest work associate.

Gabrielle and Vaughn placed the table against the wall, and she brushed her hands on her skinny jeans. Again, today, she was dressed down—at least for her. The lemon-colored camp shirt with rolled sleeves, jeans, and leopard-print heels that were only two inches instead of her usual three-inch stilettos must mean it was another hands-on workday for her. Just looking at her shoes made my feet hurt, but she always wore heels. I had a feeling she could run a marathon in them without blinking an eye. She placed a hand on his arm. "Vaughn, honey, how are you doing? We're so sorry about Klea. Were you close?"

Vaughn had been at the school as long as I could remember. With his thin silver hair, bushy gray eyebrows, and wrinkled face, he certainly had to be near retirement age, and was probably at least fifteen years older than Gabrielle, but he responded as I'd seen almost every other male respond to her. Like a bee attracted to a bright flower, he focused on her, giving her all his attention. "It's very sad," he said with a shake of his head. He gave the table a shove with his foot to make sure it was secure against the wall. "But I didn't really know her. She kept to herself," Vaughn said, and moved to leave the cafeteria.

"Did she?" Gabrielle asked as we walked with him through the lobby. "In what way?"

He shrugged one of his broad shoulders as he came even with the door to the janitor's office. "She didn't talk about . . . anything personal . . . nothing about kids, husband, family, that sort of thing. Not at all like that Rosa, who worked here before her. She talked so much, she couldn't get her work done. It was a relief to have Klea. I don't think she had many friends, actually," he said. "She never talked about meeting anyone for drinks after work or traveling to meet family. She didn't jabber all day. Just came in and put her purse away, then went straight to work."

"Did you see her put her purse away Wednesday morning? You know, before the fire drill?" I asked, glancing inside the little room at the row of lockers, curious to see if he'd tell us what he'd told Detective Waraday.

"Yeah. She was here when I got here at seven-thirty-five. She'd already unlocked the doors. That's the advantage of living across the street—no traffic, she used to say. She'd kid me about being late sometimes. I live on the other side of North Dawkins," he said with a grin. Then the smile dropped off his face. "That was one of the few things we talked about, traffic. It's a shame what happened to her—ignoble, you know."

The word choice of *ignoble* surprised me a bit. It wasn't a word that usually came up in conversation, but when I glanced in the room, I saw a crossword puzzle book, folded back to a partially completed puzzle, on the round table. A hardback dictionary was propped up on the windowsill behind the table. He caught my glance and said, "I like crosswords. I had Klea hooked on them, too. Maybe that's why she didn't talk much. If we both happened to be in here on a break, we worked puzzles."

"Did she say anything that morning?" I asked.

"No, Mrs. Kirk came in with a list of things to do to prep for Field Day, so Klea and I didn't talk."

"I see." So it had been Mrs. Kirk who backed up Vaughn's statement about seeing Klea that morning. No wonder Detective Waraday hadn't seemed to think there was any issue to investigate further. You couldn't get much better than the principal of the school seconding your statements.

"Did you see her again that morning?" Gabrielle asked.

"No," Vaughn said, and I thought, with a cold feeling creeping over me, that he hadn't seen her because she had been in the storage closet. Sometime between seven-thirty and eight-twenty-five, when the announcements started, Klea had been killed. "Mrs. Kirk had a list of things she needed moved to prep for Field Day, so I went with her to the cafeteria to figure out if we had any extra tables we could move that day or if we'd have to wait until the next morning."

"But the fire drill . . ." Gabrielle said. I sent Gabrielle a warning glance, and she must have received the same warning from Detective Waraday about talking about what she'd seen in the closet as I had, because she stopped. After a second's pause, she ended with, "I mean, she wasn't there, was she?"

Vaughn shook his head. "No, and I wish I had spoken up, but I didn't want to make trouble for her. I figured she was at the other end of the school. Most of the school goes out these central doors," he said as he tilted his head toward the main doors that opened onto the covered porch, where the car circle pickup line curved in front of the school. "But there are several classes that go out the south doors," he said, referring to a set of doors at the end of one hallway that opened to the area near the bus circle.

Vaughn lifted his powerful shoulder again. "I thought she was over there. And then it was a false alarm. . . ."

"Yes, it was," I said, and realized Gabrielle was sending me a significant look. When I didn't respond—because I had no idea what she was trying to convey—she rolled her eyes.

"Who set off the alarm? That's the question, isn't it?" Gabrielle said.

Even though the question wasn't addressed to Vaughn, he answered. "One of the fifth-graders, most likely. We have that problem during the last weeks of school. High spirits, you know." He rubbed his hand across the back of his neck, then said, "A false alarm is nothing unusual this time of year. No, what bothered me was the trash can. I sure didn't like that, when I heard about it."

"What do you mean?" I asked.

"Well, she was a janitor. Was it some sort of statement? You know, was someone insinuating that she was trash, or does someone have it in for janitors?"

"Like it was some sort of . . . serial killer?" Gabrielle asked, her expression incredulous.

Vaughn immediately looked like he wished he could take the words back. "I'm not saying that's what happened, but you got to wonder. At least, I do. A janitor is killed, and her body is found in a trash can. You got to wonder." He shifted around us. "Excuse me, I've got to get back to work."

"Wait, Vaughn," I said before he got too far away. "Do you know where the trash can went missing from?"

"Oh sure, it was from the main office. The detective showed me a picture of it, and I recognized it right away. It had a streak of yellow paint on the handle from when the office was painted last summer. It usually sits in the corner by the cubbyholes in the main office." He caught sight of Mrs. Kirk coming out of the office and moved away quickly.

Gabrielle and I did the same. I headed for the checkout

computer in the main office, noticing that a new, smaller trash can stood by the row of teacher cubbyholes. Gabrielle followed me, signing out after I did.

As I headed out the main doors to the overflow parking lot, I heard Gabrielle calling me. "Ellie, wait."

I'd arrived early this morning, so my van was fairly close, and I was opening the back of the van so I could stow the chair and my tote bag by the time she caught up with me. As Gabrielle hurried over, she waved the sheets of paper at me. "You forgot your portion of the list."

"Gabrielle," I sighed, not sure where to start. "I know you want to get this thing cleared up, and I understand that you're worried about your clients, but I don't think you need to worry about being a suspect."

"No? Are you sure? Did you think you'd be a suspect last time? I bet you didn't. I don't want to be blindsided."

She flapped the papers at me. "Come on, Ellie. At least take a look."

"And," I continued as if she hadn't spoken, "I know Detective Waraday would not be happy for you to be poking around in his investigation."

"But we'd be helping him," she said, her eyes wide.

"Trust me, he doesn't want our help."

"Well, whether or not you help me, I'm doing it. You don't even have to talk to anyone. Just *look* at the list. Please," she said, drawing out the word like Livvy did when she asked if a friend could stay for a sleepover, but my impassive face must have gotten across the message that pleading wouldn't work with me. I had years of practicing that *it's not going to happen* expression with the kids.

Gabrielle glanced around the empty parking lot and her voice went completely serious as she took a step closer. "I'm not going to stand around and wait to show up on the evening news. And I promise you that if I show up on

the news, you'll be next, because who was with me when I
saw the body?"

"I wasn't with you."

"You were there on the scene."

On the scene. Detective Waraday had used those same
words, and they echoed in my head.

"I'll make that very clear to anyone who asks. You were
there."

"That's blackmail," I said.

She grinned. "No, don't think of it that way. It's just a
little motivator."

I blew out a breath. I couldn't tell her what Detective
Waraday had said about the investigation focusing on
Klea's personal life—he'd asked me not to talk about that—
so I couldn't use that as an argument to convince Gabrielle
to back off.

Gabrielle waved the papers again, her expression expec-
tant and hopeful. The phrase *a dog with a bone* came to
mind. She was as persistent as Rex when he wanted a treat.
Gabrielle wasn't going to give up. I sighed again and took
the papers. "I will look through them, but I am *not* chas-
ing down half the parents from Muffins with Mom Day
and asking them for an alibi."

She must have sensed that she wouldn't get any more
out of me today because she said quickly, "That's okay. I'll
do all the asking. I just want you to read over them, see if
anything pops out. You know more of the parents than I
do." She gave my upper arm a quick squeeze. "Thanks,
Ellie. I knew I could count on you. I'll call you later so we
can compare notes." She marched off, her heels clicking
across the asphalt of the parking lot.

I stood there for a second, scanning the list in my hand,
then let out a snort. She hadn't given me half of the list. Of
course not. Once I'd agreed to look it over, she'd given me

the *whole* list, a complete printout of every parent or volunteer who had signed in from when the doors opened at seven-thirty until the eight-twenty-five bell rang on Wednesday. Hundreds of names. I stuffed the list in my tote bag, then put it in the back of the van, along with my lawn chair and closed the hatchback door.

"Excuse me, Mrs. Avery," said a voice behind me, and I turned to see Detective Waraday.

Chapter Seven

"Oh, hello," I said. "I didn't see you there." I glanced around, looking to see if Gabrielle was still in the vicinity, but she was already motoring out of the parking lot in her compact SUV.

"Do you have a moment?" Detective Waraday asked.

I checked my watch. It was only a little after noon. "Yes. I have some time." It was noon, but I didn't have any other plans, except to go home and work on an ad for Everything In Its Place, my organizing business, and to clean house. Everything seemed fine at the school, and although part of me wanted to camp out in the workroom all day, I knew that realistically I couldn't do that.

"Good. I have a request." Detective Waraday looked away, squinting as he gazed across the tops of the cars. "I'd like for you to look at Mrs. Burris's house."

"Um—why?" I'd been braced for questions that would rehash everything that Detective Waraday had asked me yesterday.

"Mrs. Burris lived alone. You saw her house a few weeks ago. I'd like to know if it is in the same state it was when you saw it."

"Oh. Sure." I paused uncertainly. "Um, should we walk?"

"If you don't mind."

"No. It's not far." Leaving my stuff inside the van, I clicked the button on the key fob to lock it, then pocketed the keys and fell into step beside Detective Waraday. We crossed the parking lot and walked on the grassy verge outside of the chain-link fence that ran along the side field, stepping over a few rutted tracks where the tires of a car had dug into the soft turf. This morning, when Field Day began, each side of the street had been lined with cars parked parallel, bumper to bumper. Parents who had arrived to find the overflow lot full had wedged their cars in somewhere on the surrounding residential streets. The extra cars were gone, and only one class was having recess as students ran back and forth across the field.

Klea's house was about halfway up the block, and we glanced up and down the now-quiet street before crossing to the other side. Klea's Craftsman bungalow looked a little rough around the edges. The white trim on the porch pillars was peeling, and the grass in the small yard was ankle high. A paved driveway ran down the right side of the property to a carport that listed to the side, following the sloping line of the ground, which plunged from Klea's property to a rainwater drain set into the grass on her neighbor's property a few feet below. A huge oak tree, with a trunk so thick that my fingers wouldn't touch if I tried to put both arms around it, threw a blanket of shade over the entire front yard.

"You said she lived alone. Was she a widow?" I asked, thinking of what Vaughn had said about how Klea never mentioned family. "I knew her from school, but not that well," I explained.

"She was getting a divorce." Detective Waraday looked at me sharply as he stopped so that I would walk in front of him along the little strip of concrete to the wide set of steps at the foot of the porch. "I'm surprised you didn't know that."

"I'd only talked to her a few times, really. I saw her around the school a lot, but we were acquaintances, not close friends. We didn't know each other well. When I came for the consultation, we talked about organizing her things and that was all."

Now that I thought about it, that was rather strange. There is something about looking through a person's possessions that is very intimate. By the end of most organizing consultations, I usually knew quite a bit about the person. Analyzing clutter typically led to at least brief mentions of family members and situations. I often knew a potential client's background and life situation—kid going off to college, or death of a relative who had left them furniture or boxes to shift through, or even mundane things like the hobbies and interests—because it was often stuff related to those very things that the client wanted help with.

One husband had called me hoping I could settle a dispute between him and his wife about how they should use an extra bedroom. He wanted to store his vintage record collection there. She wanted to turn it into a darkroom for her hobby of taking pictures with vintage cameras and developing the film herself. Those were details that I normally wouldn't have known about near strangers. But Klea hadn't been chatty or forthcoming, I realized, now that I thought about it.

"And that seems odd to you?" Detective Waraday said as he took out a key ring and unlocked a dead bolt on the front door.

"At the time, I didn't notice it, but it does now, since I've thought about it. Most people chat and tell me about their life. And seeing their belongings, well, you always learn things about people from their stuff."

"And what did you learn about Mrs. Burris from your appointment?" Detective Waraday switched to another key and unlocked a second dead bolt.

"Hardly anything," I said slowly. "She said she'd bought the house about a month ago and had too much stuff. She was downsizing." I thought back over the meeting, then shook my head. "No, I think that was it. That was all she said about herself."

He nodded. "From what I've found out about her, that was typical. She was a loner. Didn't have any kids. Her parents were both dead. A relative—a sister—lives in Missouri, but she didn't keep in close touch with her."

"What about friends?" I asked, thinking of Vaughn saying that Klea kept to herself.

"I can't find anyone she kept in touch with regularly. Except for her work, she didn't have contact with many people."

"That's so sad," I said, wishing that I had taken the time to talk to her and gotten to know her a little bit.

"Some people don't want lots of social interaction." Detective Waraday pushed the door open and stepped inside. I followed him in, and he closed the door behind me, but didn't flip the dead bolts. The air was stale and muggy in the little house. The blinds were drawn, and with the heavy shade from the tree outside, it was so dark inside the house that it almost felt like night.

Waraday opened the curtains in the front room and crossed to a floor lamp, which he switched on. The front door opened directly into a living area, which was so filled with boxes that I could only see a couple of inches of the golden oak floorboards. A bit of breathing room had been carved out for a couch, a coffee table, and an older television at one end of the room.

"Look around," Waraday said as he moved into the dining room directly behind the living area and turned on more lights. As he went into the kitchen at the back of the house, he called out, "Tell me what's changed."

I felt a bit like I was looking at one of those Find the Hidden Item books that the kids liked so much as I scanned the room. "Not much in here . . . I think," I said. I remembered the room being filled with boxes. I reached for my phone. It had been a while since I'd been there and I couldn't remember exactly what was in each room, but—like Gabrielle—I often took pictures of rooms to help me jog my memory.

I found the pictures I'd taken of Klea's front room and compared them to the room as it was now. "She opened some boxes that were stacked here by the wall," I said to Waraday as he came back into the room. I showed him my phone. "Look, you can see the fireplace now, and it was totally blocked by boxes when I was here."

Detective Waraday nodded. "I'd like a copy of those." He handed me a business card. "You can text them to this number."

"Okay," I said. "I would have mentioned them yesterday, but I didn't think about them—that you might be interested in them." I tapped on my phone as I spoke, sending the images. "I only have this room and a few pictures of the spare bedroom."

"Anything will be helpful." Detective Waraday's phone dinged, and as he checked it, he pulled at the collar of his polo shirt. "Got them. Thanks. It's stuffy in here. Let me see if there's central air." He walked off down the hall. A low rumble sounded, and he came back with a shake of the head. "Just window coolers. I turned one on, but I doubt it will do much good out here."

"Yeah, I love the architecture of these homes—they have plenty of charm—but I don't think I could get by without air-conditioning here in Georgia."

Mitch and I had lived in what we'd come to think of as our antique starter home during his last assignment in Washington state. We hadn't had air-conditioning there. It had been bearable, but only because the summers were so short. I looked toward the window at the front of the house, thinking of all the times I'd opened windows in Washington and set up fans in an effort to get a cross breeze. Except for the windows with the AC units, Klea's windows were painted shut, and in addition to the old sash locks that had been painted over, all the windows had an extra set of what looked to be brand-new bolt locks. Not a speck of paint marred their shiny silver surface, unlike the rest of the windowsills, which had thick coats of paint on them.

I moved into the dining room. A large cabinet stocked with antique china and a dining room table with eight chairs filled the small space. "She did a lot of work in here. There were boxes stacked all along that wall, but they're gone now. The table looks . . . about the same," I said.

Klea had been using the dining room table, a huge rectangle of dark wood that was too big for the room, as a desk when I'd come through for the appointment. I remembered that her laptop had been at the head of the table, with piles of papers, folders, notepads, and bank boxes arranged around it. The paper stacks and the boxes remained, but the laptop was gone now. The police had probably taken it to examine it.

"Can I look in the boxes?" I asked.

Detective Waraday waved his hand. "Go ahead. We've already fingerprinted everything and removed what looked significant."

I peered in a few of the bank boxes, which had their lids

off. They contained old bills and file folders of tax returns from prior years. "There were boxes on the table that day I was here. Klea and I talked about going through them, throwing away old paperwork, and setting up a filing cabinet to store the records she needed to keep. I recommended using the extra bedroom into an office."

I picked up a lid from the seat of a nearby dining room chair and replaced it. I could only suppress my instincts to tidy things for so long. Klea must have used the box lid as a notepad because it had scribbles all over it. The word "dentist," along with a time and next Tuesday's date, filled one corner.

I ran my finger over the indentations the pen had made in the cardboard, thinking how sad it was that her life had been cut off so abruptly and how fragile all our connections were. Klea had been moving through her days, planning for next week and next month with no idea that everything would end so abruptly. I let my finger trail over another jotted note for her to buy a shredder, which had been checked off; then I paused at a list of names.

"What is it?" Detective Waraday asked.

"This list of names. I know the first person, Mrs. Harris, and the last four, Ms. McCormick, Mrs. Kirk, Peg, and Marie—they all work at the school—but I don't know who Alexa Wells is." Her name was second on the list and bracketed in parentheses. A question mark was written to the side of the names. Did Klea have some question about the whole list or one person in particular? Or was it only a doodle, something she had randomly written while waiting on hold when she was on the phone? "I wonder why one name is set off from the others in parentheses? Maybe she's a new teacher, and I just don't know her."

"Or maybe a parent," Waraday said, looking over my shoulder. "It's probably nothing." He seemed more interested in a phone number jotted down across one corner and made a note of it.

After checking some of the papers on the table and the contents of some of the boxes, I said, "It looks like she was working her way through the boxes, sorting which things to keep and which to get rid of." I pointed to the different stacks on the table. A paper shredder sat by the table, its bin full of confetti.

I stepped away from the table, and Detective Waraday gestured for me to go ahead of him through the kitchen door. "Klea said she didn't like to cook and didn't need any help with organizing or de-cluttering the kitchen so I didn't even go in here—"

I glanced into the tiny galley kitchen, which was old-fashioned and decorated in lime green, but what caught my attention was a piece of wood in the window over the sink, where a pane of glass should have been. "But I would have noticed if that window was broken. It wasn't like that."

A faint smile crossed Detective Waraday's face. "That's another reason I asked you to look around. We found the window broken when we checked the house yesterday. It must have happened Thursday, after she was killed. I doubt she would have gone off to work without putting something in the window or making a call on her cell phone or a search on her computer for glass repair. Someone's been in here. It looks as if they tried the back door, but couldn't get in that way—there are scrapes and scratches around the frame—but these old houses are pretty solid."

I studied the back door, which opened onto the carport and driveway, for a second. It looked as if it was more than the craftsmanship of the home that had kept the intruder out. Like the front door, the back door also had two thick dead bolts.

Someone had swept up the big pieces of the glass from the counter and sink, but tiny shards speckled the Formica. Two partial prints from the sole of a shoe marred the clean surface of the white sink. The treads were bumpy and patterned like the sole of a tennis shoe.

"They only came in for a look around, it seems," Detective Waraday said. "No fingerprints, nothing identifiable, except those shoe prints. The only thing I can figure is that someone wanted something from this house." Waraday put his hands on his hips and looked back toward the living room. "The question is, what? Nothing obvious is missing—no jewelry, no valuable electronics—the laptop was still here—and the neighbors didn't notice anyone coming or going. I thought you might be able to tell us more about Mrs. Burris's possessions. Did she mention any sort of collection or anything valuable at all?"

"No. Nothing like that came up." I heard a faint ringing, and recognized the school bell. I checked the time, but saw it wasn't the last bell of the day. I still had some time before I had to get back to pick up the kids. I wasn't surprised that you could hear the school bells from inside Klea's house. Since she was right across the street, she probably got so used to them that she just tuned them out.

Detective Waraday didn't seem to notice the school bell and went on. "It was a long shot. She didn't seem the type of woman to own jewelry or valuable decorative things. Why don't you take a look in the bedrooms?"

"Okay," I said, doubtfully. "But I was only in those rooms for a few minutes." Now that I knew why I was here, I felt overwhelmed. It had been weeks since I was in this house, and I hadn't been looking at and memorizing each individual thing. I'd focused on the big picture, the clutter, and tried to figure out how to help Klea get it under control. I retraced my steps through the dining room and the living room, and down the short hallway that branched off the living room to the two bedrooms.

The first bedroom was Klea's. The window unit was pumping out cool air. I shivered as I walked into the room, but it wasn't because of the temperature. A pair of flats was discarded in front of the closet, and a jumble of earrings, lipstick, and a phone-charging cord covered the dresser. It looked as if Klea had stepped out and would be back at any moment.

I swallowed and moved to the closet. "Nothing's changed in here that I can see. Klea showed it to me so I could see how much storage she had in this room and the other room, but I told her she was better off using this for clothes and converting the extra bedroom to an office with storage in there." As I glanced around the room a final time, I noticed that in addition to the regular sash locks, each window had shiny new metal locks.

Detective Waraday nodded and stepped back from the doorway, where he was waiting. I moved by him to the last room. It was still a mishmash of extraneous stuff that Klea hadn't known where to put: packing boxes, unhung pictures, a coat rack, folded lawn chairs, and a treadmill filled the room. I looked from the pictures on my phone to the room and sighed. "I don't think anything's changed in here, but I'm not sure at all. I measured the room and tried to help Klea imagine what it would look like without all the clutter." After a quick survey of the room, my gaze stopped at the window. It, too, had the new, extra locks installed.

Detective Waraday noticed what I was looking at. "Security seemed to be a high priority for her," he said.

"Yes. Now that I think about it, I do remember that it was a nice day—unusually cool—when I was here, and I said something about how it was pleasant enough that I'd opened some windows at my house to enjoy the cool air. She said she never did that, and when I came inside, she locked both dead bolts on the front door. At the time, I thought it was a bit strange. The multiple locks seemed like something out of a television show—you know, something you'd see on a show set in a rough, downtown area, but I didn't think about it again until now," I said as I followed Detective Waraday back down the hall to the living room.

"Did she have a security system, too?" I asked.

"No." His gaze went from lock to lock on the windows in the front room. "It looks as if she wanted one—there was a search on her computer for home security companies—but I think she probably couldn't afford to have one installed. Her finances were . . . um, tight after purchasing the house."

"I know that feeling," I said, thinking of all the unexpected expenses that pop up after buying a house.

"It looks like the locks were her cost-effective alternative to installing a whole house-monitoring system," Detective Waraday said. "So nothing stands out to you?"

"Except for the locks?" I frowned and looked around the small rooms with their thick trim, coved ceilings, and freshly painted white walls. "No. The only thing I'm sure of is that some boxes in here and in the dining room are gone."

Detective Waraday said, "I doubt the person who broke in here did it to steal cardboard boxes, but I'll check. There is a stack of flattened cardboard boxes in the carport—probably boxes that Mrs. Burris had gone through, as you indicated. I'll have my team compare your pictures to the boxes out there. I have a feeling that they'll be a match. Well, thank you for taking a look, Mrs. Avery," he said as he walked me to the door. "I won't keep you any longer. I have to turn everything off and lock up, but you don't need to stay."

He thanked me again for my help, which was a rather odd thing for me—I was used to Detective Waraday warning me off or even accusing me, not thanking me. I walked down the street and back to the school parking lot, wondering why Klea had needed so many locks.

Despite being packed with activities, the weekend was uneventful. Soccer games for Livvy on Saturday took up most of the day, and Sunday, after church, we had a birthday party for one of Nathan's friends, which left enough time to run home and prep lunches, wash clothes, do the bath and bedtime routine. Then I called the parents who had signed up to bring food on Monday for Teacher Appreciation Week and remind them of their commitment to bring a breakfast-type food. The rest of the week was planned, and each day had a menu. Tuesday was snacks and desserts, Wednesday was catered sub rolls for lunch, Thursday was breakfast again, and then on Friday we had a catered barbecue buffet scheduled for lunch.

Another mom, Mia, and I had coordinated the whole thing, but her twins had gotten into poison ivy. She'd said, "My life is all about calamine lotion and oatmeal baths. Can you handle this week on your own? They're both very sensitive to it and taking prescriptions to help, but the doctor says it could be a week before we're back to normal."

I told her not to worry, that the hard part—getting parents to sign up to bring food or donate money—was done. All I had to do was make reminder calls and make sure the food was put out and later cleared away each day. It would actually be a great way to unobtrusively check in at the school every day.

With the kids in bed, I settled into my favorite overstuffed chair for some downtime. Rex was sprawled on the floor, snoring so loudly that I wondered if he'd keep the kids awake. I had the television on more for company than because I was interested in the sitcom rerun. Without Mitch around, the house always seemed a little empty, so I liked the low murmur of the television show in the background.

I read the first chapter of the novel for the book club, which the back cover described as "hauntingly evocative and moving," but I couldn't get into it, so I put it aside. I'd try it again later when I wasn't so . . . what? Edgy. Despite being tired from doing the parenting thing solo for several days, I felt twitchy and unsettled. I knew it was Klea's death and the questions around it that had me feeling off. This was the first time I'd slowed down all weekend, and of course my mind went directly to Klea.

I thought of her stuffy, deserted house and its abandoned air. I shifted in the chair, reaching for the list of parents who had signed up to bring food this week for Teacher Appreciation. I scanned down the list of names. The unfamiliar name of Alexa Wells tugged at me. I didn't remember seeing that name on the list, but I had been more focused on getting the calls made than concentrating on names. I ran my finger down the lists for each day of the week, but there was no Alexa Wells.

I uncurled my legs and went to find the list that Gabrielle had pressed on me. I hadn't had time to look at that list either and studied it as I walked back to the chair. It was much longer—several pages—but I reached the end of it without seeing the name Alexa Wells there either. I frowned over the list for a while because I knew that Gabrielle would ask me about it the next time I saw her, but I couldn't for the life of me see how we could use this list of names to figure out who had killed Klea.

Yes, all the people had been at the school that morning, but unless we planned to interview each person and trace their movements around the school—and I knew Gabrielle and I couldn't do that—it wouldn't do us much good. No, those were tasks more suited to someone like Detective Waraday. He could interview everyone and plot movements, and I was sure he already had a copy of the list. I turned off the television and gave Rex a rub on his belly before I went to switch off lights around the house. Somehow I doubted Gabrielle would see it the same way.

Organizing Tips for PTA Moms

To keep from getting roped into doing more than you're able, choose the type of volunteer activities that work best with your schedule. If you are juggling a job outside the home as well as volunteering at school, pick one-time events like a field trip or yearly events like Field Day or holiday parties. If you have the ability to be at the school more often, you could volunteer to help in a certain area on a recurring basis, like in your child's classroom or in the library.

Chapter Eight

"What are you talking about?" Gabrielle asked the next morning, her eyes wide. "That list is *the* key."

A group of second-grade boys walked through the school lobby, their gazes fastened on Gabrielle and me. She rotated her shoulders and lowered her voice. "We have to use it."

"How?" I asked.

I'd arrived at the school early to help set up food for Teacher Appreciation and had run into Gabrielle on my way into the office to sign in. She was on her way out the door, a stack of papers tucked into her elbow, and had nearly collided with me. I'd sidestepped and managed not to drop the bag of paper cups, the gallon of orange juice, and the platter of breakfast biscuits I'd picked up on the way to school.

"What do you mean, how?" Gabrielle said. "I told you. We ask everyone where they were that morning. If they were in any other hallway besides the blue hallway, then we mark them off the list."

"And what if they were in several hallways, like me?" I shifted my grip on the cold orange juice container, which was already beaded with condensation. "I visited Nathan and Livvy's classrooms."

"Then we'll put them down for both. We'll need a spreadsheet. You can take care of that, right? I have a meeting today with the school board to update them on the progress of the implementation." She smoothed a hand over the lapel of her black suit jacket. With her black skirt and heels, she looked much dressier than most of the teachers and parents at the school.

"And what if they lie?" I asked.

"Lie? Why would they lie?" she asked, her tone indicating I'd suggested something as impossible as snow in Georgia, a very rare occurrence.

"Lots of reasons . . . maybe just to be difficult. But it will only confuse the issue, if we try and do it. It's something Detective Waraday should do, and I bet he already is. People don't have to talk to us, but they do have to answer to the police."

She frowned at me a moment, then said, "Ellie, you are as obstinate as a mule, do you know that? You could argue with a wall and win. Just because this was my idea . . ."

"No, that's not it, Gabrielle," I said quickly. "I think we can use our time in a better way."

She narrowed her eyes. "How?"

"By focusing on the things that Detective Waraday won't see or overhear. He'll get the official story, but we're in the school with the parents and teachers in a way that Detective Waraday can't be. We're here every day—or it seems like I'm here every day right now. We listen and pay attention. That's all we can do."

"Listen and pay attention," she said slowly as if those were foreign concepts. "I don't know. It seems kind of . . . vague." She pursed her lips to one side, then said, "Okay, I don't like it, but we can try it—for a bit. If it doesn't work . . ." She looked at her watch and gave a little shriek. "Oh, I have to get on the road to be at the district office on time."

She swept off, her heels clacking over the tile floor. As I walked inside the office and set the food and drink down on the counter to sign in, Marie followed me in, looking a little breathless. "Hi, Ellie," she said as she hurried around the end of the counter to her desk. She patted her fluffy blond hair into place. "I know better than to wait until after seven-thirty to leave. I just could not get out the door this morning."

"Hi, Marie," I said over the clatter of the little printer as it spit out my volunteer sticker, glad to see Marie's friendly face, which was such a contrast to Peg's usually sour looks. Abby had told me that Marie's husband had worked for an accounting firm that went under because of a financial scandal several years ago. He'd had a heart attack shortly after he lost his job, and Marie had found herself on her own without a retirement plan or investments because they'd lost everything when his company shut down, and up to that point she'd been a part-time employee. Abby said Marie had switched to a full-time position the next year, and I admired Marie for always being upbeat, despite having had a rather rough time, and wondered if any of her sunny disposition would ever rub off on Peg.

I peeled the sticker off the paper and attached it to my shirt. "How was your vacation? Did you go to the beach with some friends?"

"No, just me."

"Oh," I said, surprised and a little saddened for her.

"Don't feel sorry for me. I shopped a lot and read two novels, and started knitting a new sweater," she said as she plucked a sticky note off her wooden cube calendar. Still standing, she read the note and looked up at me. "So, no second round of fundraising?"

I paused, the platter of food balanced in one hand and the juice dangling from my other hand. "Oh, right. I'd completely forgotten about that note. I left it for you last week when I found out the second fundraiser was off the table."

Marie nodded and tossed the note in the trash. "Glad to hear it. There's enough going on during the final weeks of school. The last thing we need is another fundraiser." She flipped the wooden blocks around so that the combination of numbers reflected the correct date, then took off her pink cardigan and draped it over her chair. She gave a quick glance around the office, then lowered her voice as she sat down in her rolling chair. "Of course, you didn't hear that from me."

I smiled conspiratorially at her. "Hear what?"

Marie shifted her chair closer to the desk and punched her computer to turn it on. "Where's Peg? I want all the details about what happened to Klea." We both looked at Peg's desk, which was cluttered with papers, interoffice envelopes, and a folder. A mug of coffee steamed to one side. "She must be around," Marie said. "Probably in the workroom, running copies. I swear she spends half her day in the workroom."

"Really? I never see her in there, and I'm in there a lot."

Marie raised one eyebrow. "Well, that's where she tells Mrs. Kirk she is." Mrs. Kirk's office light was on, but the room itself was empty. I'd seen Mrs. Kirk a few minutes ago when I dropped the kids off, so I knew she wouldn't be back until after the tardy bell rang.

Marie waved a plump hand with pink nails. "You'll have to tell me." She came around the counter and picked up the juice. "Let me help you with this, and you can fill me in on the way. Teachers' lounge?"

I nodded, and we headed out of the office, Marie's pale pink skirt swishing as she walked beside me, her pumps tapping out a sturdy beat as we crossed the lobby, dodging kids streaming in from the drop-off as they hurried to class, their backpacks thumping against their backs. I was in my usual mom uniform of jeans, a casual T-shirt, and boat shoes. I didn't make a sound as we walked along.

Once we'd cleared the lobby and the door to the teachers' lounge swung shut behind us, Marie said, "I heard the news about Klea as soon as I got back in town last night. I couldn't believe it. Poor Klea. What happened?"

I shrugged. "No one knows. The sheriff's department is investigating."

"And she was found during Field Day?"

I nodded as I arranged the paper cups. I summarized what had happened, skipping over Gabrielle's sighting of the body in the closet, as Marie found paper napkins and set them on the table. I removed the cover from the food, and she shook her head as she picked up one of the biscuits and put it on a napkin. "It's shocking, that something like that could happen here at the school." She shook her head again and muttered, "Just shocking," again before taking a bite. I agreed and wadded up the plastic wrap and dusted a few crumbs from the table.

"I bet it was her ex." Marie pointed the half-eaten biscuit at me to emphasize her point.

"Her ex?" I asked. "Why do you say that? I thought she was in the process of getting a divorce."

Marie waved floury fingertips. "All but done. Only a few more days and the papers would have been filed. I heard her telling Mrs. Kirk in the office the other day. Klea was already calling him her ex even though it wasn't official yet. He is apparently quite a character. In fact, you probably know him—or would recognize him. You've heard of Ace Burris Auto Sales?"

"You mean Screaming Ace? That guy that runs commercials on the local channels?"

Marie nodded as she polished off the last bite, then mimicked the announcer's voice, but in a quieter tone than the one I'd heard on the commercials, "Get a screaming good deal from Burris Auto!" Marie's voice returned to normal. "Yep, that's Klea's ex. Or was her soon-to-be ex."

"Really?" I asked, amazed. "I never would have pictured them together. Klea was so quiet and reserved." At the end of every commercial, "Screaming Ace" gave a loud "yee-haw" before his signature pitch line.

"It just goes to show, doesn't it? I don't know the whole story—Klea was a very private person—but I do know that she had a restraining order on him. He wasn't allowed on school property at all."

"Wow. That's kind of scary. I wonder what he'd done."

Marie glanced quickly at the door. "I think—I don't know this for sure—but I think he beat her up."

"Oh, that's terrible."

Marie nodded as she wiped her fingers on the napkin. "It was. Klea came in to work one day, and she was moving stiffly. Mrs. Kirk noticed. You know what Mrs. Kirk is like when she focuses on something. Mrs. Kirk must have suspected something because she had Klea in her office with the door closed as soon as the announcements were over. Klea came out, her eyes all red, and Mrs. Kirk said she'd be out of the office for a few hours. She bundled Klea into her car. Klea took some vacation days, and I didn't think anything else about it until a parent, Mrs. Hudson—

she had a daughter in fourth grade at that time, I think—
she came in a couple of days later for something at the office, and she asked how Klea's ribs were doing. She's a
nurse at the urgent-care walk-in clinic over on Tyler Av-
enue. Mrs. Kirk came flying out of her office and got Mrs.
Hudson out of the office quick as a duck on a June bug.
Nothing else was said, but about a week later, I heard that
Klea had moved into an apartment. It was right after that
happened that Mrs. Kirk told me and Peg that Mr. Burris
was not allowed on school grounds, and if we saw him we
should call the school district's resource officer."

"When was this?" I asked. No wonder Klea had sturdy
locks all over her house and Detective Waraday said the
investigation would focus on off-campus issues.

"Let's see, she put that offer in on that cute little house
across the street a few months ago, so I think this was
about six months before that. Last fall sometime, anyway.
There's the second bell. I have to get back. Let me know if
you hear anything else, will you?"

Peg opened the door and held it so another mom could
walk in with a plastic container of fruit salad. Another
mom followed her in with a breakfast casserole. Marie
and I moved to the door as I said in a quiet voice, "I'm
sure the sheriff's office will keep Mrs. Kirk updated. You'll
probably hear any news before me."

She patted my arm. "But you somehow always manage
to find things out. It must be your knack for organizing
that lets you put it all together. Keep me in the loop."

Abby came through the door, spotted the food, and
said, "Oh, isn't this sweet? I love Teacher Appreciation
Week. So thoughtful of everyone." Her smile included me
and the other moms who had put out food. A group of
teachers arrived and picked up paper plates, commenting

on how good everything looked. The word was out that the food was here, and I knew the room would be busy until the eight-twenty-five bell, with teachers slipping down for a quick bite to eat.

Abby filled her plate and came back to stand by me on the side of the room. "So how are things in the classroom? Are the kids worried or scared?" I asked.

"They are doing okay for the most part. I've had a few kids who have been more clingy than usual, but that's all I've noticed."

"What about the teachers?"

Abby sipped some juice, her face thoughtful. "Well, it's certainly a topic of conversation, but no one seems to know anything specific about what happened. I have heard a few . . . I don't know what you'd call them . . . insinuations, I guess, that Klea was probably poking her nose in where she shouldn't have."

"Really? I hadn't heard that. Only that she was very private."

Abby popped a grape in her mouth and chewed while a group of teachers passed us. When they were clear, she said, "Klea did keep to herself, but there was once that I came back to the school for something I'd left here—a jacket or something like that—and when I walked into my classroom she was at my desk and jumped. She said I'd startled her, and I apologized. We had a laugh, but"— Abby paused, her forehead crinkling into a frown—"I had the impression that she was closing one of my desk drawers when I came through the door."

She took a bite of a biscuit and shook her head as she chewed. "I could be totally wrong. That's why I didn't say anything, but I made sure I didn't leave anything on my desk—or in it—that I didn't mind anyone seeing. I've gotten the impression from a few other teachers that they were . . .

let's say, a little wary of her." Abby frowned again. "Or someone. There's a definite atmosphere lately of tension."

"That's understandable with the circumstances."

Abby tossed her empty plate in a trash can as she said, "No, it's more than just generally being worried. Something is up—and it has been for a while. Klea's death has magnified it—or perhaps given it a focus, would be a better way to say it. I can't put my finger on exactly what it is, but there's definitely an uneasy atmosphere around here." Abby glanced at the clock on the wall. "I have to get back. Thanks for breakfast," she said, and turned to leave.

"Oh, Abby, wait. Do you know Alexa Wells?"

I probably wouldn't have noticed Mrs. Harris, except she was standing directly behind Abby in my line of sight. When I said the name Alexa Wells, Mrs. Harris's whole body went completely still. She had been leaning over the table, scooping a spoonful of the fruit salad onto her plate. But at my words, she froze, the spoon suspended in the air.

Abby's face split into a grin. "I don't know her, but I know *of* her."

Her words broke the spell around Mrs. Harris, and she glanced around with the same expression I'd seen on Nathan's face when I mentioned Rex had suddenly taken to digging holes in the backyard. I hadn't thought the divots in the grass were Rex's doing, but Nathan had confessed that he and Charlie had been pretending they were pirates. Mrs. Harris's face had that same guilty cast to it for a few seconds; then she dumped the fruit on her plate and moved to stand close to us. She kept her gaze focused on the windows, but I had the feeling she was listening intently to every word we said.

"So Alexa Wells doesn't work at the school?" I asked. "Her name sounded familiar, but I couldn't place it."

"Because we talked about reading her book for the book club," Abby said.

"Oh, right," I said as the light bulb went on. "Alexa Wells, the author. Super steamy."

Abby cocked an eyebrow. "More than that. Erotica, actually."

"Oh, is that what she writes? I got a phone call when we were discussing which book to read next at the book club and missed the discussion." I'd returned from my phone call to find that the Alexa Wells title was off the table and the group had agreed on the evocative and haunting women's fiction book that I'd tried to read last night.

"Are you thinking about picking up a copy?" Abby asked. "If you do, I'd keep it out of Livvy's sight. I know what a voracious reader she is. You might not want to have to explain some of the things in there to Livvy."

"No, it's not that. I saw the name on a list that Klea had written." I didn't mention where I'd seen it. I thought it would be better to keep my visit to Klea's house quiet. "The weird thing is that the rest of the list was names of teachers and staff from the school."

Mrs. Harris was standing just behind Abby's shoulder, facing slightly away from me. She had been eating chopped fruit with mechanical movements, but she suddenly sprang to life, tossing her plate that was still half-filled with food into the trash can and striding out of the room. Another teacher was on the way inside and backed out of the doorway as Mrs. Harris motored through.

Abby hadn't noticed Mrs. Harris's abrupt exit.

"Well, maybe Klea wanted to read one of her books and jotted the name down," Abby said.

"But it was in the middle of a list of names, not just scribbled randomly on the page." Right under Mrs. Harris's name, I thought to myself, but didn't say aloud.

"Weird," Abby said in a tone of voice that indicated that it was nothing significant. "Got to run," she said. "Will you be around today?"

"Yes, I think so," I said, already trying to think of when the best time would be to get a minute alone with Mrs. Harris.

Chapter Nine

It was lunchtime before I saw Mrs. Harris again. I'd hung around in the workroom for about an hour, intermittently cruising up and down the first-grade hallway a few times, but Mrs. Harris was always busy moving from student to student, along with the teacher, so I went back to the teachers' lounge and cleaned up the breakfast spread, left the campus and ran a few errands, then returned to the school with two Subway sandwiches and surprised Nathan when I joined him for lunch. He was still cool with his mom sitting beside him in the cafeteria. I wasn't sure Livvy would be too excited about me eating lunch with her, but I'd offer to bring her lunch later in the week and see how she reacted.

As I said good-bye to Nathan when his class left for their after-lunch recess, I spotted Mrs. Harris moving down the hallway toward the workroom. I scooted along and followed her into the empty room. She stood at the copier, one veined hand holding down the lid, while pages whirred out into the bin. She saw me as I walked into the room and she froze again like she had in the teachers' lounge for a second. The copier ejected the last page with a click, then went silent.

I couldn't transfer the questions that had been bumping around in my mind into words. Standing there in her plain white cotton top, sensible dark knit pants, and flat-soled loafers, she looked like the last person in the world who would know anything about Alexa Wells.

She cleared her throat and nodded at me as she opened the copier lid and picked up a book. "Mrs. Avery." The ends of her gray bowl haircut brushed at her cheekbones as she reached down to retrieve the copies from the bin.

"Mrs. Harris, there's something—"

"Let's go outside for a moment," she said, clasping the papers and the book to her flat chest and marching by me.

I turned and followed her through the lobby and out the heavy doors. She glanced around the school's empty porch, then moved to benches that lined the covered area, taking a seat on the one farthest from the school building.

She sat down and balanced the papers and books carefully on her knees. I'd barely had time to sit down beside her on the metal bench before she said, "You want to know why I reacted so oddly in the teachers' lounge this morning when you mentioned Alexa Wells."

I shifted a bit uncomfortably on the bench. "Yes. You seemed to be shocked or startled to hear the name."

She looked at me for a moment, her dark eyes studying me, reminding me of the sparrow that was hopping around the patch of grass behind her. Finally, she said, "And I assume this list that you saw my name on was at Klea's house?"

"How did you know about that?" I asked.

She shifted her dark gaze to the side field and pointed. "Klea's house is just over there. I was on the side field last Friday during recess when I saw Detective Waraday speak to you in the parking lot. Then you walked with him to Klea's house and were in there for quite a while."

"He asked me to look around her house because I'd been inside a few weeks ago for an organizing consultation," I said, figuring that if I shared some information she might return the favor.

"Ah, I see." She squinted across the parking lot, then nodded her head decisively. She turned to me and tilted her head to one side. "I am Alexa Wells."

I blinked. "Oh."

"You half suspected it, didn't you? From my reaction when you mentioned the name."

"The thought crossed my mind—fleetingly. You looked so . . . well, guilty, is the word that comes to mind. But then I thought I must be mistaken."

"Because an old woman like me could never write"—she leaned forward, her eyes twinkling—"erotica?"

I opened my mouth, but she leaned back, a smile on her face, and waved away my response.

"Perfectly logical explanation. Nice old ladies don't write erotica," she said in her normal tone of voice. "Usually. Except in my case. You see, years ago, my husband was diagnosed with a degenerative disease. Eventually, he couldn't work." She gazed at the field surrounding the school, but I could tell her thoughts were turned inward. After a second, she breathed out a little sigh and said, "We'd been fine with both our incomes, but even with insurance, it was difficult to make ends meet on my salary alone. After he passed away, there was a bit of a pension, but it didn't amount to much. Being a teacher's aide doesn't pay well, so I had to either find a way to supplement my income or find a new job. But I do love working with the children here so much that I hated to leave. And everything else I looked into paid a pittance as well. If I was going to be on my feet all day, I'd rather be here at the school with the children than in a department store or something like that."

She straightened the edges of the papers stacked in her lap. "So I decided to try my hand at one thing I've always loved—books. I wrote a historical novel first. It was one of those sweeping family sagas, an epic that covered three— no, four—generations. I sent it to a few agents and the verdict was that it was well written, but nobody wanted epic family sagas. Too dated."

Her laugh lines creased the skin around her eyes. "I put it on the top shelf of my closet. I thought that was that. I should move on to something more practical, but then I heard about erotica and how well some authors were doing. I thought, why not? I'd give it a try. I could write under a pen name and no one would know it was me. That's how things are now. You can be a totally different person on the Internet, and no one has a clue. Well, unless you slip up."

My mind was reeling. I pushed down the many questions that were crowding to the front of my thoughts and focused instead on her last words. I didn't think she was talking about me. "So Klea found out?" I asked.

Mrs. Harris nodded, her face clouding over. "I was foolish. I'm so careful. I never bring anything to school with that name on it—no manuscripts to proofread or anything like that. I never open any of my accounts with that name on any of the school's computers. I always tried to keep Alexa separate from my life here, but I do have a Facebook account in my pen name. I forgot my phone in the workroom one day—set it down while I was making copies and walked off and left it."

Mrs. Harris smoothed back a strand of hair that the breeze had teased across her face. "Klea found it. I'd remembered I'd left the phone and went rushing back to get it, but she'd picked it up and opened the Facebook app, thinking that was the fastest way to see who the phone belonged to." Mrs. Harris's voice became practical. "Very smart of her. Our phones have so much information on them, but sometimes the hardest thing to find is the owner's name."

She lifted a shoulder. "So Klea knew my secret. She'd heard of the books. I could see it in her face when she looked from the phone to me, but she was kind about it. She handed back my phone and said, 'Is this yours? I wasn't sure who it belonged to.' But of course she knew. My picture was right there at the top where you can choose which profile you want to use to post. Next to my public profile about me as everyone knew me, Mrs. Harris, was the profile . . . with a much racier picture for Alexa Wells."

My thoughts skipped ahead. I knew that Mrs. Harris wouldn't want the school to know about her side job. No matter how sweet Mrs. Harris was, there would be some parents who wouldn't want her working with their children. So Klea had to be a threat to Mrs. Harris—whether or not Klea seemed inclined to keep Mrs. Harris's secret. But Mrs. Harris, a murderer . . . ? No, I just couldn't see it.

"Now, I know you're smart and can put two and two together," Mrs. Harris said. "I did, without a doubt, have a reason to silence Klea if I was afraid she'd tell my secret, but I didn't do that. I didn't like that she knew, but I wasn't worried that she'd talk about it. She never mentioned it again, and she wasn't a gossip, so I felt I had nothing to worry about."

"When did this happen? Do you remember?"

"I believe it was right after spring break last year. April or May. I have no idea of the exact date." She waved a hand, brushing away that detail, but I thought it was important.

If Mrs. Harris were worried about keeping Klea quiet, why would she wait nearly a year to kill her? That didn't make sense at all. I breathed a little easier at the thought.

"I have let you in on my little secret for a reason," Mrs. Harris said, her voice brisk. "I know you have an aptitude for finding out interesting things. I could tell from your face this morning that I'd given myself away. And I know you, Mrs. Avery. You're not one to let questions go unanswered, so I decided to take you into my confidence in the hope that you will keep my identity as Alexa hidden."

She held up a finger as I was about to break into her speech. "I know what you're going to say—that this is something that can't be kept from the people investigating Klea's death, and you're absolutely right. I will contact the sheriff's department today and tell the detective in charge the whole story."

One corner of her mouth quirked down. "I had hoped it wouldn't have to come out, but I will certainly explain everything and ask for the investigator's discretion. The detective in charge seemed like a nice young man. I understand that he is interested in the time from seven to nine on Wednesday morning. Fortunately, I have you, Mrs. Dunst, and a whole classroom of six-year-olds who can vouch for me during that time."

"How do you know the times?" I asked, surprised at her exact knowledge.

"Oh, that tidbit was one of the first details to circulate through the school's grapevine after the police began interviewing us. The detective talked to all of us, every teacher, asking each of us about our movements during that time. It wasn't that difficult to deduce when they think Klea was killed."

I nodded, but didn't say anything, thinking that Detective Waraday must have widened the window he was asking about so he wouldn't give away the exact time of death. I knew from talking to Vaughn and being with Gabrielle when she saw the body that it was the time before school started that mattered the most, seven-thirty to eight-thirty. Mrs. Harris had arrived at school Wednesday morning the same time I had. We'd walked into the school together. She didn't realize it, but I was her most critical alibi.

She picked up the papers and pressed them to her chest. "Mrs. Dunst is probably wondering what happened to me. I have to get back. Can I count on you?"

"As long as you tell Detective Waraday, I won't say a word."

"Thank you, Mrs. Avery." She tensed to stand, then stopped and swiveled toward me on the bench. "I have begun to think about retiring. My knees are not what they used to be. All the time sitting crisscross applesauce with the children is taking its toll, but I would like to be the one to make that decision and not have it made for me."

"I can understand that," I said. I hesitated for a second, then said, "Mrs. Harris, can I ask you a question?" She nodded. "Are you doing all right with your writing? No financial worries?" I asked because I'd discovered that some people were really good at hiding their problems. If she needed help, I wanted her to know that she had plenty of friends who would be happy to step in, as well as several resources in the community, like the local food bank, where I sometimes volunteered.

For the first time since we'd begun talking, her shoulders relaxed completely. "I said I was thinking of retiring, didn't I? I wouldn't—or couldn't—do that without my little side business." She winked as she stood to go back into the school.

After she'd left, I sat on the bench for a few more minutes, my thoughts whirling. I wasn't sure what was going on at the school, but one thing I knew for sure was that Klea's list of names *did* mean something.

Organizing Tips for PTA Moms

<u>Timeline for Planning an Event</u>

- Get permission from school/principal
- Decide on date
- Coordinate with room moms to recruit volunteers
- Announce event:
  —PA announcements
  —Flyers posted around school
  —Banner for hallways/drop-off area
  —Social media
- Send reminders to volunteers one week before
- Send reminders to volunteers one day before
- Thank volunteers after the event

Chapter Ten

The next morning, Tuesday, I drove up to the school drop-off line, and Mrs. Kirk slid the van door back. "Bye, kids," I called as they scrambled out.

Mrs. Harris was on car line duty today, standing between the two lanes of one-way traffic, waving cars through or motioning for them to stop to let kids walk through the crosswalk to the building. I waved to her as I went by, and she sent me a cheery smile. Mrs. Harris was Alexa Wells. I still had trouble taking that news in.

I spun the steering wheel and accelerated slowly, mentally shifting my thoughts to the rest of my day. I had an appointment with Margo Wilkins, a mom I knew through the school. She was remodeling her kitchen and wanted me to help her plan the cabinet and pantry layout of her new kitchen so she'd get the most storage out of the space, but before I went to her house, I exited the car circle, then parked on the grassy verge by the side field and walked back into the school.

I stopped by the office to sign in and said hello to Marie and Peg. Marie had walked into the office a few steps ahead of me, and as she stowed her purse beneath her desk and reached over to flip the calendar blocks to the new date, she raised her eyebrows and asked, "So ... any news? Heard anything?"

"Nope," I said, mentally adding, *not that I can talk about.*

She sat down and tilted her head, looking at me out of the corner of her eye. "You're not holding out on us, are you?"

"Of course not," I said quickly.

She turned on her computer, then flicked open a file on her desk. "I only ask because you always seem to find out things," she said with a smile. "You're always in the know."

"Not really. I usually feel like I'm in the dark," I said lightly. "Sometimes people just tell me things," I added, thinking of Mrs. Harris and how she'd spilled the whole story of her secret pen name without me hardly having to ask her anything. She must have been longing to talk about it with someone. It would be hard to have a whole separate life and not be able to share it with anyone. It was only because I'd seen her face at a critical moment when she'd given herself away that I had discovered her secret ... well, that and the fact that she'd wanted to head me off at the pass, so to speak. She'd taken the direct approach and volunteered her secret in the hopes that I would keep quiet. If she'd kept up her end of the bargain with Detective Waraday, then I certainly wasn't going to say anything to Marie about it.

"People trust you," Marie said with a nod. "And I bet you're a good listener." She dropped the file into a metal bin and looked up at me, her face serious. "Don't keep everything to yourself. That could be dangerous."

Peg, who hadn't said a word, let out a snort, and both Marie and I looked toward her. She turned from the cubbyholes, where she had been depositing papers. "Like a mom is going to uncover some deep, dark secret in the school that could endanger her life."

It was the first time Peg had said anything to me that wasn't directly related to school business.

"Peg!" Marie said, her tone scandalized. She shot a quick glance at the door that opened into the lobby, but none of the students were near the door at the moment. "A staff member has been killed," she said in a whisper. "*Someone* did it."

"I thought you were sure it was her husband," Peg said as she banged a stack of papers on the counter to align the edges.

Gabrielle, attired in casual work clothes, an oxford shirt, and khaki pants, came through the door from the lobby as Peg finished her sentence. Gabrielle sang out, "Morning, ladies."

Peg and Marie ignored Gabrielle.

"How did you—?" Marie shifted her glance toward me. I gave a tiny shake of my head to indicate that I hadn't said anything to Peg about what Marie had told me about Klea's husband. Marie spun her chair so that she faced Peg directly. "You were listening at the door to the teachers' lounge." Her voice was accusatory. "I can't believe you would do something so low as eavesdrop."

"I did not eavesdrop." Peg said. "If you don't want people to hear what you have to say, you shouldn't talk about it in a public place where people come and go constantly." She tucked the papers into the crook of her arm and strode out the door of the office, causing Gabrielle to have to sidestep around her.

"Well, I never," Marie said.

Gabrielle watched Peg walk out the door, then swiveled back to face Marie and me. "What's going on?"

Marie waved a hand dismissively at Peg's desk. "Just ignore her. She's having one of her snits. She does that. No big deal."

"What's this about a husband?" Gabrielle asked, her face eager as she looked from Marie to me. "You're not talking about Klea's husband, are you?"

"Why would we be talking about Klea's husband?" Marie said quickly.

Gabrielle dropped her expensive leather purse with heavy gold embellishments onto the tall counter with a *thunk*. "Because Klea is all anyone is talking about." She looked over her shoulder and amended, "Well, when the kids aren't around. But it is the main topic of conversation." She stepped closer and hunched her shoulders over the counter. "Come on, give. What do you know?"

Marie said, reluctantly, "I don't know anything for sure, except that Klea's soon-to-be-ex-husband, Ace Burris, was a first-class louse. He's *got* to be the prime suspect. It's always the spouse, right?"

Gabrielle reared back from the counter. "Ace Burris? But he can't be the prime suspect."

"Why not?" Marie asked in a challenging tone.

"He was at a chamber of commerce breakfast meeting on Wednesday."

"How do you know this?" I asked, thinking that the whole school system and everyone associated with it must have figured out that the time of Klea's death was Wednesday morning.

"Because I'm a member—you really should get involved, Ellie. It will do wonders for your networking," Gabrielle said in an aside. "Anyway, Ace was on the agenda to speak, but I absolutely had to be *here* to do my organizing work, you know, so I had to miss it. But one of my other clients, Crissy Monroe—she's in the chamber, and she went. I talked to her yesterday about the meeting. She said Ace was there. As I said, he was the speaker."

"How long do these meetings go?"

"Let's see, the breakfast meeting starts at seven-thirty and ends about nine or nine-thirty. Since he was speaking, he'd need to be there early. Crissy said he had a Power-Point and everything. He would have had to get there early to set it up. There's no way he could have . . ."

A student walked into the office with a slip of paper. Marie hopped up and took the paper. "Thank you, Holly," she said, and the girl left.

Gabrielle waited until the girl was in the lobby, then said, "There's no way Ace murdered Klea. He couldn't have."

The three of us looked from one to the other. "That's not good news," Marie said.

I agreed. I wanted Klea's murderer caught, and I wanted it to be someone not associated with the school. All through yesterday afternoon and last night, what Mrs. Harris had told me had been on my mind. I'd managed to convince myself that it didn't really matter that Klea knew a secret about Mrs. Harris that the teacher's aide wanted kept quiet.

I'd turned on the news this morning, hoping—half expecting—to hear that an arrest had been made. Not that I expected Mrs. Harris to be arrested, but I'd hoped that Detective Waraday might have turned up a suspect in his original line of investigation that he'd hinted involved someone off campus.

After learning about Klea's soon-to-be ex and the restraining order, and seeing firsthand Klea's DIY security measures at her house, the logical conclusion would seem to be that the murderer was Ace Burris. But if Gabrielle was right and he did have an alibi—and it sounded like an airtight alibi, at that—then it was looking more and more likely that the murderer was associated with the school. Vaughn and Detective Waraday had said Klea kept to herself. Without any close family or friends, where else could the murderer have come from but the school? Everything seemed so normal this morning at the school—kids crisscrossing the lobby, their high-pitched voices filling the halls, the aroma of Tater Tots wafting out from the cafeteria, and the faint sound of basketballs smacking against the blacktop as the first P.E. class of the day began. A cold feeling of dread washed over me at the thought that someone here at the school was a murderer.

Gabrielle leveled her gaze at me. "This listening and waiting isn't working," she said in a low voice. "We need to get serious and find out who killed Klea. The police don't seem to be doing anything."

"You know that's not true," I said to Gabrielle. "They're working on it. They're just not keeping us updated on their progress."

Gabrielle gave an impatient toss of her head and returned to her normal tones. "But it amounts to nothing. Have they arrested anyone? No. What are they doing? Who are their suspects?"

"If Ace is out of the running, I don't know who else could have done it. It's not like Klea had . . . enemies," Marie said.

Mrs. Kirk entered the office and our group immediately broke up, Marie moving to her desk, and Gabrielle going to sign in. I went to the teachers' lounge to check on the food for the day, and was happy to see that the parents on the Tuesday Teacher Appreciation crew had come through. Snacks and drinks were spread across the table. A tray of homemade brownies tempted me, but I resisted, promising I'd treat myself to a Hershey's Kiss. They were my Achilles' heel when it came to chocolate, but at least they were small doses of chocolate.

Ms. McCormick was helping herself to one of the delicious brownies, and I thought of the list of names Klea had written down. Mrs. Harris's name had been on it, along with her pen name, something she wanted to hide.

Ms. McCormick's name had been on that, too. Maybe Ms. McCormick was hiding something as well? Her blue dress looked nothing like a ball gown, but with her blond hair up and the color of her dress making her eyes look even more intently blue, she reminded me more than ever of an illustration of a fairy tale princess.

She caught sight of me as she took a bite of the brownie. She put a hand over her pink lips and looked a little embarrassed. Swallowing quickly, she said, "I know it's early, but I just couldn't wait. They looked so good."

"I'm not throwing stones," I said, picking up some napkins that had fallen on the floor and throwing them in the trash. "I love chocolate. And the food is here for you— you're supposed to enjoy it."

"Thanks. I can't believe that the parents bring in food all week. This really is the nicest school. The one I was at before didn't do anything for Teacher Appreciation. Not even a card."

"Really? I thought this was your first teaching assignment."

For a second, a stricken look crossed her face and I had the funniest feeling that internally she was muttering a curse word. Moments later, her face transformed as she smiled brightly at me. "Oh, it is." She picked up a few almonds and added them to her plate. "I mean, it is my first teaching *job*. I was a substitute before."

I took more napkins out of a cabinet and placed them on the table. "Where was that?"

"Oh, it was in another state. Look, someone made a fruit tart—I just adore those." She moved a wedge of the tart onto her plate. "So you're"—she checked my name tag—"Livvy's mom. She's great."

"Thanks," I said, noticing how fast she'd changed the subject. She really didn't want to talk about her other job.

"I enjoy having her in my math class."

"How is everything going . . . after Klea, I mean? Do you think the kids are okay?"

"Oh, yes. Now that we're back in a routine, the kids are fine. Well, you know what I mean. It's hard to have a routine the last weeks of school, but I think they feel safe and that's the important thing."

"Yes, it is. That's what we all want, to feel safe, but I can't help worrying. Did you know Klea?"

"No." She shook her head and leaned back against the counter as she cut a bite of the tart. I could have sworn she looked completely at ease. She didn't mind discussing Klea at all. "So horrible what happened to her. I mean, I never even talked to her, but to think about that happening . . ." She shivered.

Gabrielle poked her head in the door. "Ellie, there you are," she said in an accusatory tone, as if I'd been hiding from her. Peg followed her into the room and picked up a plate.

Ms. McCormick stiffened, and her face changed back to a guarded look. She gave me a quick nod. "Nice chatting with you," she said, and left the room. I glanced between Gabrielle and Peg. It seemed that just the arrival of one of the women had caused Ms. McCormick to leave the room immediately. Which one was it?

"I had to check and make sure everything was set up here," I said to Gabrielle. Peg didn't say anything, just filled her plate and left the room without looking at either one of us.

Gabrielle watched her go. "Well, she must have gotten up on the wrong side of the bed."

"I'm glad I don't work in the office." I glanced at the clock on the wall. "Speaking of work, I have to go."

Gabrielle held up a hand. "Oh, no. You can't just run out of here. We need to talk. What have you found out? I'll walk with you."

"Gabrielle—" I sighed. "I don't have anything to tell. It seemed like Klea's husband might be . . . involved, but apparently not. That's all I know." I wasn't about to tell her about Mrs. Harris's pen name, and the only other bit of information that I'd picked up—the list of names—was so vague that I didn't want to mention it. Gabrielle was the sort to charge ahead without thinking, and I didn't want her to do anything that would endanger herself—or make Detective Waraday angry with me. "All we can do is try and find someone with a connection to Klea—someone who was either angry enough or scared enough of her to want her dead."

Gabrielle had been walking with me as we spoke in low voices. We paused in the lobby, and she sent me a frustrated look. "There's got to be more we can do."

I decided the only way to deal with Gabrielle was to handle her the same way I did when the kids were determined to help me do something—usually with something that I didn't want their assistance with, like painting a room. "Okay, here's something. See if you can find out if anyone at the school was close to Klea. As far as I can tell, she didn't have any friends."

"Not have any friends? How could that be?"

"She kept her distance."

"That's . . . weird," Gabrielle said. Clearly keeping people at a distance was a foreign concept for her. "Okay, I'll ask around."

The faint sound of a horn honking repeatedly filtered through the closed doors at the front of the school as someone's car alarm went off.

"Well, weird or not, that's how she was," I said. "See if you can find anyone she talked to or confided in."

Gabrielle nodded. "I can do that."

"Subtly," I said.

"Pshaw," Gabrielle said with a wave of her hand, and moved down the hall.

I'd never actually heard anyone use the southern expression *pshaw*, except in old movies, and I wasn't exactly sure what it meant, but I had a feeling from Gabrielle's attitude that it translated loosely to something along the lines of *don't be an idiot*.

I shook my head and went into the office to sign out. Peg was there, her plate of food on her desk. She didn't look up from her monitor. Marie, on the other hand, smiled at me as I signed out. I motioned to her with a tilt of my head, and she hopped up from her chair and walked with me across the lobby. "Do you know anything about Ms. McCormick?" I asked as I pushed open the heavy door. Humid air swept inside and the volume of the car alarm, which was still going on, increased.

"No, just that she's from somewhere out of state."

"Is this her first teaching job?" I asked, to see what Marie would say.

"Yes, I think so. I can do a . . . little digging, see what her application says. Discreetly, of course."

I smiled at her, knowing that she would keep anything she found to herself. "That would be great. I don't know anything, but I have a feeling it might be important."

"Gotcha. Check in with me tomorrow."

"Okay. Thanks."

Marie tilted her head and looked over my shoulder out the door I held half open. "Isn't that your minivan?"

I turned. The taillights of the van were flickering on and off in time with the honking horn. "Yes. How embarrassing." I felt my pockets for the key. "I probably pressed the panic button on the key fob somehow."

I found my keys, clicked the button, and silence fell for a moment until the school bell rang. I waved to Marie and headed across the school property to walk along the chain-link fence by the side yard, but when I rounded the side of the van, I stopped in my tracks. A spider web of cracks covered the driver's-side window around a gaping, concave hole.

Chapter Eleven

Idon't know how long I stood there, stunned by the vandalism. This was a nice, safe neighborhood. Things like windows getting broken—especially in the middle of the day—didn't happen. I shook myself out of my frozen state and took a few steps closer to the door. I peered inside the van though the hole radiating out from the hole.

I didn't touch anything because a network of jagged cracks radiated out from the hole, but I saw that a brick rested on the driver's seat. Tiny chunks of glass pooled around it, glittering in the sunlight like diamonds. I twisted around and scanned the street and surrounding houses, but the front yards were empty of neighbors—not a single person moving a sprinkler or weeding a flowerbed. Faint shouts from the kids at recess were the only sounds.

With a sigh, I took out my phone. I'd already rescheduled once with Margo when Gabrielle convinced me to search the school with her on the morning of Muffins with Mom. Now I called Margo to tell her I needed to postpone our appointment again.

*   *   *

"Random vandalism?" Mitch asked later that night, disbelief heavy in his voice.

"I know," I said. "I don't really believe it either." I sat down on the bed and held the phone in place with my shoulder while I tied the laces of my tennis shoes. Dinner was over, the dishes were washed, and the kids were in their rooms doing the last bits of homework. There wasn't much homework at this time of year, but the teachers were still sending a few assignments home for the kids to do in the evening.

Rex was prancing back and forth letting out low-level whines, sensing that a walk around the neighborhood was imminent. In Rex's mind, footwear signaled a trip around the block, which was what I had planned, but the walk could wait while I talked to Mitch. I had no idea when he'd be able to call again.

"Ellie," Mitch said with a sigh in his voice, "what *have* you been doing?"

I flopped back on the bed and stared at the ceiling fan. "Just all the usual stuff—running the household, taking care of the kids, *trying* to meet with clients."

"All the usual stuff," Mitch repeated, "which, I know, means that you're also keeping your eyes and ears open for anything that might be a tad off or strange. And possibly dropping a few questions here and there. Am I right?"

"Since we're not on a video call, I should tell you that I'm rolling my eyes."

"I know you are." Mitch's chuckle came over the phone. "Do I know you or what?"

"Yes, and that is both a blessing and a curse," I said.

"I wish I was there with you," Mitch said, his tone becoming more serious.

"I know. That would be really nice. How many more

days?" Mitch was much better at keeping track of how many days he had left on his trips than I was. His constantly changing schedule was hard to keep up with, to begin with, and if he was gone on a long deployment, it was easier for me if I didn't focus on the exact number of days until he came home. Anything over a week was a little depressing to contemplate. It was usually easier to roll with the punches until the trip was over.

"Ten days until I'm back, and we can have your delayed Mother's Day celebration." Mother's Day had actually been last Sunday, but because of Mitch's rather unpredictable schedule, we celebrated events and special days when we were together and that wasn't always when those days showed up on the calendar. Since Mitch's training exercise happened to fall over Mother's Day, we postponed celebrating that day until he got back. We did the same with birthdays and holidays.

"I'm looking forward to it," I said.

Letting out another round of low whimpers, Rex pressed against my leg. I rubbed his side with my foot.

"So back to the car," Mitch said. "Did you call the police?"

"Yes, and the insurance. It's all covered. I have a copy of the police report, but the officer spent about as long on it as Livvy did on the first draft of her science report."

"So about ten minutes."

"Yep. Even after I told him about Klea's death. He said he'd mention it to Detective Waraday, but I could tell the officer didn't think it was related. Like I said, random vandalism was his assessment."

"I don't agree. Have you heard or seen anything that could make someone nervous?"

"Possibly," I said, thinking of Mrs. Harris. But she'd told Detective Waraday her secret—hadn't she?

I should ask Detective Waraday and make sure she had followed through with him. But even if she hadn't talked to Detective Waraday, I couldn't see her throwing a brick through the van window any more than I could see her strangling Klea. Without giving away her secret or mentioning her pen name, I gave Mitch an outline of what Mrs. Harris had told me.

"And you don't want to share names or specifics?" Mitch asked.

"No, I can't. I promised, but I will check with Detective Waraday and make sure he knows. If he does know about the situation, what would be the good of tossing a brick at my car? The secret is already out—to a limited audience, granted—but it's not totally hidden anymore."

"Maybe this person changed their mind and regretted telling you the secret. Maybe it was a warning to continue to keep quiet. You know, no talking to the other teachers."

"Kind of an unspecific way to do it." Rex walked around to the foot of the bed and poked his nose over the edge, fixing me with the saddest brown-eyed expression that I'd seen since yesterday at this time.

"Oh, I think they got their message across." Mitch paused a moment, then said, "Or maybe it was a completely different person. Any other tidbits you've heard or prodding questions you've asked?"

"Ms. McCormick is hiding something, I'm sure of it. But I don't know specifically what it is." I recounted my conversation with her as Rex kept his gaze fastened on me and whined a few times just to make sure I didn't forget about him.

"Breaking car windows after a conversation like that would be going to quite an extreme," Mitch said, "but it looks as if you've made someone nervous."

"Or I've been the random victim of senseless vandalism."

"Odd that I actually like the sound of that better. Look, there's a chance this exercise may get cut short. Weather issues. I could be home in a day or two."

"That would be great," I said. "And you don't have to say it. I'll be careful."

We said good-bye, and I hung up. "Come on, Rex, let's go."

With a joyful spasm that shook his whole body, he pranced to the back door.

When we returned a few minutes later, I punched in the code to open the garage and then walked by the van. The new window had been ordered and should arrive tomorrow. But, for now, a clear piece of plastic covered the window, a temporary fix that the repair shop had put in place in case it rained, which was always a possibility in Georgia. After the police had finished, I'd gone back to the school and found Vaughn, who'd brought a cardboard box for me, along with a dustpan. We'd cleaned up the glass from inside the van, then scoured the grass, looking for any tiny pieces that we might have missed, but it seemed all the glass was inside the van, not outside it.

I went inside the house, hung up Rex's leash, and then quizzed Livvy on the words for her last spelling test of the school year. An hour later, the kids were tucked in bed and I had an old movie playing on television, the barely audible dialogue filling the quiet house. I was seated at the dining room table going over my "homework" with Rex curled up under the table at my feet. I rubbed my foot along his back as I flipped from one page to the next in Nathan's homework folder, dutifully scribbling my initials on each page near the letter or number grade.

Tuesdays were homework folder days, which meant the kids brought home their work for the week, and I went over it. I thought it was absurd that the teachers required that the parents initial each paper. I didn't need a threat to keep up with my kids' homework, but it seemed that some parents did because some teachers dropped students' grades if they didn't return the homework papers with their parents' initials.

I had already gone through both Livvy's and Nathan's folders earlier in the evening while they were with me, going over the questions that they'd missed and praising them for their good grades. I signed Nathan's last homework paper, slid them all back into the pocket, and flipped to the front of the folder, where I recorded the date and signed my John Hancock on one of the last lines of the form. I was glad it was the end of the year and the avalanche of paperwork was tapering off.

I slapped the folder closed, then pulled Livvy's folder to me and worked my way through this week's stack, signing off on all papers. Finished, I stacked the papers and slid them back into the pocket, but something blocked them. The sheaf of papers wouldn't go in all the way. I removed them and pulled out a folded note that I must have missed earlier.

It was a piece of white copy paper, folded in thirds and held together with a piece of tape. Folded and taped notes placed in take-home folders were not a good thing. Usually, they were a message from the office about some sort of problem. Livvy and Nathan were both good students. They kept up with their work, mostly, and behaved in class, so we didn't usually receive notes from the office.

I smoothed the wrinkles out, worked the tape free, and unfolded the note, expecting it to contain a list of Livvy's overdue library books or something along those lines, but it was only a few lines of text, carefully hand printed. It read, *Back off. Klea was nosy and look what happened to her.*

Organizing Tips for PTA Moms

Staying in touch with other parents is critical and it's easier than ever with digital tools. Yahoo Groups allows you to create a group and invite members, then share information through emails and a group calendar. Companies like SignUpGenius and Volunteer Spot provide free online volunteer sign-up forms and reminders, which are sent through emails and texts. The advantage to this type of system is that the contact list is maintained for you through the site. You can easily send an invite to members of the list and not have to weed through long "reply all" emails.

Chapter Twelve

Detective Waraday placed the note inside a plastic sleeve. "How much did you handle it?"

"Quite a bit, I'm afraid. It got pushed to the bottom of the folder, and I ran my hand across it to flatten out the wrinkles."

Detective Waraday made a "hmm" sound and read over the note again.

Rex, now fully awake, was sitting by my knee at the table, keeping a sharp eye on Detective Waraday.

"And you found it when?" Detective Waraday asked.

"Just now. I dropped it and called you."

Well, I'd actually dropped it on the table and contemplated doing several things, from ignoring it to burning it, but in the end, I'd known I had to call Detective Waraday. I was glad the kids were asleep—and they had to be or they would have popped into the living room at the sound of a deep male voice, expecting to see Mitch, whose job had him arriving and departing at all hours. I was relieved I didn't have to explain why a detective was at our house.

Detective Waraday pointed to the folders with their lines of signatures on the outside. "Tell me about these homework folders. Who has access to them?"

"Livvy is in fifth grade and those students change classes for different subjects, but they have a homeroom class-room. That's where each teacher sends all the papers for the week. Either the teacher, the teacher's aide, or a parent volunteer sorts the papers into the files for each student. Once a week, the papers are transferred from the files to a folder and the kids bring them home. I sign off on every-thing, and it all goes back the next day. I did it last year for Nathan's class." It was a fairly mindless volunteer job, but I actually preferred other ways of helping out, like helping with the book fair or Field Day, which were more active and not so monotonous.

Detective Waraday tapped the plastic sleeve with the note on the table. Rex's ears pricked at the sound. "And the classrooms aren't locked during the day when students are out of them for recess or lunch." He looked up from the paper. "I found that out last week when I was at the school."

"No, they're not."

"So anyone—teacher, staff, or student—could have written this note and slipped it in your daughter's folder, knowing that it would go home to you today. I'll send it to the techs, but there probably won't be any distinguishable prints on it since it has been handled so much. But we'll check." He rubbed his hand across his forehead as he said, "Someone is not happy with you, Mrs. Avery."

A statement like that would have normally "gotten my back up," a description I'd heard members of Mitch's very Southern family use, but Detective Waraday said it in a flat tone, not as if he was laying blame. The bags under his eyes made him look almost mature, and the way he'd wearily dropped into the chair at the table indicated that he was tired. I wondered how many hours he'd worked today.

"I really don't know who it could be," I said. "Ms. McCormick did act kind of strange today when I asked her where she taught before she came to North Dawkins. But other than Ms. McCormick and one other person . . . I'm not sure . . . were you contacted . . . ?"

"A certain person from the school got in touch with me and told me about her . . . um"—a smile flickered at the corners of his mouth—"literary activities, let's call them. I don't think this note has anything to do with that."

"That's good. I was wondering because, if she had changed her mind and hadn't talked to you, then this could have been from her, but since you know about the situation . . ."

"Yes, the cat is out of the bag, at least where the investigation is concerned. She came forward voluntarily, so I doubt she'd double back and attack you. She doesn't seem the sort to regret her actions."

"No, I agree."

"This Ms. McCormick you mentioned who acted odd— what happened?"

I told him how she'd hadn't wanted to talk about her other job and how the general impression at the school was that this was her first job. "But when I asked her about it today, she said it *was* her first teaching job—that she'd only been a substitute before. I got the impression that she wasn't telling the truth . . . or not the whole truth."

Detective Waraday raised his eyebrows, looking energized for the first time that night. "A possible lie, then. Lies are always interesting. And her name was on that list you spotted in Mrs. Burris's house." He didn't say anything else, but he wrote something in the notebook that he removed from his pocket. "Anyone else upset with you?"

Noting that he seemed to have changed his opinion about the list from Klea's house, I said, "No, not unless you count my client I keep canceling on or Peg in the school office, but she seems to be upset with everyone all the time."

"An Eeyore," he said with a nod.

"I'm sorry?"

"I met her the other day when I interviewed all the teachers and staff. She's an Eeyore. We have had one at our office. Generally gloomy disposition and always looking on the dark side."

"Yes, I think that's a good description of her."

"Melancholy," Detective Waraday said. "So I don't know that we should mark her down as an enemy of yours just yet."

"She was on Klea's list."

"As was Marie Ormsby."

"That's true," I said, "But I don't think Marie is upset with me."

Detective Waraday didn't reply, just made another note, and I had a feeling that he would be chatting with both Peg and Marie tomorrow.

"I did ask Marie what she knew about Ms. McCormick," I said, hoping that getting that fact out there now might pre-empt any recriminations from Detective Waraday later. "Marie said that Ms. McCormick was from out of state."

Detective Waraday nodded as he studied the note in the plastic sleeve. He tilted it toward me. "Do you recognize the handwriting?"

I'd had plenty of time after I made the call and waited for him to arrive to study the note. "No. It's so perfect, it's almost like it was printed on a computer." Each stroke of every letter in the hand-printed note was made with precision. None of the letters were higher, lower, wider, or fatter than the others. None of the letters had a stroke that trailed off below or soared above the others. "It does remind me a little of the printing I've seen on architects' drawings, but those have some style . . . or flare to them with some of the strokes extended or angled. This writing is even more precise than that."

"Presumably done to disguise the handwriting."

"Why wouldn't someone just have used a computer? Why go to the trouble of handwriting it?" I asked. It was one of the many questions that had been going through my mind while I waited for Detective Waraday.

"Maybe they didn't have time. If someone wanted to get a note into the folders, they'd have to slip in the classroom when it was empty. Maybe the person saw their opportunity and took it—a spur-of-the-moment kind of thing. And then there is also the fact that most documents created on a computer are traceable even if they are deleted. Perhaps the person knew that and didn't want any record of these words on their computer, which would be pretty far thinking. But it would also be very wise. With all the school computers linked to the school district's database, it would probably be more difficult to make sure no record of the words existed."

He inched his chair back from the table. "After we check for prints, I'll send it off to the state crime lab, see what they can come up with related to the handwriting. And then there is your car. I got the message about it this evening. Mind if I have a look?"

"No, not at all." I stood, and he followed me to the garage. I flicked on the light, and he moved around to the driver's side, where he examined the doorframe. I waited in the doorway. Rex positioned himself by my leg.

"It was a brick, you said?"

"Yes. It was inside the car."

"Where is it now?"

"Probably in a Dumpster at the school." I told him how Vaughn had helped me clean up.

Detective Waraday nodded. "Perfectly reasonable for the officer who arrived in response to your call to assume it was random, but in light of this"—he held up the note—"well, maybe not so random. The brick probably wouldn't hold fingerprints very well, but I'll send someone out to look for it tomorrow and canvass the street to see if anyone saw anything."

"Thank you. That would make me feel a little better."

He came inside and headed for the front door. I locked the door to the garage, then followed him to the front door, Rex at my heels. "The brick through your car window could have been random, but this"—he raised the paper and the plastic sleeve caught the reflection of the porch light—"is a threat, directed specifically at you. I suggest you lock up and keep your head down. The farther you stay away from the investigation, the better off you'll be."

"I know. Don't worry. I'm not asking any more questions. It's too dangerous."

And that was my intention. I'd had plenty of time to think things over while I stared at the note, jumping at each little creak the house made. It was just too dangerous to keep asking questions. I had two kids to think of. For their sake, I had to back off. I knew Gabrielle wouldn't agree, but she'd have to deal with it.

Despite knowing that Detective Waraday had the note and that the brick-throwing incident was being investigated more thoroughly, I didn't sleep too well. The next morning, I was afraid that the bags under my eyes rivaled Detective Waraday's.

With the temporary plastic covering on the driver's window pulsating as I drove, I dropped the kids at school, then went to the glass repair shop. It was next door to a shopping center, which contained a gym and a newly opened boutique that sold decorative knickknacks and personal items. While my window was being fixed, I walked over to the boutique to look for Teacher Appreciation gifts for the kids to give to their teachers. I'd been so busy with everything going on at the school that buying gifts for the teachers had fallen completely off my to-do list. I found several cute notebooks embellished with different school themes—math and science problems and the titles of classic children's stories—and purchased one for each of the teachers, along with some cool pens.

As I walked back to the window repair shop, the repairman, a guy in his mid-twenties, stepped into the parking lot. He waved and crossed the lot to me. "All fixed. We're running it through the car wash and will have it out here in a minute. You can pay at the desk inside," he said, handing me an invoice.

"So have you had a lot of these types of repairs lately?" I asked as we walked to the office portion of the shop.

"Vandalism, you mean? Nah, you're the first we've had in, oh, probably two or three months. We see mostly chips and cracks from rocks hitting cars while they are on the road." He opened the door for me.

"Thanks," I said, and went in to pay my bill. Since this was the only repair shop in this area, they'd know if there had been an uptick in vandalism of car windows. It looked more and more likely that the brick through the window had been a random incident.

I powered the new window up and down a few times to make sure it worked, then set out to mark off the rest of the items on my to-do list, putting thoughts of Klea, bricks through windows, and threatening notes out of my mind. I ran by an ice cream shop, bought some gift cards, and tucked them into each notebook. I'd have the kids wrap them tonight—well, gift-bag them—and we'd be set.

Then I ran home, switched the load of laundry that I'd started that morning to the dryer, and tossed in a new load to wash. I hit the road again to pick up today's food for Teacher Appreciation. It was Wednesday, so that meant sub sandwiches were on the menu.

I swung by the sub shop to pick up a platter of sandwiches, glad that Mia had coordinated all the details, even the payment, beforehand. All I had to do was take the sandwiches and chips to the school.

A few minutes later, I parked in the school parking lot, as close to the main doors as I could get. I wouldn't be parking along the chain-link fence anymore. My phone rang. I saw it was Gabrielle and braced myself. "Gabrielle, I'm so glad you called," I said. "Quite a bit has happened—"

"For me, too, honey. That's why I called. You won't believe what I found out. Talk about juicy gossip—"

"I'm not really interested in gossip," I said quickly.

"But it's not any old gossip. This has to do with the school. There are some mighty shady things going on at that school."

"Gabrielle, before you say anything else, you should know that I'm done with poking around, trying to find out what happened to Klea."

Gabrielle's rich chuckle sounded through the line. "I don't believe that for a minute."

"Well, it's true. A brick was thrown through my van window, and I got a threatening note. I can't continue to ask questions and snoop around. It's too dangerous."

"What did the note say? Did it demand money?"

I'd gotten out of the van, slid the side door open, and reached to pick up the sandwiches, but I paused. "Money? No, of course not. The note said I should back off and that Klea was nosy and 'look what happened to her,' to be exact. It was a threat."

The line was silent a few beats. "Oh. Well. That is a bit disconcerting," Gabrielle said quietly. Then her voice changed to a more upbeat tone. "But I know you. You won't let that sidetrack you."

"No, I'm afraid it has. I'm done."

"Of course you're not. You only think you are. Now, I have a meeting starting in two minutes, so I can't talk any longer, but I want to get together with you and discuss this info I have."

"Gabrielle—" I sighed as the buzz of the disconnected line sounded in my ear. I picked up the sandwiches, dropped my phone into the van's console, and locked the van. I'd only be in the school for a few minutes and didn't need to bring in my purse and phone.

I was backing though the main door, using my shoulder to open it as I balanced the tray of sandwiches, when a voice near my ear said, "There you are." I nearly dropped the tray.

Marie, today in a pink shirt and white short-sleeved sweater, reached out to steady the tray of sandwiches. "I've been watching for you all morning. You said you'd check with me first thing this morning about . . ." She stopped speaking abruptly as a line of students walked through the lobby. Ms. McCormick, the skirt of her blue shirtwaist dress swishing, was in the lead. As she passed us, she glared at me, and instinctively I fell back a step. She looked nothing like Livvy's description of a fairy tale princess. Instead, with her angry face, she looked more like an evil villainess.

As Ms. McCormick disappeared into the cafeteria, Marie let out a whoosh of breath. "I'm glad I wasn't standing any closer to you. We'd both be in cinders if looks could kill."

"Why is she mad at me? What's happened?" I asked.

"Detective Waraday was in first thing this morning, asking all sorts of questions about Klea," Marie said. "He started with me and Peg in the office. Why didn't you tell me about the note you received?"

"Detective Waraday told you about the note?"

"Showed us a copy, even."

"Oh." I hadn't expected Detective Waraday to show the note to anyone at school, but of course that was silly. How could he question people unless he mentioned the note? And if he showed them a copy he could watch their reactions.

"Of course we were floored," Marie continued. "But then he wanted to speak to Ms. McCormick, which I thought was odd. Why her, of all the teachers? But now that I've done that little bit of research for you, I think I understand."

It didn't seem odd to me. Mrs. Kirk, Marie, Peg, and Ms. McCormick were the four people left on Klea's list, but of course Marie didn't know about the list. Although why Detective Waraday would include Marie in his questioning, I didn't understand. Marie had been out of town the morning Klea died, but I guessed he was just being thorough.

"Oh, it's sub sandwiches today," exclaimed a teacher coming out of the cafeteria, and I said to Marie, "I'd better get this set up."

She nodded. "Meet you back here in a jiffy."

I put the tray in the teachers' lounge and set up bags of chips alongside it, with napkins and paper plates, then headed back to the lobby. Marie emerged from the office with some papers, which she handed to me. "Look at this."

The page on top was a job application form.

"Ms. McCormick's job application? How did you get this?" I asked.

Marie smiled. "I have my ways."

She was the longest employed person at the school. She'd been here even longer than Mrs. Kirk, so I supposed she knew how to get a hold of files. "Remind me never to cross you," I said with a grin.

"Wouldn't be wise. Now, look at that." She pointed to the job history.

"It's blank . . . but she said she worked before. Even if it was only substitute teaching, shouldn't she have put it down as prior experience?"

"Yes, she should have," Marie said as I quickly scanned the rest of the form. Ms. McCormick had a degree in elementary education from a university in North Carolina and had listed her address as an apartment in Charlotte.

I thought of Detective Waraday's comment about Ms. McCormick and a potential lie.

"There's more," Marie said.

I flipped to the next page and realized it was a wage and earnings statement. I pushed the papers back into Marie's hands. "No. That's too personal."

Marie frowned at me. "This has nothing to do with the amount of money she makes. Look here, at her name. See how it's spelled?" Marie pointed to the wage form.

"Jill McCormick," I said, not seeing her point.

Marie flipped back to the other page. "And here, on the job application? I don't think you looked at it very carefully."

She pushed both papers back at me, pointing to the names. I *had* read them too quickly. The name on the job application had an extra letter. She'd listed her name as "Jill MacCormick."

"So the job application has MacCormick, but her wage and earning statement has McCormick? Which one is right?"

"Her name is Jill McCormick. I checked the database. We have to verify everyone's name with a government-issued ID, so I'm pretty sure that's her real name," Marie said.

"So the name on the application must be a typo," I said. "It looked like it was filled in on one of those online application systems. It would be easy to make a mistake. She probably caught it when she was hired."

"I don't think so. I know the process. The job application is the basis for the background check. Jill *Mac*Cormick would have been the name that was checked, not her real name. Once an individual clears the district's background check, and they're hired, then they fill out all the tax paperwork. I was curious what a background check on the name 'Jill McCormick' would bring up in North Carolina, so I did a little searching online on my own this morning."

She handed me the last sheet of paper. It was a printout of a newspaper article. I recognized Ms. McCormick's face under the headline, which I whispered, " 'Teacher arrested in drug bust'? *Ms. McCormick* was involved in a drug arrest?"

Marie nodded, her lips pressed together.

"Oh, this is not good," I said, looking at the ceiling. While parents might not like a teacher writing erotica, a teacher with a drug arrest in her past was a completely different level of complication. Just for starters, the school district held Red Ribbon Week, which taught students the dangers of drugs and warned them away from them, every year. Everyone—the parents, Mrs. Kirk, the other teachers—would be upset at the news about Ms. McCormick.

Marie said, "You can see why she changed her name. Just one little letter, and she becomes a whole new person. The background check doesn't show anything—no drug bust—nothing." Marie pointed to the name of the newspaper. "That's actually in South Carolina, so I assume she put North Carolina as her permanent address, hoping to confuse the issue even more. I found a record of a Jill McCormick employed at an elementary school in Lexington, South Carolina."

"Which didn't show up on the background search because the name that was checked was spelled with an extra 'a.'"

"Right. And then once she had the job here, she gave us the correct name and Social Security number, probably hoping that the district wouldn't check into it again. And, of course, they didn't. We can't afford to do yearly background checks." Marie fiddled with a rubber band that was around her wrist. "Do you think Ms. McCormick had anything to do with Klea?"

"I honestly don't know, but this is quite a secret."

Marie nodded. "Something worth killing for." She lowered her voice. "She'll lose her job, for sure, once this comes out. And then what will she do? She won't be able to find work again."

"Well, she found this job, didn't she?" I said grimly.

Marie's forehead wrinkled. "Do you think she could do it again? I don't know. I think she was lucky. Someone should have cross-checked her ID with the name on the background check and her application. If Klea found out somehow . . ."

"How could she have known?" I asked.

Marie shrugged. "I don't know. Klea was always going through the trash. She was supposed to just dump it, but I saw her, digging around in the papers. She liked to know things. If she *did* find out about Ms. McCormick . . ."

"Have you shown this to Detective Waraday?" I asked.

"No, I didn't dig into it until after he asked to see Ms. McCormick this morning when he finished talking to Peg and me."

"So did he talk to Ms. McCormick?"

"No, she was in the office and told him that she had classes to teach, but she could talk to him during lunch. We're shorthanded today. Mrs. Kirk has already had to call for another substitute for a second-grade teacher who got sick. Mrs. Kirk is actually covering the class until the sub arrives."

"But this must be Ms. McCormick's lunch," I said. "Remember, she just went into the cafeteria."

"That's her students' lunch. She stays with them until they go out to recess, then she gets a thirty-minute lunch while they are outside." Marie glanced at the hall clock. "I'm sure she'll be along shortly."

A sheriff's car pulled up into the drop-off circle and parked in front of the main doors. "There's Detective Waraday," I said. "You better make sure he sees those papers before he talks to her."

"Me? But you asked me for it. Remember, you wanted me to do a little digging?" She pushed the papers toward me.

"No." I held up a hand. "I can't. You heard about the note. I'm out. No more questions. It's too dangerous. I told Detective Waraday last night that I'm done. I can't go running up to him with all this now. You found it. You should be the one to tell him about it."

A car door slammed, and Marie went a shade paler. "I'm not supposed to be in these files. I could lose my job."

I looked at her, trying to imitate Rex's pleading look. "You're retiring in—what?—two weeks. What can they do to you?"

"My pension may be tiny, but I want it." She flapped the papers. "Say you found them on the counter with your name on them. A little bird left them for you. Please, Ellie." She looked at me beseechingly. "I need that pension."

"Oh, all right."

She pressed the papers into my hands and twirled away, her pink skirt flaring out as she skittered back to the office.

I turned toward Detective Waraday. As he came in the doors, I held out the papers. "You know what I said about not being involved anymore? Well, turns out it's not so easy to bow out. People know I'm involved. I was given this today."

Detective Waraday frowned as he took it. "Did this person have a name?"

"Yes, but they would prefer you didn't know it came from them."

Detective Waraday scanned the documents. "Well, we'll see if that is possible. Depends on what . . ."

He must have picked up on the discrepancy in the last names because he looked back and forth from the first two pages for a few moments, then went on to the last page, the newspaper article. He looked up at me. "What did I tell you? Lies are always interesting." He went into the office, and a short time later, Peg came out of the office and went into the cafeteria. I went into the teachers' lounge, checked the sub platter, put out more napkins, and cleaned up a plate with crumbs someone had forgotten. When I left, I automatically headed for the office, but realized I'd forgotten to sign in in the first place.

I'd barely cleared the threshold of the office when Peg burst in, bumping into my shoulder and causing me to stumble. "Ms. McCormick is gone."

Chapter Thirteen

I caught the counter and steadied myself.

"What do you mean, she's gone?" Detective Waraday asked.

Peg drew in a breath. She'd obviously been hurrying through the hallways. "She's not in the cafeteria or the teachers' lounge or her classroom."

Mrs. Kirk came out of her office. "What is the problem?"

"It's Ms. McCormick," Peg said. "She's gone."

"Gone?" Mrs. Kirk said. "She didn't schedule the afternoon off." She scowled. "And I just got a substitute in for second grade."

"She's probably in the restroom," Marie said.

"No. I think she left the campus," Peg said. "Her purse is gone. I checked when I was in her room."

"Why did you do that?" Detective Waraday asked.

Peg, whose face had been bright with excitement, suddenly looked uncomfortable. "I'm not sure . . . except when I walked in there . . . it felt like she was gone. The lights were off in her room. No one turns their lights off except when they leave for the day. I know she keeps her purse in her desk—most of the teachers do, and I've seen her put hers away. So I checked. Bottom left drawer. It's gone."

Marie turned toward the windows. "Her car is a little blue one."

We all moved to the windows and spotted a blue Ford Fiesta as it careened along the aisle, then turned at the exit. Its brake lights flared for an instant, contrasting with the royal-blue bumper sticker that read, KEEP CALM AND MATH ON; then the car surged out of the parking lot and went down the residential street, breaking all the school-zone speed limits.

Detective Waraday ran out of the office, and in a few seconds, we heard the wail of his siren as he pulled away from the front doors of the school. His car disappeared down the street. With the sound of the siren fading, we all looked at each other for a few seconds. Then Mrs. Kirk said, "What could have happened?"

I caught Marie's eye, then let my gaze fall on the papers that I had given to Detective Waraday. He must have set them down on the counter while he was waiting for Ms. McCormick and forgotten them when he left to pursue her out of the parking lot.

"I think it had something to do with these papers." I pushed them across the counter to Mrs. Kirk. She marched across the room and swiped them off the counter so quickly that the papers snapped. Mrs. Kirk read over the pages, her frown of irritation transforming into an expression of alarm. Marie hovered behind her shoulder, her hands linked together at her waist in such a tight grip that her knuckles showed white. Peg moved back around the counter to her desk, but her pace slowed to almost non-movement as she strained to get a glimpse of the papers.

Mrs. Kirk reached the last page, scanned it quickly, then briefly closed her eyes. She opened her eyes, noticed Peg and Marie hovering, and folded the papers in half. Peg and Marie retreated to their desks as Mrs. Kirk said, "Let me know the moment Detective Waraday returns."

"Do you think he'll be back?" Peg asked.

"I'm sure of it," Mrs. Kirk said, and braced her shoulders. She turned back toward her office. "For now, we must do something about Ms. McCormick's classroom." She looked at the clock. "Recess will be over in five minutes. I believe she has her planning period after this period. I can ask Mrs. Cross to cover for her after that, but we are already stretched quite thin today." She sighed and then a speculative look came into her eye as she turned her attention to me. "Mrs. Avery. May I impose on you for an hour of your time?"

"What?"

"I believe your daughter, Livvy, is in Ms. McCormick's class, correct?"

"Yes."

"And you've volunteered in that classroom before, haven't you?" Mrs. Kirk's voice was becoming more upbeat as she spoke.

I had a feeling I knew what was coming. "A little, yes. But it was before Christmas break—"

"Excellent. You have already done so much for the school that I hate to ask for anything else, but we're in a sort of emergency situation right now. Could you monitor Ms. McCormick's classroom for the next hour until Mrs. Cross can take over? I'd do it myself, but"—she glanced at the papers—"I have some calls that absolutely must be made, and then I'm sure Detective Waraday will return and need to speak to me as well."

"Mrs. Kirk," Peg said, pointing out the windows, where the sheriff's car was pulling slowly to the curb. "There he is now."

"I can give you an hour," I said, partially because I wanted to see what happened, but also because Mrs. Kirk looked more frazzled than I'd ever seen her. She was always upbeat and encouraging, and exuded an air of calm competence. Seeing that the school had hired someone with a drug arrest in her past, Mrs. Kirk had been shaken. I was sure she was wondering what the fallout would be.

Detective Waraday came into the office. "She had too much of a head start for me to catch her, but the county and the city police will be on the lookout for her." He spotted the papers in Mrs. Kirk's hands. "I'll need to take those with me."

"Yes, I assumed so," Mrs. Kirk said, her shoulders braced again. "And I believe you have a few questions for me as well?"

"Yes."

Mrs. Kirk nodded and handed off the papers. "Fine. If you'll wait in my office, I'll be right with you. I must get Ms. McCormick's class settled."

The bell rang, indicating the end of the period, and I knew the fifth-grade students would be trudging in from recess.

Detective Waraday frowned and looked as if he was about to protest, but Mrs. Kirk said, "I assure you, Detective, I will not go AWOL. It is important that I speak with Ms. McCormick's class. I don't want to have any rumors circulating. Well, any more than are already going around."

She motioned for me to come with her, and I followed her across the lobby to the fifth-grade hallway. I let her enter Ms. McCormick's room first. Students were milling around and talking. The volume level dropped immediately when they caught sight of Mrs. Kirk. Students quickly slid into their seats.

"Something unexpected came up, and Ms. McCormick is not here this period. Mrs. Avery has kindly agreed to fill in for her and monitor your class today." She looked toward the board. "I see your assignment for the day is listed. I suggest you get to work. Mrs. Avery, if you'll see me at the end of the hour?" She looked toward me, and I nodded. Then she ran her gaze over the class. "I'm sure you won't have any problems because fifth-grade students are really so grown up and responsible." She nodded her head and exited the room.

Every head in the class swiveled to look at me, except for Livvy, who had her attention focused on her stack of textbooks. She looked like she wanted the floor to open up and swallow her.

I glanced at the board. "Well, let's get on with this. Chapter ten, lesson seven," I said, reading the board while mentally estimating how far away Abby's classroom was in case a question came up that I couldn't answer or a riot broke out. Moving so slowly that they reminded me of the sloths we'd seen on a recent visit to the zoo, the students took out textbooks and flipped pages.

Remembering Livvy's mention of the computer game in Ms. McCormick's classroom, I said, "And if you get your lesson done and there is still time left, you can take turns playing the game on the computers." Monitors lined the back wall of the classroom, their screens dark. A murmur of what sounded like halfhearted approval ran through the room and several students, including Livvy, bent over their desks.

Ms. McCormick's desk was at the back of the room. I went and perched on her chair. I checked the clock. Only forty-seven minutes to go.

I swiveled in the chair and studied the desk, which was covered with papers, sticky notes, pens, and books. An aloe vera plant in a clay pot perched on one corner beside the computer. A couple of framed pictures were also propped up on the desk, including one of an older couple on a golf course, whom I supposed were Ms. McCormick's parents. Another showed Ms. McCormick with a man with longish brown hair who looked to be about her age. They stood on a beach, smiling happily and holding up sand dollars. Several sheets of stickers were scattered around the desk. Lots of them were happy faces of many varieties, along with stars, rainbows, and several sheets that proclaimed, *You're a Star!* and *Good Job!* The graded papers were liberally spotted with the stickers and plenty of hand-drawn happy faces and exclamation points.

I debated for a moment, knowing that poking around in the desk drawers was snooping, but then I thought of Klea's body in the woods. I inched open each drawer and found nothing more exciting than extra office supplies and a stash of gummy bears at the back of a lower drawer.

I closed the last drawer and sat back in the seat, wishing I'd brought my phone with me, but it was locked inside the van in the parking lot. I watched the kids for a bit. Most of them had settled down to their task and were working through the problems.

Livvy looked back over her shoulder at me. I smiled at her, then crossed my eyes. She grinned before she could help it and quickly turned back to her paper.

More out of habit than anything else, I tidied the desk, sorting papers into stacks and dropping paper clips and rubber bands into the pencil tray. Most of the papers were easy to sort—obvious homework papers or memos from the office, but there were a couple that I frowned over.

One was a schematic of some sort. A hand-drawn sketch, it was filled with lines that traveled from one geometric shape to another. *It must be some sort of flowchart,* I decided as I tried to make out the notes inside the shapes, but the words—whatever they were—were abbreviated and I couldn't decipher them. There were four similar sheets and the only words I could actually read were across the top of the pages: *Undersea Exploration, Mayan Temple, Egyptian Pyramid,* and *Jungle Trek.*

I fingered the sheets, paging back and forth. They all began with the same set of shapes running in a smooth line down the left-hand side of the page, but after a few shapes, the lines branched off in different directions without a pattern that I could see repeated anywhere among the four sheets of paper. Perhaps it was some sort of quiz or puzzle for her class?

A whisper of conversation floated my way. I got up and paced up and down the rows of desks, and the room fell silent again. Most of the students had made at least some progress on the problems and several were near the end. The minutes were ticking down in the class. I wandered around the classroom and even helped a few students get unstuck on their problems.

One student finished his last problem and hopped up. He dropped the paper into a basket on a table at the front of the room, then looked at me questioningly as he pointed to the computers.

I nodded, and he headed to the back of the room, where he logged in and was soon playing a game. Livvy was the third student to finish and headed for the back of the room. Soon, all the chairs around the computers were full, and I had instituted a ten-minute limit so that everyone could have a turn. Low groans and cheers sounded from around the computers as the kids moved through the bright images on the screen, cartoony versions of a deserted island or the jungle.

The bell rang and there was a scramble for backpacks and a surge for the door. Livvy gave me a little raised-eyebrow look with a lift of her head, which I took to mean *Bye, Mom,* and then the room was quiet.

Ms. McCormick had a schedule taped to her desktop and it showed that the next hour was her planning period, so there wasn't a flow of kids coming in for the next class. I walked around the room, picking up a stray pencil and a page of homework that hadn't been deposited in the basket. I shut down the computers, then walked back to Ms. McCormick's desk and paused, looking over it, taking in the framed photos and the plant and the super-cheerful stickers and notes. Could this really be the desk of a killer?

I shook my head and was about to leave the room when the flowchart pages caught my eye again. It must have been because I was standing a little distance away and looking at them upside down that I noticed it. I wasn't trying to read them individually, but looking at the page as a whole, I could see what I hadn't noticed before—that the printed abbreviations on the flowchart page were made with precise, even strokes. The perfectly spaced letters looked exactly like the printing on the threatening note I'd received.

Organizing Tips for PTA Moms

<u>End-of-Year Tips</u>

- Write a thank-you note to your children's teachers.
- Get contact information for your child's friends so you can stay in touch over the summer.

- Have a plan for sorting the reams of paper that will come home as the school year ends, deciding which papers or artwork to keep.
- Have an end-of-school ritual like a trip to get ice cream or a visit to a pool to mark the last day of school and celebrate the beginning of summer.

Chapter Fourteen

I hurried over to the desk, and compared the writing on the flowcharts, which was careful and exact, to the flowing writing on the graded papers. They weren't exactly the same, but they were similar enough that it looked as if the same person had written both things. When Ms. McCormick wrote on the graded papers, her letters were printed and small, but not nearly as perfectly formed. Those notes looked as if she'd been in a hurry, jotting down short notes to the students and scribbling the grades quickly across the top of the papers. The painfully exact lettering on the flowchart looked like the printing on the note I'd received in Livvy's take-home folder.

I snatched up one of the flowchart papers and dashed out the door. Once I entered the hallway, which was a mass of kids and bumping backpacks, I had to slow down. I spotted Livvy at the other end of the hallway. She stood outside the door to her science classroom, talking to another girl. I waved, catching her eye.

Her easy stance shifted so that she looked as stiff as one of Nathan's action figures. I waved for her to come to me, figuring that would be slightly less embarrassing for her than me going into her classroom. After a second of hesitation, she motored down the hall to me.

"*Mom*," she said, drawing out the syllable and infusing it with as much chagrin as any tween can. "What is it?"

"Did you ever see Ms. McCormick working on papers like this?"

"Sure," Livvy said without a moment's hesitation. "It's for the game," she said easily, and then her eyes widened. "I wasn't supposed to tell."

"Tell what?"

Livvy clamped her lips together and sent me a mulish look.

"This is not the time for secrets, Livvy." I said it so sharply that, after a sigh, Livvy nodded, then looked up and down the hall. "It's Ms. McCormick's secret project, her game," she said in a voice that made me lean close to her to hear. "She was letting us test it, but didn't want us to tell anyone." Livvy pointed to the words at the top. "See, this one is for the Egyptian Pyramid." Livvy's finger traced along the line of shapes. "They all start out this way, with a really easy problem." She paused over the first geometric shape, then traced the line on down the page. "But they get harder."

"Did you ever see her actually writing on these flowcharts? Is this her writing?"

"Sure," Livvy said, back in her normal voice.

"It's very different from the way she writes on your homework papers."

Livvy shrugged. "She says math is exact and you have to be neat when you're working problems. Ms. McCormick said that writing stuff for the game is the same way. You should see her when she works problems on the whiteboard, it looks like something from a computer."

"You said it was her game. Did Ms. McCormick have early access to the game, or was it actually her game?"

"It was her game. She was making it up as she went along. That's why she wanted us to play it, so that she could make it better before she told everyone about it." Livvy looked around the almost empty hall. "Mom, I've got to go."

"Of course. I'll see you after school."

Livvy scooted down the hall and into her classroom. She made it before the bell rang. I went slowly back into Ms. McCormick's room. I stopped inside the doorway and looked at the lesson that was printed on the side of the whiteboard. The letters were exact. They did look like a computer printout . . . just like the flowchart and the printing on the threatening note.

"I don't know why I didn't see it right away," I said to Detective Waraday.

After Peg fled, he must have gotten a search warrant because when I stepped out into the hall to track him down and share the news about the handwriting, he was already in the hallway, leading a group of crime scene technicians to Ms. McCormick's room. As the technicians worked around us, Detective Waraday and I stood at the whiteboard where Ms. McCormick had written the day's lesson.

Detective Waraday slipped the papers with the flowcharts into plastic sleeves. "It's not surprising. You weren't looking for it. I'm sure you were only thinking about keeping the kids in line for fifty minutes, which is enough to occupy anyone's mind."

One of the crime scene techs was going through Ms. McCormick's desk while another had opened the storage closet and was removing items one at a time and examining them. Detective Waraday had looked disgruntled when he arrived with the crime scene technicians. If Ms.

McCormick was the murderer, then she'd had plenty of time to get rid of any evidence that might have been left behind, but it looked as if they were going to go over the room inch by inch.

Detective Waraday pointed to the flowchart. "You say this had something to do with a game?"

"Yes. My daughter—she's in Ms. McCormick's class—I asked her about the paper, and she told me just now that it was a secret. Apparently, Ms. McCormick was designing a game about math and was letting the kids play it on the computers. Livvy had mentioned the game before, but not that Ms. McCormick had created it."

"And that was the word your daughter used, 'secret'?" Detective Waraday asked thoughtfully. "Something like that wouldn't be allowed on school time?"

"I don't know. You'd have to ask Mrs. Kirk, but Livvy said they only were allowed to play it if they finished their schoolwork, so it wasn't like Ms. McCormick was ignoring the kids or their studies."

Detective Waraday said, "Perhaps there would be some sort of conflict of interest with the school district or her contract or something."

"I suppose that could be a possibility," I said. "If Ms. McCormick left those papers out on her desk—and they were out today—and Klea saw them and realized what they were . . ."

Detective Waraday frowned. "Did you know what these were?"

"No."

"And you'd actually heard of the game. I'm not sure someone not associated with the class would make that assumption. In fact, I think most people wouldn't know what these were."

The sound of a voice came from the doorway. "Oh, sorry, I didn't realize . . ."

Abby stood uncertainly. "Sorry," she said again. "I heard that you had to wrangle Ms. McCormick's class, and I popped down to make sure you were okay." Her gaze traveled from Detective Waraday to the crime scene techs going through drawers and closets.

"No, that was last period. It went fine," I said. I turned to Detective Waraday. "Do you need anything else from me?"

"Not at this time," he said. He closed the door behind me as I left.

"What is going on in there?" Abby asked in a whisper as I fell into step with her in the quiet hall, which was as still as a library on Friday night.

"Detective Waraday wanted to talk to Ms. McCormick, but she bolted. Left her class and drove off campus right after lunch. I think she wrote the note."

"What note?" Abby asked.

"That's right—I haven't had a chance to tell you." I quickly caught Abby up on what had happened, describing the smashed window, the threatening note, and the scandal in Ms. McCormick's past, figuring that if Marie and Peg knew about it, it would only be a short time before the word spread through the school, at least to the teachers. "That should probably be confidential, but I don't think there's any way that the news won't get out."

"I won't tell anyone," Abby said, then shook her head. "A drug bust?" She mouthed the words, not even wanting to speak them aloud. "How did she ever get hired?"

"It's a long, complicated story that I don't think I should go into," I said as we arrived at the door to Abby's classroom. A low murmur of conversation broke off when she peered inside, called a few names, and pointed out that they still had one more quiz left to take this week.

She turned back to me. "Call me if anything else happens, okay? I can't believe you're dealing with vandalism and threats and you didn't call."

"It was late when it happened, and you're busy," I said.

"Not that busy," she said firmly. "I'm calling you to-night to check on you."

"Okay," I said with a grin. "Hey, before I go, did you ever hear Ms. McCormick talk about a game?"

"No . . . what kind of game? Playground game or board game or what?"

"A computer game. It looks like Ms. McCormick was working on one and letting the kids test it for her. I saw her notes for it, and the handwriting looked exactly like the writing on the note."

Abby frowned at the tile floor for a second. "No, she never mentioned it, but we aren't on the same team—not even the same grade. I've only spoken to her a few times, in fact. But it sounds like you should steer clear of her."

I sighed. "I vowed I was going to stay out of all this, but that's not going so well."

"Hmm. Well, you do have a way of getting at the truth, so perhaps it's not all bad, especially if it was Ms. McCormick." She shivered. "I hate to think that she . . . hurt Klea. I mean, that's what the detective must think since they're going through her classroom."

"Well, I think they have to check into it since she ran off campus instead of talking to Detective Waraday. Just doing that by itself looks suspicious. It is possible that Klea found out what Ms. McCormick was doing with the game or maybe Klea found out about that thing from Ms. McCormick's past," I said, being intentionally vague since we were standing at the door of Abby's classroom, even though I was speaking softly. "You aren't the only person I've heard say that Klea was nosy. Maybe Klea figured out Ms. McCormick's secret—at least one of them."

"And Klea threatened to expose Ms. McCormick, so Ms. McCormick killed Klea?" Abby whispered. "Ugh. I don't even like to think about it." She glanced at her watch. "It can't already be one-thirty," she said. "And we haven't even started going over homework. I've got to go. I'll call you tonight."

I waved at her, distractedly. One-thirty. I had a bad feeling that I had something on my calendar today at one-thirty. "Oh, great," I muttered as I remembered my schedule for the day. I half walked, half ran down the hallway. I could not postpone my organizing appointment with Margo *again*.

Fortunately, Margo lived in the neighborhood that surrounded the school. I was only a few minutes late when I rang the doorbell of her brick rancher. I'd met Margo once last year when her youngest was still at school with my kids, but he was now at the middle school, so I hadn't seen as much of Margo as I used to. I'd been surprised to hear from her a few weeks ago when she filled out the online contact form on my website. She wanted to use one of my *a la carte* services, a one-time consultation to help work out the cabinet design of her kitchen remodel.

When she opened the door, she looked just the same, slender with a sprinkling of freckles across her cheeks. She taught yoga at the local gym, and I'd always seen her in workout clothes, which was how she was dressed today. She had a phone tucked between her ear and her shoulder, and mouthed *hello*, and then raised a finger. *One minute.*

I nodded, and she waved me inside, motioning for me to go down the hallway to the kitchen. She followed me into the small square of space that was walled off from the living room as she wrapped up her conversation.

She ended the call and ran her hand through her short red curls. "Well, here it is. It will be completely gutted, and we'll start from scratch." She waved her hand around the kitchen. Formica countertops, faded linoleum, and a dropped ceiling with fluorescent lights showed the house had been built in another era. She motioned to the wall that separated the kitchen from the living room. "That wall will come down to open up the room. And in here—" She took a few steps into the breakfast nook next to the kitchen and moved to the wall of windows that overlooked the backyard. "We're blowing out this wall to give us more space. This whole area"—she circled her hand around the breakfast nook—"will actually be where the sandbox is now."

"Wow. That's a big job," I said.

She ran her hands through her curls again. "Don't I know it. I'm lying awake at night, trying to figure out whether to put in a lazy Susan or those rollout shelf things. That's when I decided to call you. If you can help me configure the cabinet design, then I'll only have to worry about the tile, counters, fixtures, hardware, and lights," she said with a grimace.

"What are your thoughts right now?"

Margo pointed to the round table in the breakfast nook. It was covered with sketches on grid paper, as well as glossy brochures featuring gorgeous kitchen cabinets and paint chips. We settled into the chairs, and it was a relief to focus on organizing and debate the pros and cons of drawer depths and dividers. After about thirty minutes, we had roughed out a way to maximize as much storage space in the new kitchen as possible. I was usually limited by what the client had in place. It wasn't often that I had a blank slate to work with, so to speak, and I had a great time exploring possibilities.

It was also nice to leave all the questions and problems surrounding Klea's death behind, and I wasn't even thinking about any of those things when Margo said, "I can't believe everything that's going on at the elementary school. So scary. I never thought I'd say this, but I'm glad my kids are at the middle school." She refolded brochures and shuffled them into a stack. "Of course, there's always been rumors about sketchy stuff going on at the elementary school, so I shouldn't be so surprised, I guess."

I handed her the list of cabinetry and organizing items I'd made while we were talking so she could order them. "Sketchy stuff? Like what?"

Margo waved a hand. "I shouldn't have said anything. I don't know anything for sure. Just rumors."

"Margo, my kids are there every day. I'm in and out of the school all the time, and I've never heard anything."

"Well, you wouldn't. You're not the type to have any problems."

"What do you mean?"

Margo wrinkled her nose. "You know . . . you're happily married—at least you seem to be. You're not the type to get yourself into a sticky situation and be . . . vulnerable."

I stared at her a moment. "I'm not sure I'm following you," I said, but I was afraid I did know what she was hinting at.

Margo sighed. "I've really put my foot in it now. Oh, well. It's all rumors, anyway." She scrubbed her hand through her curls. "It's probably totally wrong, but I heard that one of the moms who had been fooling around got a note from the office in their kid's take-home folder, demanding she pay a certain amount of money or her husband would be contacted."

I fell back against the chair. "A blackmail note?"

"Yes, but, as I said, it's all rumor."

"What did she do?"

"Paid it, I guess." Margo shrugged. "Since she didn't end up getting a divorce."

"So you know who it was?"

"No, not really. I mean, not one hundred percent. I

think I know, but I'm not sure. It was one of those things that you hear third-or-fourth person, so I have no idea if there's even a bit of truth in it."

"Wow." I blinked, stunned that something like that was going on in the school—if it was true. But then I thought of Gabrielle's call this morning and her juicy gossip about something shady going on at the school. And Gabrielle had asked if the note I received demanded money. . . . Maybe there *was* some truth to what Margo had overheard.

"Wait," I said as I sat forward. "You said it came from the office."

"Did I?" Margo looked flustered. "I hadn't realized . . ." She gazed off into space, then said, "But I think that's right."

"How would someone know it came from the office?" As Detective Waraday and I had worked out, almost anyone could slip a note into the papers that went into the take-home folders.

"I don't know." Margo shrugged and looked like she wished she'd never brought up the subject. "I suppose someone said it was one of those folded and taped notes. Isn't that how all the notes from the office look? I know whenever I got one of those, it was from the main office."

"That's true, but it could be someone imitating that. It's not hard to fold a piece of copy paper in thirds and put tape on it. It could have been from anyone in the school— a teacher, the staff, or even another parent."

She closed a folder with a thump. "I probably shouldn't have said anything at all."

"No, it could be very important. Will you tell the sheriff's department about it? I can give you the name of the detective—"

"Oh, no. I could never do that." She looked like I'd asked her to rob a bank. "In the first place, Dave would not like it," she said, referring to her husband. "And, in the second, it's just a rumor. I'm not even sure who mentioned it. It came up after a yoga class. I overheard a couple of the moms talking as I was cleaning up the room. It was a tight little group, and I don't even remember all the names of the people who were there. It was last year, too, so it's probably nothing to do with anything this year." She pushed her chair back. "Would you like a cup of coffee?"

The subject was closed, and I could tell she wasn't going to give an inch, so I declined the coffee and gathered up my organizing materials. I gave her an invoice and left, wishing that we hadn't ended on such a strained note.

Chapter Fifteen

The next morning, I was the first person to pull into the school parking lot, and my conversation with Margo was still on my mind. I'd debated calling Detective Waraday yesterday, but in the end, I just couldn't see telling him about the rumors and then expecting him to take them seriously when I couldn't give him a single name or solid fact, especially since Margo refused to talk to him.

I was still second-guessing my decision as I parked near the main doors to the school. I must have arrived even before Vaughn, who was supposed to be here a few minutes early to open the doors for me. I was here to meet Joy Peel, the owner of the catering company providing the breakfast buffet for today's Teacher Appreciation.

While we had some parents who wanted to bring homemade food, there was another set of parents who were just as happy to write a check and let someone else bring the food. We'd sent home a letter with the students a month ago and asked for either sign-ups to bring food or a donation to purchase catering. The donations had provided enough money to cover Thursday's breakfast and Friday's barbecue lunch. The only glitch was that the catering company had two events this morning. If we wanted our food, someone had to be at the school at seven to make sure Joy was able to get inside and set up. Abby had offered to help me by bringing the kids with her at eight, and I'd taken her up on the offer, figuring it would be easier to coordinate the food if both kids weren't underfoot.

The catering van lumbered into the parking lot, followed by Vaughn, who pulled into the drop-off line and unlocked the main doors for us before he went to park his car. I grabbed my phone, hopped out of the van, and went to prop open the school's door. Then I flipped on the lights in the lobby and the teachers' lounge. Joy was a military spouse who I knew through the squadron's spouse club. She came through the doors, carrying a container of muffins. "I figured I better get right to it, since I've got to run."

"That's fine. Through here," I said, directing her to the teachers' lounge. We ferried the rest of the food inside, arranged it, and then set out coffee and juice. I could hear Vaughn's keys jangling as he moved through the school, unlocking doors.

Joy put the last tray in place and removed the cover.

"Looks great," I said.

"Excellent. Thanks for the business," Joy said before departing. "I'll close that main door on my way out. Anything else?"

"Nope."

I tweaked the card with Joy's company name so that it was more visible, then noticed a book with a flowery cover on one of the tables. It was a datebook. When I flicked the cover open, I saw the name Hillary Cross, one of the fifth-grade teachers, on the first page. She must have forgotten it here yesterday, I thought. I had some time. I'd run it down to her room and drop it off.

As I paced through the empty halls, I could hear Vaughn bumping around in the janitor's office, but other than that, it was quiet. The calm before the storm, I thought. In about twenty minutes, the halls would be flooded with scurrying kids and teachers.

Mrs. Cross's room was one room beyond Ms. McCormick's, and I couldn't help but glance in as I approached the door. I'd almost expected to see crime scene tape sealing off the room, but the door was open and the swath of room that I could see as I passed looked completely normal. Detective Waraday must not have found anything significant enough to warrant sealing the room. I dropped the datebook on Mrs. Cross's desk, then returned to the hallway, again looking into Ms. McCormick's room as I approached.

A flicker of movement within the room caught my eye, and I veered toward the door. I had thought for a second I'd seen Ms. McCormick, but that couldn't be right. It was probably just another teacher with a slender figure and blond hair—the substitute teacher for the day, most likely.

But as I paused by the door, I saw it wasn't someone else. It *was* Ms. McCormick. She was bent over the desk at the back of the room. She glanced up and saw me an instant after I spotted her. I suppose if I had been smart I would have ducked out of the door as quickly as I could, but I was so shocked to see her that my feet stayed planted to the floor. For a second, I wondered if everything had been cleared up. Perhaps the newspaper article and the two different names were some sort of mix-up that had been explained, and she was back at work today.

But after one look at her haggard face, I dismissed that thought. She looked like one of the kids when they come home from a slumber party where they didn't sleep at all. Ms. McCormick's makeup looked like she had stayed up all night, with her eyeliner smudged and her mascara flaking off, making the dark circles under her eyes look even worse. Her dress was wrinkled and creased, and I realized it was the same dress she had been wearing yesterday. Her golden hair was in a lopsided ponytail, and her lipstick had been chewed off. She looked like a weird, distorted modern-art version of a cartoon princess.

She stood there a moment, her eyes wide. "What are you doing to do? Call the police on me again?"

"I had nothing to do with that. I didn't call the police," I said.

"But it's your fault. You wanted to know about my other job. No one else *ever* asked about that. You set everything in motion. You and your questions." She slammed a drawer closed, rifled through the papers on the top of the desk, then stood back and scanned the rest of the room.

"Where are they?" she demanded.

"What?"

"My notes for the game." She came around the desk, fingering the zipper on the cross-body bag that was slung over her shoulder. "I *know* you were in here yesterday. If you want to know anything that's going on in a school, just follow some of the kids on social media. They have no filters and post about absolutely everything."

I did not have a good feeling about her hostile tone. Was anyone else in the school besides Vaughn? And where was Vaughn? I listened, but didn't hear the jingle of his key ring. "But if you knew that the kids were so unguarded, I'm surprised that you would let them play the computer game. It was supposed to be a secret, right?" I asked.

She gave a sharp nod. "You're right. I shouldn't have let them see the game, but I was stupid. I needed their help to get through beta. I figured the risk was worth it. I *need* those notes. That game is all I have."

I was about to make some excuse and slip out of the room, but her words surprised me. "What do you mean, it's all you have?"

"You're kidding, right? Even I understand that I'll never get another job at a school again after all this comes out. My teaching career is over, but the game—the kids like it. It has potential. I can upload it and sell it myself. No one will care that I happened to be too stupid to realize a friend had put *her* drugs in *my* car. One mistake. I made *one* mistake."

She rotated her shoulders, relaxing them slightly. "But that's over. No more trying to hide my past. I'm a game designer now, and I need those notes. They're critical for the app version."

"I'm sorry, but I don't know where they are. They're not on your desk?"

"No, they're not on my desk," she said, raising her voice. "They're not *anywhere* in this room." She pulled a gun from her bag. "Now, what did you do with them?"

I put my hands up, palms facing her, and backed away. "Ms. McCormick—"

She laughed, but it wasn't a normal laugh. The sound had a slightly hysterical edge to it. "You don't have to look so terrified. It's not a gun. Not a real one, anyway." She twisted her hand for a second so that I could see the gun from the side. "It's a Taser," she said.

It was boxier than a real gun and seemed to be made of plastic, I realized and calmed down a bit.

She shifted it back so that it was aimed it at me. "Handy to have. I got it when I was in college for those long walks across the campus after my night class. Who would have thought that the first time I would use it would be in my classroom?"

I was pretty sure that even mace violated the school's

no-weapons policy, so a Taser would definitely be against the rules, but I wasn't about to mention that at this moment. Instead, I moved an inch toward the door.

"It won't do you any good to run. The range on these things is quite impressive," she said. "Now come inside the room. Yes, that's good," she said, indicating that I should stop between two of the rows of desks.

I kept my eyes on her face, which was now a bit flushed, as I listened for the sound of the first teachers arriving. Surely it wouldn't be long before there would be several teachers in the hallway and surrounding classrooms.

I swallowed, going back to the issue that seemed to have set her off. "If your papers aren't here, then Detective Waraday probably took them."

She lowered the Taser an inch. "Why would he do that? Why would he even care? He's investigating Klea's death. My game has nothing to do with Klea."

"Well, then you'll get the papers back, no problem. You're sure Klea didn't know about the game? Or . . . anything else?" Were those footsteps echoing down the hall?

"My past, you mean," Ms. McCormick said. "Oh, no, it wasn't Klea who knew."

She put a slight emphasis on the name Klea. "But someone else knew," I said slowly, working it out as I remembered Ms. McCormick's comment when Klea was discovered in the woods and the way Ms. McCormick had stiffened when Peg and Gabrielle came into the teachers' lounge and then departed as quickly as she could. "Peg. Peg knows?" I asked, dropping my hands to my side at the thought. The footsteps faded, probably a teacher going into another room closer to the main hall, but I only half noticed.

Ms. McCormick's shoulders sagged. "I think so. It's someone in the office, that's all I know for sure. Peg always has a sort of superior smirk on her face when she sees me, so I think it's her. But that's hardly evidence."

My thoughts were churning. If Peg knew about Ms. McCormick's past, why hadn't she said anything? But then I thought of the rumors Margo had mentioned—the rumors that focused on someone in the office. "You were being blackmailed," I guessed.

Ms. McCormick closed her eyes for a second, then snapped them open and tossed her head. "I suppose since it's all out now, it doesn't matter anyway. I might as well take her down with me. Yes, I was being blackmailed, and I do think it was Peg."

"Not Klea?" I asked just to be sure.

"No, of course it wasn't Klea. It couldn't have been her."

"Why?"

"Because the note that said I had to pay up came from the office. It thoughtfully included an envelope that I was to fill with my cash and then return to the office in one of those inter-office envelopes—you know, the kind with the lines on the side and the string tie to hold down the flap. Who sorts the inter-office mail? Peg. It *has* to be her."

It did sound logical. Peg handled the paper that came into the office, as well as distributing the papers that went out. She was always over at the pigeonholes, shifting paper into the slots for teachers to pick up.

"I knew I shouldn't pay, but what else could I do? The envelopes came like clockwork every other Monday," she said with a bitter laugh. "And I filled them with cash and returned them."

"How long has this been going on?"

"Since the week after I arrived." Her arms were now sagging, and she shifted over so that she could prop one hip on a student desk, suddenly looking drained.

Some of the tension had eased out of me when Ms.

McCormick lowered the Taser, but she still held it in her hand, even if it wasn't aimed at me right now. I decided that I wouldn't make any sudden moves. I didn't want to startle her now that she seemed to be calming down.

"You thought I hurt Klea?" She dropped the Taser to her lap. "I would never do that. Besides, when would I have had time? I was with my class all that morning."

It was a good point, except that the critical time wasn't during the Muffins with Mom; it was earlier, when teachers were moving around the hallways before the students and parents arrived in the classrooms. It wouldn't be hard for a teacher to slip out and strangle someone unnoticed at that time of the morning, especially if the murderer caught Klea going either into or out of the closet and attacked her there, then left her body in the closet until it could be moved. With a jolt, I realized that that line of reasoning meant that Mrs. Harris could still be a suspect, too. She could have arrived earlier, then returned to the parking lot to remove the food from her car. I hadn't seen her arrive at the school, only met her standing in the parking lot.

"It had to have been Peg who did it," Ms. McCormick said, interrupting my thoughts. "I mean, everyone knew Klea liked to snoop in drawers and files and stuff. She must have found out what Peg was doing, and Peg killed her."

"Why didn't you tell Detective Waraday that instead of running away yesterday?"

"Because how could I tell him what was going on without telling him about the blackmail? And I have no proof, only my suspicions."

"You don't have any of the envelopes or the original note? Did you get a note every time?" I asked, my thoughts swerving all over the place.

"No, only that first time. Believe me, the envelope was sufficient for me to know what was being demanded."

"And that first note?"

"I burned it on the barbecue grill at my apartment complex. So, no evidence, just Peg's smug looks."

"Still, you should tell Detective Waraday. You can talk to him about your notes for the computer game at the same time. I'm sure that you can get them back, at least a copy, especially since they don't seem to have any relation to Klea's death."

She jumped up from the desk where she'd been perched. "No. I'm not talking to him. I have a criminal record. He's not going to believe anything I say, especially after—" She stopped speaking and looked down at the Taser, fidgeting with one of the little flap-type things that covered the end of the barrel.

Watching her pick at the flap of the Taser made me nervous—it was still pointed loosely in my direction—but the guilty cast of her face looked just like Nathan's when I pointed out to him that I knew from the crumbs all over the counter that he'd had a snack when I told him not to.

"That wasn't the only note," I said. "There was also the note you wrote to me."

Her head popped up. "You can't prove that."

"Oh, I'm afraid I can. Or, at least, Detective Waraday can." I glanced at the handwritten lesson that was still on the whiteboard. "You left a sample of your handwriting here on the board as well as in the game notes. Why did you write that note to me, if you didn't kill Klea?" I asked, realizing that despite all her lies and misdirection, I really did believe her when she said she hadn't killed Klea.

Ms. McCormick swiped at a strand of hair that had fallen over her forehead. She pushed it back. "It was stupid. I see that now, but I thought if I could just get you to keep quiet and not ask any more questions . . . then it

would all be okay. No one had been interested in my previous job—or whether or not I'd even *had* a previous job.
If I could get you to leave it alone, it would all be fine."

I'd been so focused on what Ms. McCormick was saying that I hadn't been paying attention to what was going
on in the hallway outside the door, but we both realized
that there were several sets of footsteps ringing out on the
tile.

"I have to go," Ms. McCormick said quickly. "Tell that
Detective Waraday everything I told you, okay?" Ms.
McCormick moved across the room. As she flitted by me,
she stuffed the Taser back in her purse, but kept her hand
around the handle, inside the bag. She reached the door at
the same time that Mrs. Kirk appeared. They almost ran into
each other, but Mrs. Kirk stepped back, her face shocked.
"Ms. McCormick! What are you doing...?" She trailed
off as she took in Ms. McCormick's rough appearance.

Ms. McCormick pushed by Mrs. Kirk and hurried down
the hall. I rushed into the hallway and grabbed Mrs. Kirk's
arm to help steady her. Ms. McCormick had pushed her
off balance, and Mrs. Kirk had half-fallen against the wall.

She righted herself and we both started after Ms.
McCormick, but she was too fast for us. By the time we got
to the end of the hallway where it met the lobby, all we
could see of Ms. McCormick was a glimpse of her blue
dress as she disappeared out the front doors of the school.
We hurried to the doors and saw Ms. McCormick's little
blue car already bumping over the dip at the exit of the
parking lot and accelerating into the street.

Organizing Tips for PTA Moms

<u>Social Media and Schools</u>

If your school doesn't have social media accounts and you enjoy social media, volunteer to create and maintain a profile for your school on one of the social media websites. Facebook probably has the widest reach so it would be a good starting point.

Use the account to post information and reminders about upcoming events, link to volunteer signup opportunities, and promote school spirit with images and reports about events, but check with your school district about their policy on photography releases before posting any images of students.

Chapter Sixteen

Mrs. Kirk shook her head. "I can't believe it . . . that she showed up here." She turned and went into the main office. I followed her more slowly, my thoughts spinning. Should I tell Mrs. Kirk what Ms. McCormick had told me—her suspicions about Peg? Ms. McCormick was sure it was Peg who was blackmailing her, and it seemed like that was the logical conclusion, but what if Ms. McCormick was wrong? What if it was someone else who worked in the office . . . ? Marie and Mrs. Kirk worked in the office, too.

I didn't want to go there—not even in my thoughts, but all three women worked in the office . . . and then there was Klea's list as well. After discovering that Mrs. Harris was writing under the name Alexa Wells, I couldn't help but wonder why the other names were on the list with those two. Could it be that everyone on the list had something to hide? Ms. McCormick certainly did. And now it appeared Peg did as well. Marie and Mrs. Kirk's names were on that list, too . . . so perhaps keeping the news to myself until I could tell Detective Waraday about it was the better call.

I went to the main office and headed for the computer, intending to sign out before I left the campus, but I realized I hadn't signed in at all, which was getting to be a bad habit. It was the second time I'd forgotten to sign in, but the shock of spotting Ms. McCormick had pushed everything out of my mind.

Mrs. Kirk was in her office, on the telephone with the door closed, but she saw me through the glass panel that ran along the side of her door. She stood and walked to the door, but kept the phone pressed to her ear. She tilted the lower portion of it away from her mouth as she said, "Ellie, you're not leaving, are you? I'm on the line with the sheriff's department. I'm sure they'll want to speak to you."

"Yes, of course," I said. Of course Mrs. Kirk would call Detective Waraday. He needed to be informed that Ms. McCormick had shown up at the school. I sat down on the long wooden bench, mentally kicking myself for not immediately telling Detective Waraday about the rumors Margo had mentioned. There was definitely something shady going on in the school.

Peg's desk was off to the side and, despite the tall counter that blocked Mrs. Kirk and Marie from my view, I could see Peg. She sat at her desk, tapping away on her computer, looking completely calm, occasionally taking a sip from her coffee mug. Could she be a blackmailer? A stack of orange inter-office folders sat in a basket on the corner of her desk. I wished I could get a peek at them, but that was crazy. I shifted on the bench, recrossing my legs in the other direction. I was too nosy. Maybe Gabrielle was right that even if I wanted to leave the questions around Klea's death alone, I just couldn't do it.

I glanced back at Peg. When I'd first met her, I'd wondered if she was shy because she hardly ever spoke to anyone and only answered if she was asked a direct question, but as time went by, I'd decided she wasn't reticent because she was nervous or embarrassed. I'd realized that there was a sullenness to her personality that came through in every interaction we'd had.

She must have felt my gaze on her because she looked over at me and raised her eyebrows. "Did you need something?" she said, her tone sharp.

"No, nothing. Sorry."

I took out my phone and checked my calls, then noticed a message had come in a few minutes ago through my website, a request for an organizing consultation. The person, Marguerite, had left the section for the last name blank. She wanted to meet this afternoon and had checked off kitchen and closets as the areas she wanted help with. I ran over my schedule in my mind. I'd planned on stopping at the office supply store, but I could put that off. It would be best to get in as many appointments as I could before summer hit and the kids were home all the time.

A strange sound—a half gulp, half gasp—made me look up, my mom senses on full alert. I knew that sound. It was the prelude to someone throwing up. Peg, one hand clasped over her mouth and the other over her stomach, lurched to the door and disappeared into the restroom across the hall.

I stood up and looked at Marie. "Do you think she's okay?"

"I better go see." Marie bustled around the tall counter, her sky-blue shirt swishing with every step.

I waited a moment, then decided that Peg didn't need a second person hovering over her in the bathroom and sat back down. My phone buzzed with a new text. It was from Abby, letting me know that she and the kids had arrived at school.

I went into the lobby in time to catch the kids and say hello to them. They answered distractedly and hurried on to the cafeteria, where they could talk quietly with their friends until the bell to go to class sounded. I turned to Abby. "Everything go okay?"

"Oh, sure. We had a short panic when Charlie couldn't find his math homework." She rolled her eyes. "I really should get you to organize his room. It's a disaster."

"I could do that. This summer?"

"Yes, please." She shifted her feet, and I knew she wanted to get to class, so I said quickly, "Have you ever heard any rumors about . . . well, shady things going on here at the school?"

She went still and tilted her head. "What do you mean, shady?"

Two teachers passed us, and I waited until they were in the teachers' lounge before I said, "There's really no way to phrase it subtly. Have you heard anything about people being blackmailed?"

I'd expected Abby to look shocked and immediately say how crazy that thought was, but she didn't. She shifted her gaze around the lobby, where more teachers were entering the building. She grabbed my arm and pulled me down to the turn where the second-grade hallway branched off the lobby. "What have you heard?"

"You mean it's true?" I asked.

"I don't know, but I have heard . . . rumblings . . . nothing concrete—that's why I didn't say anything to you. I figured it was just some moms exaggerating."

"It was moms—parents—you heard talking about it?"

"Two moms. I walked into the workroom one day and heard what I thought was the word 'blackmail.' The two women shifted their conversation to something else right away, and I decided it was just too absurd. I must have misheard them."

"Who were they?"

"I don't know. Not any parents I've come in contact with before, but the school is pretty big. There are lots of parents that I don't know. And people are always moving in and out, coming and going. I don't know everyone. But you've obviously heard something, too—something more than the word blackmail."

"I've heard a couple of things—"

The bell rang, and Abby sighed. "I'm late. I have car circle duty today. I have to go, but we have to talk later."

I nodded and went back to the office, passing Mrs. Kirk. "Detective Waraday is on his way," she said. "He does want to speak to you." She moved to the main doors, her walkie-talkie in hand.

A runaway teacher might have returned unexpectedly, but the routines of the school day, like monitoring morning drop-off, continued.

"I'll wait in the office," I said, and returned there to find Marie making a *tsking* sound as she picked up the stack of papers Peg had been working on. Marie dropped them in the basket on top of the inter-office envelopes, and carried the whole thing over to her desk. She went back to Peg's desk and switched off the computer, then picked up her coffee mug. Marie took it to the back of the room, where there was a little bar-type sink in the counter next to a coffeepot. She dumped the coffee, rinsed out the mug, and returned it to Peg's desk. "I just hope none of the rest of us come down with it."

"Oh, no. What does Peg have?" I asked.

"I hope it's food poisoning. She said she had a fast-food breakfast roll on the way to work today. Otherwise, we're all in for it."

"I hate to wish food poisoning on anyone, but I hope that's it and not something else contagious," I said, thinking of how quickly viruses and flu bugs spread through the school.

Marie moved back to her desk. "I told Peg to go on home. She didn't want to, but she looked as green as the grass out that window. No use her sitting around, spreading germs, if she is contagious."

"And she seemed fine a few minutes ago."

"You know how those things are," Marie said. "They come on sudden."

Marie attacked the pile of papers she'd transferred to her desk, and I went back to my phone, automatically tapping out a reply that I could meet my new client at two o'clock, wondering if it was too much of a coincidence that Peg had become ill and had to leave the school shortly after Ms. McCormick returned. Had Peg somehow overheard what she'd said? I bit my lip, trying to remember how busy the hallway had been. A few people had been moving around—teachers, I'd assumed, going to their classrooms. But from the point when Ms. McCormick mentioned blackmail, I had been so focused on her that I hadn't noticed anyone in the hall.

I supposed Peg could have been hovering outside the room listening to part of the conversation. I couldn't be sure, so I sent a long text to Detective Waraday, summarizing what Ms. McCormick had told me, and sat back to wait, hoping that Marie might get called away, and I could sneak a look at the basket of inter-office envelopes.

Chapter Seventeen

"I was caught completely off guard," Mrs. Kirk said. Mrs. Kirk, Detective Waraday, and I were in Mrs. Kirk's office with the door closed. It was close to noon. I had spent the morning hanging about the school, waiting for Detective Waraday. I had lingered for a good hour in the office, but Marie hadn't left her desk once.

After retrieving my laptop—which I'd gotten into the habit of bringing with me because I could get a lot of work done while waiting in the car circle line at the end of the school day—from the van, I'd finally moved down to the workroom and cleared my email inbox, then created a checklist for a client who was moving soon.

Detective Waraday had arrived, and I'd been called to the office shortly before noon. I'd thought it might have taken him so long to arrive because he had gone to Peg's house to speak to her, but he'd explained that he'd been delayed because a report had come in that he had to investigate. Ms. McCormick's car had been spotted at a park on the other side of North Dawkins. It had been abandoned, and there'd been no sign of her, but a search of the surrounding area had to be made.

Mrs. Kirk tapped a pencil on her desktop. "I find it very disturbing, Detective, that Ms. McCormick returned to the school this morning and slipped in before the students arrived."

"I can understand your worries," Detective Waraday said. "I've instructed an officer to be here from the time the doors open until the school is locked at night. He should arrive soon. I've told him to check in with you, but I doubt Ms. McCormick will return to the school. I understand that what she was looking for wasn't here," he said, glancing at me.

Mrs. Kirk sat forward, her surprised gaze fixed on me. "She spoke to you? Why didn't you say anything?"

"You had drop-off, and with Peg getting sick . . . there was so much going on, I thought I'd tell you both, at once."

Mrs. Kirk frowned. "Well, what did she want?"

I looked at Detective Waraday, and he gave a nod of his head, indicating I should tell her. "The notes for her game."

Mrs. Kirk's chin came down, and she looked at me with raised eyebrows. "She came back to the school for a *game*?"

I was surprised that Detective Waraday hadn't told Mrs. Kirk about the game. He'd definitely known about it yesterday and could have informed Mrs. Kirk about it then.

Detective Waraday said, "Yes. It appears Ms. McCormick was creating a computer game. I think Mrs. Avery can explain it better than I can." He motioned that I had the floor.

I gave Mrs. Kirk a quick summary of the game, noticing that while Mrs. Kirk's attention was focused on me, Detective Waraday was watching her intently. I said, "So Ms. McCormick wanted those notes, the flowchart schematic thing. That's what she was looking for today."

Mrs. Kirk shook her head. "Of all the things . . ." She

picked up a pencil and tapped the pencil's eraser on the desktop rapidly. "And they weren't there? She didn't find them?" Mrs. Kirk's voice had an edge to it. She wasn't happy that I hadn't informed her of all this before Detective Waraday arrived.

"No," Detective Waraday said, "I have them."

"I see," Mrs. Kirk said, and gave him a long look that I was sure made the kids squirm in their chairs, but it didn't seem to bother Detective Waraday. After a second, Mrs. Kirk went on. "Well, creating a game on the school's computer system and using students to beta test it, as you called it, is certainly something she should have run by me."

The beat of the eraser increased, then stopped abruptly as Mrs. Kirk replaced it in a pencil cup. "But, as we all now know, Ms. McCormick had quite a few things that she preferred to keep to herself, things that she should have informed me of." She inched her chair back. "If that's all you need from us, Detective . . . ?"

He said, "That's not quite all. Do you have an extra classroom where I can speak with Mrs. Avery?"

I had been wondering if I should launch into the whole blackmail story of Ms. McCormick's in front of Mrs. Kirk. It seemed that Detective Waraday wasn't sharing all the details of the investigation with her, and I didn't want to give anything away.

Mrs. Kirk stared at him a moment, a frown on her face. "At the moment, no, there is not a free classroom, as we have a substitute in Ms. McCormick's classroom today, but you may use my office."

She stood and left, closing the door behind her.

Detective Waraday looked at the door for a moment, then turned back to me. His expression seemed to say, *I'm not getting any bonus points here, thanks to you.* He cleared his throat and adjusted his sport coat as he shifted in his chair so that he was fully facing me. Today he wore a dress shirt, tie, and jacket with his khakis. I wondered if he'd had to testify in court or attend some other important meeting. "So, blackmail?" he asked.

"I know it sounds crazy, but that is what Ms. McCormick said."

He took me through Ms. McCormick's story, then circled back and asked me about certain points again. Finally, he put his notebook and pen away. "It would make this whole situation much easier if she'd kept the note demanding money from her," he said.

"Do you think it could be true?" I asked. "I've heard some other . . . rumors. Nothing substantial, but . . ."

He took out his notebook again, and I recounted what Margo had told me without mentioning her name. "And then Gabrielle Matheson called me and told me she had some juicy gossip about something shady going on in the office, but I haven't heard back from her, so I don't know exactly what she was talking about." I frowned. "In fact, it's odd that she hasn't called me back. That's not like her."

Detective Waraday's chest heaved with a silent sigh as he added Gabrielle's name to his notebook. "I wouldn't worry about it. If there is one person who knows how to look out for herself, it's Mrs. Matheson."

I raised my eyebrows. "That's true."

He rubbed his hand down over his face, muffling his next words. "That was an inappropriate comment. I'm putting in too many hours, if I'm not censoring myself."

"I suppose something can be inappropriate but still true," I said with a grin.

"If that means I can count on you not to pass that comment on to Mrs. Matheson, then thank you." He stood and moved to open the door for me, but paused with his hand on the doorknob. "I thought you were giving up sleuthing," he said.

I threw up a hand. "I'm trying. It's not like I was camped out, waiting for Ms. McCormick to come back to the school. And about the blackmail, what M—" I cleared my throat, realizing I'd almost given away Margo's name. ". . . my friend told me about the rumors . . . well, I'm sure you can imagine what the number-one topic of conversation is among people connected to the school—Klea's death—so it's not like I'm seeking this out."

Detective Waraday nodded. "Right. Just be careful. The possibilities are narrowing. That's got to make the murderer nervous."

"Are you narrowing things down?"

"Oh, yes. We may have this resolved shortly. About the note and the handwriting samples . . . I have a local consultant—a person I've used a few times. I called her in, and she took a look at the two samples before I sent everything off to the state crime lab. She's confident the same person wrote both the note you received and the gaming flowchart."

"So Ms. McCormick did write the note that was in Livvy's take-home folder."

Detective Waraday nodded. "And probably threw the brick through the window of your van. I checked with the teachers in the rooms on either side of Ms. McCormick's room, asking them about the time period after you spoke to Ms. McCormick in the teachers' lounge. Ms. McCormick wasn't in her classroom when the bell rang for that next period. One of the teachers in the room next door to her classroom said she had to go over and tell Ms. McCormick's class to be quiet. Ms. McCormick arrived a minute or so later, slightly out of breath and with her hair windblown. Would she have known which car was yours?"

"Yes. All the teachers take turns monitoring drop-off and pickup. I'm sure she'd remember that I had a minivan. If she didn't remember exactly which one, she'd just have to look for the one with my kids' name tags hanging from the rearview mirror." The school required parents to hang laminated tags from their rearview mirror with the names of their students on it, to help keep the drop-off and pickup lines moving. "She didn't actually admit to throwing a brick at my van, but she told me she wanted me to back off."

"So now it's just a question of running down this blackmail thing, seeing if there is any truth in that," Detective Waraday said.

"But Ms. McCormick didn't think it was Klea who was blackmailing her."

"Right. But she's lied before," Detective Waraday said simply.

He opened the door, and let me precede him out of the office. Mrs. Kirk was at the counter, speaking to a teacher. Marie's desk was finally empty and the basket of inter-office envelopes sat invitingly unattended, but I thought that Detective Waraday would definitely see it as stepping on his toes if I tried to get a look at them. I settled for pointing out the envelopes quietly to Detective Waraday while Mrs. Kirk finished up at the counter. When she turned around, Detective Waraday thanked her for the use of her office, then said, "I'd like to make sure that Ms. McCormick didn't put any of her other papers in your inter-office mail. It would be helpful if I could check that. I can have the search warrant extended to include the office. . . ."

Mrs. Kirk said, "No need," and gestured to Marie's desk and the stack of envelopes. "There they are. Help yourself. You can even use Marie's desk. She's at lunch."

Detective Waraday sat down and began to unwind the string on the top envelope. I left the office and spotted Livvy's class going into the lunchroom. She had late lunch today. She waved and slowed down. "Are you here to have lunch with me?"

I checked my watch and saw that I had some time. "If you'd like that," I said, and she nodded.

I wasn't sure what had brought on the sudden change of her being okay being seen with me, but I figured I'd enjoy it while I could. I ate a lunch of watery spaghetti and heard all about Livvy's science class and their last experiment of the year, building a suspension bridge for toy cars using clothespins, paper, and yarn. Her team had built the only bridge that hadn't collapsed. Watching her animated face and listening to her and her friends describe their design, often speaking over each other in their excitement, I wished the rest of the school year could be more like the end of the year.

The end of the year—when the standardized tests were over—was when the kids got to do all the fun stuff. Instead of studying for the standardized tests, why couldn't the kids do more hands-on activities like this throughout the year? Abby and I discussed this topic often—in fact, I knew not to get her started on it unless I had plenty of time to listen.

We turned in our trays, and I said good-bye to Livvy and her friends. "See you at the end-of-school party, Mrs. Avery," one of Livvy's friends called as I left. The parties were still a week away, but the kids were already looking forward to them.

I gathered up my laptop and left the school for the organizing appointment with my new client. I wished Marguerite-with-the-last-name-left-blank had given me more details. It would have been nice to have a better idea of what she was hoping for, but she hadn't filled in any of the additional fields except the one for how she heard about me. She'd marked *From a Friend*, but that was it, except for the address.

North Dawkins was an interesting mix of densely packed stands of pines, sprawling rural areas with small ranch homes on large lots, and pockets of suburbia with street grids and modern homes. Marguerite lived in one of the more rural areas, and I was glad I had used my GPS as I turned onto the unmarked and slightly rutted lane that ran through a thick copse of pines.

The trees fell away, and I drove into a small clearing with a pale yellow frame house with a connected carport, which was obviously a more modern addition, tacked on to the side. A little flowerbed of orange and yellow flowers ringed the foundation of the house and a pair of white iron chairs were positioned at the side of the clearing in the shade of the pines.

I followed the rutted tracks to the carport and parked behind a silver two-door sedan. It was another muggy day, and the air felt heavy and stagnant as I walked around to the back of the van to gather my tote bag with all my organizing paraphernalia. Except for the faint call of a bird, the clearing was absolutely quiet and still. Not even a gust of wind ruffled the tops of the pines.

I climbed the steps to the wooden porch and rang the bell next to the door, which had a metal screen door mounted in front of it. I waited, surveying the porch swing with its flowered cushion and the hanging pots of petunias. A bee buzzed lazily from one bright pink flower to another. After a few minutes, I rang the bell again, leaning a bit longer on the button, but I didn't hear any sounds from inside to indicate someone was on his or her way to the door. Despite the car parked to the side of the house, it felt like no one was home. I knocked on the frame of the metal screen door. It clattered, sounding extra loud in the stillness, and the bee bobbed off around the side of the house.

It certainly wasn't the first time someone had forgotten an appointment with me, but it *was* unusual that someone would not show up for an appointment they'd made only a few hours earlier. With sweat already beading along my hairline, I shifted over a few steps, taking a peek in the windows on either side of the front door. Through the window on the left, I could see a dining room table and a corner cabinet with antique plates displayed. Clearly, Marguerite didn't need my help organizing that spotless room. I moved to the other window and caught my breath.

A woman lay sprawled on a couch. My hands began to shake as I reached for my phone to call 911 even though I knew it was too late to help her. There could be no mistake—with her white skin and jaw hanging open, she was dead. But what was worse was that it wasn't some stranger named Marguerite. It was Peg.

Chapter Eighteen

I don't know how long it was until I heard the low rev of an engine. I looked up and saw a sheriff's car bump down the rutted road toward me. I'd dialed 911 and then called Detective Waraday and left him a message when he didn't answer.

My legs had felt unsteady, and I'd moved over to the porch steps. I had dropped down onto the lowest step and put my elbows on my knees and my head in my hands, fighting off the surge of nausea that hit me as I thought about Peg's slack and lifeless face.

The deputy parked the car near the steps. He came out of his vehicle slowly. He was a young man in his twenties with dark hair and eyes. RAMIREZ was printed on his name tag. "You made the emergency call?"

I nodded, grabbed the step's handrail, and levered myself up. "Yes. I had an appointment here at two—I'm a professional organizer—but no one answered the door, so I looked in the window and saw her. She's on the couch," I said, looking over my shoulder to the house.

"Name?"

"She's Peg Watson. She worked at the elementary school."

"No, your name."

"Oh. Ellie Avery."

He methodically took down my name and contact information, then told me to stay where I was and climbed the steps to the porch. He peered in both windows for a moment, then went to the front door. He tugged on the screen door's handle, and it opened with a screech. He raised his hand and knocked on the wooden front door, but it swung open at the first touch of his knuckles.

He turned back to me. "Did you go inside?"

"No. I just rang the bell and knocked on the screen."

"You didn't notice that the door wasn't closed?"

"No."

He was about to enter the house when the sound of another car engine filled the air. It was Detective Waraday. He parked beside the sheriff's car and crossed quickly to the steps. He must have received my message because he said, "It's Peg Watson? You're sure?"

I nodded. "I could see her through the window." He went up the steps, paused to glance in the front window, then moved to the front door. "William," Detective Waraday said in greeting.

The deputy nodded. "Detective. I haven't been in yet." He glanced over Detective Waraday's shoulder to me. "Witness states that she didn't enter the house." He waved at the door. "It opened when I knocked."

Detective Waraday removed some plastic gloves from his pocket and handed a pair to Deputy Ramirez. "I have a feeling we'll need these." He lifted his chin toward the open door as he worked his fingers into the gloves, indicating that the deputy should move into the house.

They were in the house for about five minutes before

Detective Waraday came back outside and moved slowly down the steps, his face grim.

"You didn't enter the house?"

"No. I rang the bell and knocked. I didn't even know Peg lived here. I mean, she does live here, right?"

"Yes. This is her residence. Let's move over to those chairs in the shade." Detective Waraday pulled off the plastic gloves and stuffed them in his pocket, then wiped his forehead with the back of his hand. I realized that I was sweaty, too. Normally, I spent as little time as possible outdoors when it was hot and muggy, but the heat hadn't even registered. My shirt pressed damply against the skin between my shoulder blades, but I felt cold. The warm metal of the chair against the back of my legs actually felt soothing.

Detective Waraday sat down across from me and said, "Why are you here?"

I explained about the online appointment system and even showed him the message on my phone. "See, it says the client is Marguerite. Why would someone put in a fake name and then give this address?" I asked. I'd been pondering that question while I waited for the officers to come back out of the house.

"It wasn't a fake name," Detective Waraday said. "Not technically. Ms. Watson's full name is Marguerite Erica Watson. Peg is a nickname. When did you get that message?" Detective Waraday asked.

"This morning."

"Had Ms. Watson ever mentioned setting up an appointment with you?"

"No, never." I shook my head. "In fact, she hardly ever spoke to me . . . or anyone, really, that I saw. She was very, um, antisocial. Kept to herself."

He handed my phone back. "I'd like to have my tech people take a look at that message."

"Of course." I put my phone back in my pocket. "What happened?"

"Overdose," Detective Waraday said. "Prescription pain-killers."

"That's—that's terrible."

"Unfortunately, we're seeing it more and more—accidental overdose, I mean," he said, his face bleak.

"I had no idea that she had any sort of . . . problem like that."

"Oh, not her. I meant in general we're seeing more and more deaths related to painkillers. No, I didn't see any evidence that she was an addict. It appears that she used painkillers that were prescribed to her several months ago by a reputable local dentist, probably after a dental surgery."

I frowned. "I do remember back around January, right after Christmas break, that Peg was extra . . . um, grumpy." I cleared my throat, feeling guilty about talking about Peg this way, but it was true and if it could help Detective Waraday narrow down the possibilities, then I should tell him.

He nodded, and I went on, "Anyway, it was during that time—right after school started in January—that Marie told me that Peg had her wisdom teeth removed."

"That makes sense," he said. "In cases with addicts, it is common to find meds from these fake 'pain centers' that have popped up. We're cracking down on them, and we've made a lot of progress, but there are still some out there. It doesn't seem that was what was going on here."

"Peg was sick earlier today," I said, "but I can't imagine she would have taken a prescription painkiller for a virus or flu or whatever it was that she had. At least, not intentionally. Is there a chance that she got—I don't know—mixed up or something and took the wrong medicine?"

"I'm afraid not." He reached inside his jacket and removed a white sheet of paper that was already encased in plastic. "Suicide," he said as he handed it to me.

I blinked and scanned the typed page with Peg's signature at the bottom. I read a few lines, then looked up at him. It wasn't long and began without a salutation: *I can't stand it anymore. It's too difficult. Now that everyone will know, I don't want to go on. It's true that I took money from people, but they were so dumb that they deserved it. If they hadn't been doing things they shouldn't, they wouldn't have had anything to worry about. Same thing with Klea. If she had minded her own business, I wouldn't have had to kill her.*

The typed signature was Peg's full name, Marguerite Erica Watson, and under her name was a date, today's date. I looked up at Detective Waraday. "She says she did it—that she killed Klea," I said, amazed.

He nodded. "And admits to the blackmail, too."

"How terrible," I said again, and handed the paper back to him. I felt even colder than I had before and wrapped my arms across my waist.

Detective Waraday's phone rang, and he took the call, saying only a few words and listening for long moments. I stared at the tall pines behind Detective Waraday, my thoughts swirling—Peg, dead. It was so shocking. And the things that were coming out—blackmail at the school, not to mention murder. I thought back to the morning that Klea had gone missing. While moms were squeezing into tiny chairs and nibbling muffins with their kids, Peg had killed Klea. Something—some stray thought—flitted in and out of my mind, but before I could grasp it, it disappeared. It had been there, something that seemed important, too. But now it was gone like a wisp of ground fog that appeared in the morning, then vanished as soon as the sun hit it.

Detective Waraday hung up and shifted back to me. "Would you say Ms. Watson had been depressed or frightened lately?"

"I suppose I should say that I didn't know her well enough to answer that question, but as little as I knew her, I would say no. She didn't seem at all like someone who would commit suicide." I paused, thinking over my interactions, then said, "But Marie is who you should talk to about that." I sat forward suddenly. "Why would someone make an appointment to organize their closets, then kill themselves later that day? That just seems odd."

"I agree, but if she made the appointment, then later realized the net was closing around her . . . perhaps she decided she'd rather die than face the consequences of her actions. Could she have overheard Ms. McCormick's accusations?"

"It's possible she could have," I said. "Anyone could have been in the hallway and heard us, but I didn't see Peg. But then Peg got sick and left the school. Could it be . . . ? You're sure her death *was* an overdose, not something else? I wonder if she had some sort of medical condition. . . ."

"I'm not the medical examiner, but that will all be sorted out. There will be an autopsy. But you're forgetting about the suicide note."

"Yes. Right," I said, rubbing my forehead. "So many notes lately—Klea's note, blackmail notes to teachers and parents, and now a suicide note."

"I'm glad that's resolved," Mitch said later that night when I told him what happened with Peg. I could hear the relief in his tone. "I mean, it's a horrible situation for everyone involved, but selfishly I'm glad it's over. Especially since there's no chance of this exercise ending early. The weather's cleared and everything is back on schedule."

"Oh, that's too bad." I curled my legs under me and settled against the headboard. The kids were tucked in bed, and I was in our bedroom with the door closed. I hadn't mentioned what had happened with Peg to the kids. I'd been able to make it back to the school in time to pick them up. Then I'd been happy to throw myself into the normal after-school routine of snacks, homework, and cooking dinner. I'd debated talking to the kids about Peg later that night, but in the end, I'd decided that I would wait. The kids hadn't had any interactions with Peg, and if they knew her at all, it would only be as one of the "office ladies." I would see how the school handled it and go from there.

I adjusted one of the pillows behind my neck and settled down to catch up with Mitch. He had a gap in his schedule, and we hadn't been able to have an uninterrupted call for a few days. "I was hoping you'd be home early."

"Me too, but it doesn't look like it's going to happen. At least now I don't have to worry about you."

"You never worry," I said. "That's my department."

"I agree, you are the chief worrier in our family, but I have my moments, too. You're not one to let things go, and I know that this thing with Klea was weighing on you."

"Yeah, about that . . ." I cleared my throat.

"Ellie," Mitch said warningly.

"What?"

His sigh came through the phone line loud and clear. "I know that tone. You think something about Peg's death is off—that's it, isn't it?"

"Well, yes. I do. Several things, actually."

"I suppose you've made a list," Mitch said.

"I have." I reached for the notepad on the nightstand.

"I knew it," Mitch said, half exasperated, half joking.

"It's everything that is weird or doesn't fit."

"I don't know if you can make suicide 'fit,' " Mitch said, his tone serious again.

"I know, but these things . . . they're just strange. I mean, who makes an appointment with an organizer, then kills herself?"

"Okay, I wouldn't think someone would do that either, but you can't know what's going on in someone's head. Or maybe she made the appointment, then realized she was about to be found out. Once she knew that, nothing else mattered."

"That's what Detective Waraday said," I admitted. "But I still think it doesn't fit. And then there was her note. It was typed, which seems a little . . . formal . . . to me."

"Maybe she did most things on the computer. People don't write longhand anymore, not really."

"I know, but if that's the case, why wouldn't she just . . . I don't know . . . send a text? That's more in keeping with how we communicate with each other now. It seems odd that she'd type up a suicide note and print it out, then sign it. And the tone—I can't remember it word for word, but it wasn't sad or morose. It was almost . . . defiant," I said, finally hitting on the word I was searching for.

"So she saw her suicide as a final in-your-face gesture. There's no rule that suicidal people must be depressed," Mitch said. I could tell from his thoughtful tone of voice that he was arguing the other side of my points, but was giving serious consideration to what I was saying. "Although, taken all together, I can see what you're saying. I hope you're wrong about all this. I mean, I hope that Peg's death is exactly what it seems. You haven't talked to anyone else about this?" he asked sharply.

"Only Detective Waraday."

"And what did he say?"

"Not much. He raised some of the points that you did."

"Keep all this to yourself, okay? If you're right . . ."

I felt my insides twist. "Then the murderer is still out there."

Organizing Tips for PTA Moms

How to find your volunteering sweet spot

Here are some questions to consider and some volunteer ideas:

Do I like this type of activity?

If you don't enjoy being outdoors, then Field Day is probably not the best place to volunteer. If you love to read, the library is an obvious starting place. If you're crafty, then planning holiday party crafts or volunteering on art days could be just the thing for you.

Do I like to be front and center or behind the scenes?

A fundraising coordinator needs a specific set of skills (comfort with public speaking, to parents and students; vision casting; and the ability to get everyone excited about the campaign), while volunteers who set up or tear down for plays or events like the book fair enjoy working behind the scenes.

Do I like to work in a group or alone?

Managing the phone or text chain requires someone who likes detailed work, is methodical, and likes to work alone. Someone who loves working cooperatively would be great at planning parties, dances, or teacher appreciation events, which require the input and coordination of many people.

Do I like to have a fixed schedule or play it by ear?

If you like to know ahead of time what your schedule is, then you'll probably enjoy volunteering in your child's classroom on a fixed day of the week. If you hate feeling pinned down by a schedule, volunteer to help when your school is shorthanded or when someone gets sick.

Chapter Nineteen

When I walked into the school on Friday before lunch, I sensed a change in the atmosphere. The first person I saw was Vaughn, striding across the lobby, whistling as he pushed a rolling trash can. He nodded to me. Two teachers had paused on the side of the lobby to chat for a moment. As I passed them, I caught a few words.

". . . so horrible to know it was Peg, but I'm so glad. That's terrible to say, but it means it's over."

The other teacher nodded. "I know exactly what you mean. We can put it all behind us now. No more looking at everyone and wondering, *Was it you?*"

I went in the office and saw that Detective Waraday was at Peg's desk. He nodded and said, "Mrs. Avery," in greeting, and I said hello. Two of Peg's desk drawers hung open as he methodically picked up sheets of paper and examined them. The computer was missing, and I assumed it had been taken so that the tech-savvy investigators could search the files.

Mrs. Kirk was walking briskly toward the door, but she paused by the sign-in computer as I waited for my name tag to print. "Good afternoon, Mrs. Avery. Such a shame about Peg, and I'm terribly sorry that you were the one to find her."

"It was distressing," I said, feeling that the word was inadequate, but Mrs. Kirk just nodded.

"Of course it would be." She frowned. "The end of the year has been quite difficult, but at least we can start over with a fresh slate next fall." She glanced at Detective Waraday, who had moved on to another drawer at Peg's desk. "Thank goodness it wasn't during the middle of the school year. By the time August rolls around, most people will have forgotten what happened." She patted my arm. "Again, I'm sorry you were involved, but we can all rest easy now."

She left, and I glanced at Marie as I stuck the name tag to my shirt. She picked up a stack of papers and came around the counter. "How are you holding up?"

"Okay, I guess. I didn't really know Peg."

"Apparently none of us did." She looked through the door into the lobby and lowered her voice. "Can you believe it? Peg!"

"No," I said quite truthfully. I felt Detective Waraday look at me sharply so I didn't say anything else.

"It's made a complete difference in the atmosphere here at the school," Marie said. "Can you feel it?"

I nodded, and she added, "I didn't realize how on edge we all were, but now that we know . . . who . . . er, I mean, what happened . . . it's like everyone has relaxed."

Through the office's windows I saw a van with the words SOUTHERN BARBECUE on it arrive. It lumbered around the drop-off line circle and came to a stop at the school's front doors. "There's lunch. I have to go."

Today was the last day of Teacher Appreciation Week, and for a finale, we had a catered barbecue buffet scheduled. I met the two restaurant employees, a young man and a young woman who looked to be about college age, at the door and guided them through the sign-in process and then showed them the teachers' lounge. I had them set up the food on the counter that ran across the back of the room. They'd barely finished putting the last pan of coleslaw out when a couple of teachers poked their heads in the room. "Is it ready? It smells delicious." I waved them in, told them to help themselves, then walked the restaurant employees back to the office so they could check out.

"Will you return this afternoon for the containers?" I asked.

"No. It's all disposable," the young woman said as I walked them out the main doors. "Hopefully, there will be some leftovers for you to take home."

"I doubt that." When we had come out of the main office, the line of teachers waiting to dip a plate of food and return to either the cafeteria or their classrooms had already been out the door of the teachers' lounge.

I was on my way back inside when a car horn tooted. Gabrielle waved from the driver's seat of a compact SUV. I saw that she had upgraded her advertising. She used to have metallic signs attached to each side that read GET ORGANIZED WITH GABRIELLE, but those were gone. Now the whole car had been encased—wrapped, I think it's called—so that the same slogan marched from the front to the rear bumper in giant font. Her website and phone number were also listed. Near the back of the car, a four-foot image of Gabrielle's face smiled out at me.

The catering van pulled away, and Gabrielle punched the gas. Her car surged forward and stopped by the main door; then she hit the brakes and hopped out.

"Wow." I pointed to the side of her car. "Nice advertising. How's that working out?"

Her long hair bouncing against her shoulders, she came around to the passenger side of the car and studied the ad on her car. She was again in a nice tailored suit and heels. Today's combination was a purple jacket with a black skirt. "Great! I've only had it for a couple of days and already gotten three calls because of it."

"Good for you," I said, as I contemplated doing something similar. I was always looking for ways to grow my business, but after thinking about it for a second, I decided that the approach wasn't quite me. So far, my best advertising had been satisfied clients who told their friends. A discount coupon for people to give their friends seemed like a better idea for my business.

"I wanted to catch you before you went inside." Gabrielle took a few steps in her high heels, but only moved to the edge of the sidewalk and stopped. "You heard about Peg?" she asked.

"Yes," I said, leaving out the fact that I'd been the person to find her. I was sure Gabrielle would be upset she hadn't been my first phone call.

"Can you believe it? I always thought she was a sneaky one, but my, I never expected that. When I heard the rumors about what was going on here at the school, I never would have put it together with her."

"We didn't get to talk about that message you left for me," I said.

"I know. I've been so busy. Fitzgerald called me."

"Oh," I said, recognizing that she wasn't talking about a person, but a company. Fitzgerald was one of the big paper companies in the area. They had a paper-manufacturing plant in North Dawkins, and their name came up frequently as a sponsor of various local events like the North Dawkins Fourth of July fireworks display.

"They want my input on a couple of changes they are

considering." Gabrielle looked pleased. "I've just come from their main offices, in fact."

"That's quite a coup," I said, and for once, I didn't envy her. I didn't have a great desire to do freelance corporate work, especially if I had to dress in hose and heels on the job.

"I'm enjoying it," she said, then lowered her voice. "Anyway, I know you're up on all the news. Detective Waraday called me the other day and had all sorts of questions about the rumor I'd heard. I wasn't able to tell him much, but I did pass along what I knew—that someone was making money off people who had been naughty. But when I asked him what was going on, he wouldn't tell me anything."

"Well, he was probably still investigating," I said, not quite believing that I was defending Detective Waraday.

She made an impatient movement with her hand. "Still. He could have given me a *hint*."

"I think that might be frowned on in the sheriff's office." She looked like she was about to protest again, so I hurried on and said, "Anyway, it appears to be all sorted out now." I didn't wholeheartedly agree with that statement, but I didn't want Gabrielle insisting that we had more to investigate.

"Yes, it is good that it's all straightened out. I doubt that the executives at Fitzgerald would have called me in if they knew I was involved in what happened here." She tilted her head toward the school building. "No matter how remotely I was involved, it would be a black mark. They're such nervous nellies, these corporate bigwigs."

Her phone buzzed with a text and she checked the display. "Oh, this is Fitzgerald." She read the message and quickly sent one back. "They want me to drop by the office to clarify a few points, which is a good sign. I better get out there right away." She held the folder in her hand out toward me. "Ellie, will you be a dear and drop this with

Mrs. Kirk? Tell her I'll be by tomorrow to explain every-thing."

"Um, sure." I took the folder. Her SUV with the ad on the side was out of the parking lot before I made it to the school doors. I dropped off the folder with Mrs. Kirk, who opened it, read the title, then looked from it to me.

"Mrs. Matheson's recommendation for the digital orga-nization class for the teachers, I assume?" Mrs. Kirk said, eyebrows raised.

"I'm not sure."

A shade of disapproval came into Mrs. Kirk's voice. "I thought she wanted to go over this with me. She was very insistent."

"She had to leave unexpectedly. I'm sure she'll con-tact you."

Mrs. Kirk made a harrumphing sound as I left her of-fice. I went back to the teachers' lounge and found that about half of the food was gone, and the teachers for late lunch were lining up, their plates ready. I was glad they were enjoying the food, and I was also happy it was the last day I'd have to monitor the food. Now, all I had to get through were the end-of-school parties next week and an-other school year would be over. Mrs. Harris, plate in hand, came over to me. "This has been wonderful, Ellie. Thanks for coordinating the food."

"You're welcome. We do appreciate everything you all do for the students."

"Well, this is an excellent way to show it," Mrs. Harris said, pointing at her plate with her fork. "I'm glad I caught you," she said. "I thought you'd be interested to know that this will be my last year here at the school."

"Really? Oh, I'm . . . happy for you . . . ?" I asked with an uncertain grin.

She laughed. "Thank you. Yes, I am looking forward to

it. I can still volunteer at the school. They always need help—volunteers don't have to be parents—but I can dedicate more time to . . . other things. I'm considering trying something new . . . more mainstream, you might say."

I fell into step beside her as we left the teachers' lounge. "Well, good luck with it," I said, glancing at her out of the corner of my eye, my thoughts about Klea's list coming back to me, as well as my realization that Mrs. Harris's alibi wasn't as solid as I'd first thought. But she looked so frail and had such a kind disposition. Could she really be a murderer? Everyone seemed to think that Peg's death had wrapped up the investigation, but there were too many questions around Peg's suicide and that had me second-guessing everything. At first glance, Mrs. Harris didn't look like a murderer, but she was also very good at hiding a part of her life from nearly everyone at school. Could she be hiding something else?

As we crossed the lobby, a strange swishing sound interrupted my thoughts, but before I could look for the source, Vaughn hurried by, his heavy tread thudding loudly. With a mop and bucket in hand, he nearly ran me over. "Sorry," he called over his shoulder.

I'd never seen him move that fast. He slowed down as he approached the records room next to the main office and stepped more carefully as he paused to prop the mop and bucket against the wall. That was when I saw water rushing out from the gap under the door to the records room. As he flicked through his key ring, the water coursed over his shoes and splashed at the ankles of his pants. He inserted the key and opened the door. A flood of water rushed out, soaking him to the knees, and spread out across the lobby floor like an incoming tide.

Organizing Tips for PTA Moms

<u>Social Media Ideas for Schools</u>

Facebook
Facebook is a great platform for posting announcements and reminders, and for providing a platform for parents to connect.

Twitter
The short format of Twitter works great for announcements and reminders for events, as well as for notifications of school closures or changes in schedules.

Pinterest
Room moms can create a pinboard for party planning and invite other moms to participate in pinning ideas for food, decorations, and games.

School clubs can create pinboards for upcoming activities to gather ideas and inspiration.

A general pinboard for the school could feature events and activities, but check with the school district for their photography policy before posting images of students.

Chapter Twenty

The water slid across the floor toward me. I automatically stepped back, but it reached me and sloshed over the tops of my boat shoes. Mrs. Harris said, "Oh my," as the water soaked into her sensible rubber-soled flats. A few teachers came out of the teachers' lounge, saw the flood of water, and screeched as the water pushed toward them.

Now that Vaughn had opened the door and released the water that had been pent up in the records room, the water flowing out of the door was lower. He stepped into the room, and the water came up to his shins. It coursed down the hallway, reaching some of the classrooms. Exclamations and the scrapes of chairs sounded from the nearby classrooms.

Marie and Mrs. Kirk emerged from the main office. Mrs. Kirk took one look around and said, "I'll call maintenance. Thank goodness we have tile floors and not carpet."

Vaughn came splashing out of the records room. "It's a broken pipe in the ceiling. The sprinkler system. I'll turn off the main." He strode quickly away, water splashing with each step as he hurried across the lobby to the doors that opened to the back field. Water continued to flow out the door of the records room, but as it spread through the hallways, the level of it went down.

Marie still stood in the door of the office, an appalled look on her face. "This is awful. We should get some towels . . . or something," she said.

Mrs. Kirk reappeared. "No, that won't do us any good. There's too much water already. Marie, help me open the main doors. Let's get as much of this water outside as possible." Mrs. Kirk sloshed through the water to the main doors. Marie followed her, and they opened the row of doors.

Mrs. Harris and I moved to the doors at the other side of the lobby, the ones that opened to the back field, and propped them open as well. Vaughn, holding a wrench, was on his way back. The water was streaming out the doors and rushing across the blacktop, soaking the grass. Vaughn shook his head as he hurried by. "This is going to be a mess."

He was right. Vaughn was able to get the water turned off, but it took an hour to clear the standing water out of the school. I pitched in and helped, along with several other teachers who were on their planning period and some parent volunteers who happened to be in the building at that time. We used mops and brooms to shift the standing water out the doors, and we were all soaked to the knees by the time the worst of it was cleared out. The school district's maintenance people arrived in a van and went to work repairing the pipe in the records room.

I gave the still damp floor in the hallway a final swipe with a push broom and returned to the lobby. I paused beside Marie, who stood in the doorway of the records room. "Such a shame," she said. "All that paper, ruined."

Two maintenance men were on ladders, working on the pipes overhead. The ceiling tiles had been soaked. Some had fallen to the floor, and others hung limply in their metal grids, looking more like soaked towels than acoustical tiles. The leak had been at the back of the room, but because the door had been closed and trapped most of the water, it had backed up and soaked into the lower drawers of the filing cabinets.

"I opened a couple of the files to see how bad it is," Marie said, nodding toward several of the lowest file drawers, which had been pulled out. The file folders and papers were waterlogged, the pages wavy and the ink smeared. "They'll have to be destroyed . . . somehow," Marie said. "These are confidential files. We can't just throw them away. They have Social Security numbers and test scores on them."

"That will be difficult," I said. "But I'm sure there are companies that handle that sort of thing. Maybe the people who repair the water damage will have some suggestions, or I can ask around."

Before Marie could answer, Mrs. Kirk appeared behind our shoulders. "A team is on the way. We should have fans set up, and the tile floors dry before the end of the day." Mrs. Kirk had made an announcement that the teachers should keep the students in their current classrooms until the water was cleaned up.

One of the repairmen clattered down the ladder. "That should do it," he said. "We'll turn on the water and test it, make sure everything is okay."

"Excellent. Thank you for arriving so quickly." Mrs. Kirk looked around and spotted Vaughn, who was collecting mops and brooms from the volunteers. She motioned him over. "Vaughn will show you the water main."

The other repairman stayed on the ladder, to monitor for leaks when the water was turned back on, I imagined.

"Could you tell us what happened?" Mrs. Kirk asked. "What caused the leak?"

The repairman had been about to follow Vaughn, but he stopped and pulled a short section of pipe from the pocket of the cargo pants he wore. He pointed at the pipe with a grimy finger. "See that? That's a pinhole leak. It happens with these copper pipes sometimes. Corrosion," he said with a shrug. "These older buildings all have it. I wouldn't be surprised to see more instances of this. The district really should look into replacing it all, but—you know—the cost." He pointed to the area where they had been working. "We replaced the whole section in the ceiling to be on the safe side. You shouldn't have any more problems— well, at least not from that pipe," he said, and left to go with Vaughn.

Mrs. Kirk put her hands on her hips and surveyed the damage. "And this was all to be digitized this summer," she said. "I suppose the only good thing about this situation is that they are old files."

"Oh, they weren't current information?" I asked, thinking that was one bit of positive news in the midst of the mess.

"No," Mrs. Kirk said. "We've used digital records for years now." She tapped the card label on one of the filing cabinet drawers near her. The writing on the label was runny, but I could still read it. *A-H, 1989.* "These files were from years ago when we used a paper system—seems like ancient times, doesn't it? Well, all except for yours, Marie," Mrs. Kirk said as she gestured at a stack of banker boxes along the floor. "They'll have to be disposed of now."

"I'll make some calls and see that it's done," Marie said.

Vaughn, his head poking in the open doorway at the back of the lobby, called for Mrs. Kirk, and she strode away.

Marie reached down and picked up some sodden papers that were plastered to the floor. "If only I hadn't moved these boxes in here yesterday." She held the dripping sheet of paper away from her body. "All that work . . . just gone." She smiled bleakly. "If I'd known all my files were going to be destroyed, I wouldn't have worked so hard to get everything organized before I retired."

"That's right. I forgot, you only have a few days left."

Marie tossed the limp paper into a trash can. "All that work, for nothing." She wiped her damp fingers on her skirt. "I don't know why I'm so upset. I mean, files of fundraising activities really are trivial when you compare it to student grades."

"Yes, but it was your work. No one likes to see something they've put time into damaged." She murmured an agreement, but was moving from box to box, lifting lids and shaking her head. "No, they're all a complete loss."

"Have you had anything to eat? No? Then come have a plate of food from the teachers' lounge," I said, thinking that getting her out of the records room would do more than anything else to cheer her up. She nodded and headed in that direction. I followed her, and was relieved to see that there was still some food. I left her microwaving a plate and went back to the lobby.

I intended to go home and change out of my wet shoes, but as my shoes squished across the lobby, I saw a petite woman hesitating in the open doors as she brushed her bangs from her eyes while she scanned the damp floor and the disarray of mops and brooms propped around the walls. I studied her oval face with its upturned nose and blue eyes, trying to place her. Was she a parent? A substitute teacher?

Since she looked like she wasn't sure where to go, I said, "Can I help you?"

"Ah—yes. I'm Jane Guthrie, Klea Burris's sister."

"Oh," I said, and immediately realized she looked slightly familiar because her build was similar to Klea's—she was slender and small, and she had the same upturned nose that Klea had had. "I'm so sorry about Klea," I said. "We all are."

"Thank you. It's still—I can't quite take it in. But at least now we know who did it and can move on." She blinked and swallowed. "I stopped by because the principal—Mrs. Kirk, I think it was—contacted me and said she had some of Klea's belongings, but"—her gaze ranged around the chaotic scene of the lobby—"this doesn't look like a good time."

"There was a water leak," I said. "It's a little crazy right now."

"No problem," Jane said. "I'm here for a few days, sorting through Klea's belongings and getting her house in order so it can go on the market. I can come back next week."

"That would probably be best. I'm Ellie Avery, by the way."

"Nice to meet you," she said, then paused. "That name—you're the organizer, aren't you?"

"Yes," I said.

"Klea mentioned you. She said that you came to her house and gave her some suggestions. I think she wanted to hire you, but money was tight and then—" She cleared her throat and hurried on. "Anyway, she said you were very helpful."

"I'm glad."

"In fact, I intended to get your phone number from the school, if they would give it to me," she said with a small smile. "Or look for you online. I have a few things I need help with and thought you might be just the person I need."

Jane brushed her bangs off her forehead again. It was a

gesture that I remembered Klea making, too. On that day Klea and I had hauled the tables up to the stage when we'd finished, she'd swept her hair off her forehead and said, "Well, that was my workout for the day." We'd laughed together, and I'd said, "Who would have thought that volunteering at the school was as good as going to the gym?"

A wave of sadness swept over me. It was still hard to believe that Klea was gone. "What kind of help are you looking for?" I asked, refocusing on Jane.

"I've been sorting through her belongings, deciding what to keep and what to give away. I should be done with that soon, but next week I have to go back to Missouri—that's where I live—so I can't be here on Friday, when I have several pickups scheduled. That was the first day I could get on their schedules. A charity is coming to pick up the boxes of belongings I'm giving away, and I have a consignment shop scheduled to pick up the furniture. Could you be there to let them in and make sure they only take what I have marked for them?"

"Yes, of course. I can do that," I said, relieved that it was a simple job. If she wanted help cleaning out every room in Klea's house, there was no way I could get it done before school was out, and my time was limited in the summer.

"I'll pay your usual rate," she said.

"There's no need for that. I'd be happy to do it, no charge."

"Oh, it's not a problem—"

"No, please let me do this. I'd like to," I said.

After a moment, she nodded. "Thank you."

She suggested we meet during the weekend so she could show me which items should be picked up, and then we exchanged phone numbers. She was about to leave when I said, "There's something I was wondering about. . . . I

may not have heard because I'm in and out of the school,"
I said, mentally amending that phrase in my mind—*except
for this week*—because I'd been at the school more than
I'd been home, it seemed. "But I didn't hear about a memorial service or funeral for Klea. Will it be in Missouri? I
know the teachers and staff here will want to know what is
planned."

Jane looked away for a second, gazing across the busy
lobby. "There will be a small memorial service in Missouri.
Klea wanted to be cremated. That's already been taken care
of. I'm taking her ashes home next week."

"Oh, I see," I said quickly.

Jane sighed. "It seemed better this way. I know it's self-
ish of me, but if we planned something here, then Ace
would show up, and I absolutely will not have him conta-
minating anything to do with Klea's memory. It's so un-
fair," she said, her tone becoming heated, "that she finally
got away from him, and then she was killed. I'd wanted
her to leave him for years, even offered to help her move
back to Missouri. She could have lived with us until she
got on her feet, but . . ." Her voice changed, and the vigor
and passion she spoke with drained out of her as she said,
"She wouldn't do it."

Jane shook her head. "She had to do it in her own way.
I never could talk her into anything, not even when it was
good for her," she said with a weak smile. "Excuse me, I
should go." She hurried away, and I knew she was leaving
before she cried. I could see the tears glistening in her eyes
before she turned away.

I watched her walk along the school's car circle lane.
Then she turned and walked beside the chain-link fence.
About halfway down the block, she crossed the street to
Klea's Craftsman, climbed the steps, and went in the front
door.

*   *   *

The weekend was actually fairly quiet, except for a soccer game and a trip to the North Dawkins library for Livvy to pick up new books. The school library had closed. All books had to be returned, so she was in book-withdrawal. We returned from the library with a tower of books for each of the kids, which at first glance would seem to keep them in books all summer, but I knew it would only be a week or two before Livvy would want to make another trip because she had "read all the good ones."

It was late Sunday evening when I met Jane at Klea's house. Jane walked me through the rooms, which looked so different with all their contents stowed in boxes. She had marked everything clearly, and I didn't have any questions. Jane gave me the keys to the front door dead bolts, then said, "If you could do me one more favor, I'd appreciate it." I could tell she'd been working hard for several days, packing and cleaning. She looked exhausted and leaned against the doorframe.

I paused on the top porch step. "Sure. What do you need?"

"Well, I thought I could stay here until Tuesday, but I have to leave tomorrow. I intended to go over to the school on Monday to pick up Klea's things, but I have to be at the airport in Atlanta at eight tomorrow morning, so there's no way . . ."

"I can pick them up from Mrs. Kirk. I'll bring them back here."

"Oh, that would be a relief. Mrs. Kirk said it's nothing really significant—just some odds and ends—but they were Klea's, and I'm afraid that if something comes up at home, I may not get back here before the school closes for the summer."

"No worries. I'll take care of it." I said good-bye to her, then got in the van to get back to the kids, who were at home.

I'd called in their favorite babysitter, but I knew it wouldn't be long before I wouldn't need her services. Livvy would soon be a teenager—teenager!—and I knew that soon she would be perfectly capable of holding down the fort while I was gone. I'd even had a few moms, who were looking for sitters, ask me if she was available. I had said we weren't quite ready for that, and Livvy had countered that *she* was ready. "You may be ready for it, but I don't think I am," I'd said with a laugh, and since Livvy was more interested in playing soccer, reading, and spending time with her friends than watching other people's kids, that had been the end of the that conversation.

I glanced at the school as I crept by with my foot on the brake. Even though school wasn't in session, the school speed zone was still in effect. The school had a forlorn, deserted air with the empty parking lot and all the windows dark.

Abby had told me that Mrs. Kirk had sent the teachers an alert, letting them know that a water remediation crew would work all day Saturday at the school to repair the worst of the water damage so that school could continue until the end of the year. Then, in the summer, any large-scale repairs that needed to be done would be undertaken. Fortunately, there wasn't a lot they had to do.

"That's the beauty of tile floors and cinderblock walls," Abby had quipped. "No wood or drywall to replace."

They must have finished the temporary repairs because the school was quiet. The sun was already low in the sky, casting long shadows from the tall pines that filled the front lawns of the houses across from the school. The patches of shade stretched all the way across the parking lot and engulfed the school, the surrounding fields, and the belt of trees behind the school. I shivered, thinking of Klea's body in the wooded area. I didn't think I'd ever want to walk through that shortcut again.

As I came even with the front of the school, I thought I saw a flash of light in one of the office windows, but it must have been a reflection of another car's headlights because when I looked again, all the windows were black squares.

The next morning, the atmosphere of the school was completely different as I pulled into the drop-off line on Monday at fifteen minutes after eight. Kids, some with parent escorts, others on their own, walked toward the school. Buses inched through the traffic, then lumbered into the bus circle and disgorged kids. Cars circulated through the drop-off circle like parts on a conveyer belt that moved in fits and starts.

The kids and I were cutting it close on time today—it had been one of the those mornings when nothing goes right—so I completed the circuit, dropping the kids at the main doors so they could make it to class before the bell. Then, knowing that if I deviated from the pattern I would gum up the works of the car circle, to say nothing of making parents, teachers, and staff angry with me, I exited the parking lot. Then I returned, but this time, instead of going to the car circle drop-off line, I turned into a parking slot and went into the school, after giving Mrs. Kirk a wave on the way in. She barely acknowledged my greeting, and looked rather harried, but I didn't feel snubbed. I was sure her mind was on making sure that drop-off ran smoothly.

Since I'd promised Jane that I would pick up Klea's belongings, I wanted to do it first thing so that I didn't forget it. I hurried in the main doors along with the last of the late-arriving kids, surprised to see a square of plywood covering a section of one of the main doors.

I crossed the lobby and walked to the office. Even though Mrs. Kirk was busy outside, I was sure that Marie would know where to find Klea's things. I was surprised to see that the door to the office was closed. It was never closed.

I turned the handle and stepped inside, then stopped dead in my tracks. The office looked like a tornado had hit it.

Chapter Twenty-one

"And I thought my day had started badly," I said, shaking my head over the destruction.

Shattered glass, bits of plastic, and paper covered the floor of the office. The desks had been flipped on their sides and chairs upended. The wooden bench was overturned, and a spray-paint scrawl of curses covered the rich dark wood. In the middle of it all stood Marie, her hands limp by her sides, and expression of disbelief on her face. She saw me and started. "Did I not lock that door?" She crunched toward me and pushed the door closed. "I thought I'd locked it," she said distractedly. She flipped the lock into place. "We can't have the students in here—all this glass and . . . and mess." She picked up an inbox tray from the floor and set it on the counter. It clattered against fragments of plastic and metal scattered over the counter.

"This is awful," I said as the full amount of destruction sank in. The glass window in the wall next to Mrs. Kirk's office had been shattered. The computer monitors were gaping holes and a couple of computer towers looked as if someone had taken a mallet to them.

"Yes. Shocking, isn't it?" Marie said. "I feel like I'm in a daze." She reached down and picked up something else, one of the wooden cubes with numbers carved into the sides that was part of her desk calendar. "I'll probably never find the other one," she said. "If it wasn't against school policy, I think I might bring my pistol to school," she said.

I must have looked surprised because she said, "It's been one thing on top of the other, you know? Klea and Peg, and now this. I'm beginning to wonder if it will stop."

"I can understand that," I said. "I was just surprised that you own a gun. You don't seem to be the type, you know."

"I bought it after Heath died. I didn't like being alone in the house at night. It was silly, I know. I mean, I live in a great neighborhood, just a few blocks from here, in fact. But it was difficult after Heath passed away, especially at night, so I got a gun and went to classes to learn how to use it and everything." She looked less skittish and more like her normal, cheerful self, but then the door handle rattled, and she jumped as a knock sounded.

Marie unlocked the door, opened it a crack, then stepped back so that Vaughn could maneuver through the door with a broom and a rolling trash can. He wore a pair of thick work gloves and also carried a dustpan. It was going to take more than a trash can to clear up this mess, but they had to start somewhere, I supposed.

Marie locked the door behind him, and Vaughn set to work as he cleared a trail from the door to the counter.

"Marie," I said. "I hate to be a bother right now, but I only ran in to pick up Klea's things. Her sister was going to come in and get them today, but she had to leave town early and asked me to do it. Do you know if they were in here?" I asked, scanning the scattered pieces of office equipment and reams of paper that covered the floor. I was already dreading calling Jane and telling her that it might be a while—maybe never—before Klea's things were found.

My question seemed to give Marie a purpose and help her focus. She put a finger to her lips and turned in a circle. "Yes, Mrs. Kirk mentioned that the sister would be coming by to pick up Klea's things. Now, where were they? Mrs. Kirk had them in her office for a few days, but—ah!—you're in luck, or I guess her sister is in luck." Marie focused on a cardboard box on the back counter near the coffeepot. "Mrs. Kirk moved it out here yesterday." Marie crunched across the floor and retrieved a cardboard box. "Somehow this escaped the destruction," she said. The flaps of the box were open, and as she handed it to me I could see it only held a few items—two coffee mugs, some paperback books, a calendar made of wooden cubes, and a sweater. That weird half-formed thought . . . or perhaps impression was a better word . . . threaded through my mind, but I couldn't quite grasp it.

I realized Marie was speaking, and I blinked, refocusing on her. "I'm sorry. What did you say?"

Marie waved her hand around the room. "Whoever did this probably didn't think this"—she tapped the box— "was worth destroying . . . unlike the computers."

"It's so sad that someone would do this," I said, looking around the office. "It happened during the weekend?"

"It must have been either late Saturday night or sometime during Sunday. The crew cleaning up the water damage was here all day Saturday."

Vaughn dumped a pile of debris into the trash can. "Everything was fine when they left. I made sure before I locked up."

"And they got in the main doors?" I asked, thinking of the square of plywood that I'd noticed on my way in. Had it been broken on Sunday night when I'd driven by the school? I didn't remember it, but would I have noticed it with all the lights off inside the school and the windows dark?

Vaughn nodded. "Yep. I got that cleaned up. First thing I did today. Couldn't have the kids walking through broken glass this morning."

"And it didn't set off an alarm, or anything?"

Vaughn snorted. "No alarms in a building this old. Only the district's newer buildings have alarms." He leaned on his broom. "But with all this computer equipment, they should have alarms in all the buildings. All the schools have computers now." He straightened and poked at the remains of a shattered computer monitor with the bristles of the broom. "Someone could have had a nice haul of computers—if they'd wanted to steal things instead of destroying them."

"And nothing else was vandalized?" I asked.

"No," Marie said. "Only the office." She ran her hand over her upper arms as if she were cold. "It seems whoever did this hates the school . . . or someone who works here."

I set the box by the door and picked up one of the gnome figurines that usually decorated Marie's desk. The tip of the figurine's red hat had broken off. "I can help you for a bit," I said as I put the gnome on the counter.

"You don't have to do that," Marie said, and there was something guarded in her tone. It appeared the wariness and distrust that had been almost palpable before Peg's death was back.

Vaughn waved me off, too. "No, you don't have any gloves or the right kind of shoes," he said, pointing at my ballet flats. Marie unlocked the door for me, and I picked up the box, but before I could step out the door, Mrs. Kirk appeared and pushed inside. She looked surprised to see me in the office, but her gaze rested on me for only a second, then swept around the room.

She put a hand to her temple and rubbed. "It's utter destruction," she said in a frazzled tone of voice. "What else can go wrong? This is absolutely the worst end of a school year we've ever had."

I had never seen her look so upset. Every time I saw her, she was calm and in control. She was a steadying influence on the students. Her high expectations made the unruliest kids curb their behavior while her firm belief that her students were bright and smart and could do anything inspired and encouraged them.

The tardy bell rang, and it seemed to snap Mrs. Kirk out of her gloomy state. She drew in a deep breath and made her way carefully through the wreckage to her office. "At least the PA system wasn't destroyed. I'll make the usual morning announcements. Perhaps we can be back to normal—or some sort of version of it—by lunch."

Mrs. Kirk's voice came through the speakers. I detected a slight quaver in her first words, but after a few sentences, she was soon back to her normal tone. I paused by the door, reciting the pledge along with Marie and Vaughn; then, as Mrs. Kirk announced that the office would be closed until further notice, I picked up the box and slipped out. Marie clicked the lock into place as soon as I was in the lobby.

I hefted the box in my arms and headed for the doors, my attention drawn to the square of plywood over one of the panes. Detective Waraday stood outside the door, examining it. I picked another one of the doors farther down from him and used my shoulder to push it open; then I angled the box through. Detective Waraday came over and held the door open for me.

"Are you here about the office?" I asked, wondering why Vaughn was cleaning up if the police had been called.

"Anything that happens here, dispatch figures I'll want to know about it," he said with a faint smile.

"Then you don't think it's related to the other things that have happened?"

"Mrs. Burris and Ms. Watson's deaths? No. This is probably end-of-year hijinks."

"Hmm," I said, thinking that he might change his mind when he saw the viciousness of the destruction. "Well, I should tell you that I drove by here on Sunday night, and I thought I saw a light in one of the window."

"The light was on in the office?"

"No, I don't think so. I'm not even sure it was inside the school. It was just a flash of light. At the time, I thought it was the reflection from another car's headlights, but I suppose it could have been a flashlight."

"Did you notice the broken pane in the door?" he asked.

"No. I wasn't looking closely. I saw the flash of light as I drove by and then went on. I only mentioned it because of what happened. That's quite a mess in there."

Detective Waraday nodded, but he looked distracted, as if his thoughts were elsewhere. He put his hands in the pockets of his khakis and surveyed the parking lot. No one else was in sight. "I want you to know the autopsy of Ms. Watson is in."

"You have the results already? That was fast," I said, surprised.

"I called in a favor," he said. "The autopsy showed Ms. Watson ingested a lethal amount of painkillers. There was no sign of any medical complication either."

"Oh," I said. "I'd thought that the results might be different. There were so many little details that seemed a bit . . .

off." It wasn't that I was hoping she hadn't killed herself—if that was the case, it would only make things much more complicated and also mean that the killer was still out there—but I didn't like the rather strange details surrounding her death, like the almost hostile typed note and, in particular, the fact that she'd scheduled an organizing appointment shortly before her death.

Detective Waraday nodded. "I know the appointment she made with you troubled you. That's why I wanted a quick word with you. Our computer forensics team tracked the IP address of the computer that was used to fill out your online appointment form. It was Ms. Watson's computer, here at the school."

"Really?" I said. I hadn't expected that. I shifted the box from one arm to another because one of the flaps kept popping up and cutting into my arm.

Detective Waraday continued, "And as far as we can tell, she had no other long-term issues with prescription painkiller addiction. The amount of medicine missing from the prescription bottle correlates with what was prescribed for her after her dental surgery. It looks as if she took two pain pills shortly after her surgery, which would be completely normal, then put the pill bottle away and didn't take any more until Thursday. And her bank account also shows multiple cash deposits at regular intervals, indicating that Ms. McCormick didn't lie about the blackmail. She was right about that. Ms. Watson had a nice little side income from her activities." He reached for the door handle. "Sometimes things don't fit together in a neat pattern. I know you're all about making things neat and tidy, but people don't behave like you expect them to, especially when someone is suicidal."

"So the investigations into Peg's death and Klea's murder are closed?" The flap released again and dug into my arm.

"Yes, they are officially closed."

I forgot about the pressure of the box flap. There was something, some slight reservation in his tone, that made me frown at him. "Are you satisfied? Personally, I mean?"

He pulled open the door. "I don't think I'm ever one hundred percent satisfied that I have all the answers, no matter what the case, Mrs. Avery." He went inside, and I stood there a moment, thinking about what he'd said. Then I set the box down on the ground and tucked the flaps under each other.

A mom approached at a quick pace. A little girl, a toddler with her fine blond hair in dog ears, ambled along behind her mom. The mom wrenched open the door with the plywood panel and held it for her daughter, but she didn't follow her mom inside. The toddler, squatting with perfect form, was trying to pick up something shiny from behind the metal doorstop that was set in the concrete.

"No! Dirty!" the mom said, and backtracked. As she took the toddler's hand and moved her toward the door, the mom used her foot to sweep away the thing that had fascinated the little girl. The mom and I exchanged a look. "Why is it that whatever is on the ground is always irresistible?" she asked.

I picked up the box. "Yep, I remember those days," I said as the mom went into the door, coaxing the toddler along with her.

I transferred the box onto my hip and went over to the bed of shrubs next to the main doors. A thin shard of glass glittered in the dirt.

An uneasy atmosphere settled over the school. I wasn't in the building as often as I had been during the previous week, but the few trips I had made inside, I noticed the tension among the staff. The teachers snapped, and even

Vaughn, who had always seemed easygoing, was jumpy. I ran by the school to drop off Nathan's forgotten lunch box one afternoon and turned the corner into a hallway and bumped into Vaughn, who was moving backward as he mopped the floor. "Watch where you're going," he said sharply, then immediately apologized.

Despite the uneasiness that the adults clearly felt, within a day, the office had been returned to a semblance of order. Computers and phones had been transferred from other parts of the school. The wooden bench was now upright, the graffiti on the back turned to the wall. Mrs. Kirk had said that she had a furniture restorer scheduled to pick up the piece as soon as the school year was over. They would strip it and re-stain it. The glass panel beside Mrs. Kirk's door was back in place, and Marie had even been able to find both wooden blocks from her calendar. I'd seen a large truck with the company name SECURE DOCUMENT DISPOSAL on it parked at the school during the week, and supposed that they had been hired to remove and destroy the sodden files from the records room.

Abby, who was usually so buoyant and positive, noticed it as well. She called me on Tuesday night to see if I could give Charlie a ride to school on Wednesday morning, as she had drop-off duty. I said of course, and then she said, "It's so weird at the school right now. I'm always glad when the school year is over, but this is so different. Everyone is tense and suspicious. I don't like it."

I didn't like it either, but there were only a few days left in the school year. I'd again considered keeping the kids home during the remainder of the week, but when I floated the idea, they'd both been adamant. They wanted to go. There was no way they were missing their year-end activities, which were mostly the fun things that they didn't get to do all year, including picking up their memory books and participating in the end-of-year assembly, when awards were handed out.

Friday, the last day of the school year, the kids literally bounced out of the van when I dropped them off. I negotiated the congestion around the school and had to park on the grassy overflow area. I would be bouncing between Klea's house and the school today. I had two charity donation pickups to supervise at Klea's house, one at nine-thirty and another at two. In between those two appointments, I had two end-of-year parties to attend.

Instead of driving the short distance back and forth between Klea's house and the school, I'd decided it would be smarter to park in the school lot and walk the short distance. With all that had been going on lately, my walks with the Stroller Brigade, my neighborhood walking group, had been sadly ignored. Getting in some extra footsteps during my day was exactly what I needed.

I left the school parking lot and walked down the grassy verge next to the chain-link fence, then crossed the street and unlocked the front door to Klea's house with the keys Jane had given me. The house was again stuffy and dark with all the blinds drawn. I snapped on lights as I made a rapid survey of the house, making sure that everything was ready for the charity pickups. Once I was sure everything was fine, I went to the porch to wait. I didn't turn on the air conditioner, figuring it wasn't worth it for the short time I would be at the house. And the people loading boxes and furniture would probably prop the doors open anyway.

But I wished I had turned it on because the charity picking up the boxes arrived forty-five minutes late. The two men used dollies to ferry stacks of boxes from the house to the truck. It took them about twenty minutes to clear all the boxes, and when they left, the house seemed much emptier. One of the guys had attempted to take the box of personal items from the school, but I'd rescued it before it disappeared onto the truck. While there wasn't anything inherently valuable in the box, Jane wanted to go through it. After I'd picked up the box of Klea's belongings from the school, I'd brought it to Klea's house and left it on the kitchen counter with a note that it wasn't part of the charity donation, but the guy must not have seen the note.

Most of the furniture was going next. Jane said she couldn't afford to move all the furniture halfway across the country. The only things that were staying were a rocking chair and a small end table that Jane said had belonged to their mother. Jane would take them back with her to Missouri after her next trip back here.

I transferred the box of belongings to the seat of the rocking chair in the living room, where I could keep an eye on it while they loaded the rest of the boxes. After they finished, I had enough time to hike down to the van, go to the nearby sub shop, and have a turkey sandwich before I returned to the school to help with the parties.

Nathan's party in Mr. Spagnatilli's room involved lots of frosted cupcakes and the traditional decorating of Mr. Metacarpal, the skeleton, for summer. "It gives the kids something to do—besides run around the room and scream," Mr. Spagnatilli said.

I thought it was a very clever idea. Each of the kids had brought some contribution. Nathan's was a beat-up straw hat. By the end of the party, in addition to the hat, the skeleton was decked out in swim shorts, sunglasses, swim flippers, and sunglasses.

A more grown-up atmosphere permeated Livvy's classroom. There were still cupcakes, but no special activities or games—those were for babies, I was informed—but the kids were allowed to talk among themselves and most of the time was spent signing memory books.

As I left both parties, I promised each of the kids that I would be back as soon as the furniture pickup was over, to sign them out early. I offered to take them with me then—there was no need for the kids to stay for the full day—but they both wanted to spend the last hour with their friends so I went back to the office to sign out.

Since the sign-in computer was in smithereens, a paper on a clipboard had replaced it. *Last time I'll sign out this year*, I thought as I wrote the time I was leaving on the line next to my name. I had that funny half-sad feeling that a phase of my life was coming to a close. This was the last year Livvy would be in elementary school. We rush through our days so quickly and have so many little rituals that we do, day in and day out, but then a moment like the last day of school comes along. It's a milestone that makes a definite break in the continuum and emphasizes that one phase is ending and another beginning.

I waved to get Mrs. Kirk's attention. She was in her office, but her door was open. "Where's Marie?" I asked.

"She left early. Before lunch, actually."

"She left?" I repeated, surprised that she wouldn't stay for the whole day. "But perfect attendance has always been so important to her." I saw that the individual touches, like her block calendar, the gnome figurines, and the sweater that was usually draped over the back of her chair, were gone.

Mrs. Kirk smiled. "I guess she figured she could slack off on her last day. She's retired now." Mrs. Kirk lowered her voice. "And after these last few weeks, I don't blame her for wanting to leave early. I would if I could," she said with a mock grimace. "Anyway, Marie said something about going out of town on a short vacation to celebrate."

"How nice for her," I said, then glanced at the clock. "Oh, I've got to go."

I hoofed it back to Klea's house and turned on one of

the window coolers, in case the next pickup was delayed. But the consignment shop people were right on time and began wheeling out furniture as soon as I let them in. It didn't take long to clear the living room. The dining room was more of a challenge with the large table in such a small area. They took out the table first, then the heavy china cabinet. They removed the top of the china cabinet with the glass doors and carried it out, then returned for the base. As they tilted it on the dolly and moved it carefully out the front door, one of the men said, "Hey, look at this. Hold up." The other man paused with the dolly balanced at the top of the metal ramp they'd positioned over the porch steps.

"Did you know that was down there?" the first guy asked, pointing to something flat taped to the bottom of the cabinet.

"No," I said.

He reached down, brushed away some dust, and pried the thing off, then handed it to me. It was an inter-office envelope.

Chapter Twenty-two

The envelope was thick and filled with what felt like paper. It flexed slightly as I handled it. The envelope was so full that the flap barely covered the opening of the envelope, but the red string was tightly wound around the little bracket and held it closed.

"Might be the Declaration of Independence," the man said with a laugh, putting out his hand to steady the base of the cabinet as the other man backed slowly down the metal ramp.

"I doubt it," I said. As they loaded the china cabinet in the truck, I unwound the string and peered inside. It contained a thick stack of paper and a leather notebook. I was about to close the flap and tuck the envelope away in the box with Klea's belongings when a design on the top paper caught my eye. It was the logo for the Hoops for Healthy Hearts event, which was a fundraiser that the students participated in each year. The school had held the event last month, and Livvy and Nathan had both collected pledges for the number of basketball goals they could shoot during the event.

Still standing on the porch, I slid out the paper and scanned it. It was the final accounting form with the figures for the money the school had raised. Marie's flowing signature was across the bottom of the page, next to the total amount of money raised. My eyebrows shot up as I took in the number with several zeros. I had no idea that the kids had raised that much money. I remembered Mrs. Kirk had praised the kids for doing a good job, but she'd never mentioned a specific amount of money.

These were obviously school records and should be at the school, not Klea's house. I tipped the leather journal out of the envelope and glanced through it as the men continued to remove the rest of the furniture from the house, wondering if the journal belonged to Klea or if it belonged to the school and should go back with all the papers.

But as I flipped through the book, I saw that the handwriting looked like Marie's smooth cursive. I'd seen her handwriting so many times in the school office when she signed off on hall passes after I brought the kids back to school after a dentist or doctor appointment.

I fanned the pages of the journal. It contained a long, ledger-like list with dates, a brief description, and then amounts entered in neat, handwritten columns. I skimmed down a random page and recognized most of the descriptions as fundraisers the school had conducted. Besides Hoops for Healthy Hearts, there were entries for the school's booster club activities, like the Friday Store, where kids could purchase pencils or candy and the profits went toward purchasing more books for the library and upgrades for computers. But there were some entries that I didn't understand at all, just a row of random numbers and letters.

I reached the end of the pages with handwriting. The last entry caught my eye. It was for Hoops for a Healthy Heart and the date was last month. Like all the other entries, it had two numbers following the description. The first column was more than the second column. It was five hundred dollars higher, in fact.

I looked at the sheet of paper that I'd first taken out of the envelope and checked it again, comparing it to the final fundraising total in the ledger, thinking that I must have misread the numbers. But I hadn't. The amount reported to Hoops for a Healthy Heart was definitely the lower amount.

"We're done, ma'am."

I looked up to find one of the men holding out a paper, the receipt for the items they'd picked up. The other man was in the truck with the engine running, ready to leave.

"Oh. Great. Before you leave, let me check inside the house, okay?" I asked, belatedly remembering I was supposed to be monitoring what the men had taken. I left him holding the receipt and quickly moved through the rooms. Everything looked as it should. The rocking chair, the box of Klea's belongings, and the side table were still there, but all the other furniture was loaded. I returned to the porch, thanked him for waiting, and took the receipt.

He climbed in the truck, and it trundled away. I glanced at the school. Parents were already arriving, lining up for the car circle line, but I had some time before the school was out. If what I suspected was true . . . well, I wanted to make sure I was right before I showed any of this to Mrs. Kirk.

I went back in Klea's house and locked both dead bolts on the front door. I needed somewhere quiet and private to check the ledger and the papers. With the blinds drawn and all the bolts on the doors locked, I felt safe.

I moved the cardboard box out of the rocking chair to the floor and sat down in the rocker. I pulled the entire stack of papers out of the folder and looked through them, comparing the dates on the papers with the dates in the ledger. Many of the pages were like the Hoops for a Healthy Heart form, summary sheets of fundraising totals, and my heart sank as I looked up each one and found a discrepancy between the total on the sheets and the total in the ledger. The total in the first column in the ledger was always higher, sometimes by a couple of hundred dollars, but other times by several thousand, and it was always the smaller amount that was listed on the reporting forms.

Then there were some forms that had the school district name printed at the top, contract work requests and purchase requests. Each request had a number associated with it on the form, and that number was also recorded in the ledger—the seemingly random strings of letters and numbers. When I went through the purchase requests, I found the amounts on the forms requesting money from the district were higher than the amounts in the ledger.

I finally sat back with a thud that set the rocking chair moving. I shook my head while I surveyed the stacks of paper I'd set on the floor as I progressed through the forms. I didn't want to believe it, but Marie had been skimming money from the school, and not just ten or twenty dollars here or there. She had taken thousands of dollars. Maybe hundreds of thousands. The ledger didn't have a running total, but the amounts were significant.

I rubbed my hand over my eyes, thinking that it was awful. She had been at the school so long. Everyone trusted her implicitly—even Mrs. Kirk, who must never have suspected anything because she'd let Marie handle the money. And Marie had handled *all* the money. She collected the cash for the fundraisers and counted it. Obviously, no one else had checked her totals. As the ledger showed, she just kept some of the money and turned in the lower numbers.

I wasn't completely sure about the requests to the district, but it looked like she'd done the opposite thing there, turning in a higher amount to the district and then paying out a lower amount to the company or contractor and keeping the difference for herself. She must have been doctoring the files as well as the receipts. I suddenly thought of the water damage to the records room and the vandalism. . . . Could Marie be behind those things as well? Was it an effort to cover her tracks completely before she retired?

I closed the ledger, feeling incredibly sad and somewhat betrayed. Someone I thought I knew had been siphoning money from the school. Stealing from kids . . . that was low.

And somehow Klea had figured it out. She must have. She had all the evidence here, even Marie's ledger. How had she gotten these papers, the fundraising forms and the district purchase requests? Had she found them while she was snooping and gradually built up a stack of evidence that Marie couldn't deny? And the ledger, how had she gotten that?

I pulled my phone out of my pocket, suddenly nervous. I wasn't sure how it all fit together, but my gut feeling was that this was why Klea had been killed. Perhaps Peg had committed suicide, but this paper trail went back years and years, and I could imagine Marie killing to keep it a secret.

I was about to dial, but stopped as a thought hit me. Marie couldn't have killed Klea. Marie had been out of town Wednesday morning, the morning of the fire drill, the morning Klea was killed. Marie had been miles away on Jekyll Island.

Had she really been on Jekyll Island? I pushed my foot against the floor and set the rocking chair in motion as I considered everything. We had only Marie's word that she had been out of town. Mrs. Kirk had called her cell phone and talked to her that morning. Marie had said she was on the coast of Georgia, but she could have been blocks away or even inside the school.

What if Marie had arrived at the school Wednesday morning and either she'd caught Klea in the act of collecting incriminating papers, or maybe Klea had confronted her? I let the scenario play out in my mind. Vaughn and Mrs. Kirk had seen Klea that morning around seven-thirty. Students would have begun arriving at seven-fifty. If Marie killed Klea, she'd need someplace to stash Klea's body until she could get it out of the school. What better place than a rarely used storage closet?

And maybe it wasn't some student prankster who'd set off the fire drill, but Marie. It would be one way to clear the school. While everyone was out front on the grass waiting for the firefighters to arrive, Marie would have had a few minutes to move Klea's body out of the school. If Klea's body had been in the rolling trash can, Marie could have easily pushed it through the school and out the back doors of the lobby, then across the blacktop to the woods. It would have been harder to move the trash can over the dirt path, but it was hard-packed earth. It would have taken some effort to move it along the path, but it could have been done. With all the students, teachers, and staff in the front of the school, the building would have shielded her from their view as she moved from the school building to the woods.

Once Marie was in the woods, she could have dumped the trash can, then continued on to the other side of the woods and come out at the street on the far side of the school. The neighborhood was full of walkers and joggers. No one would give her a second glance. Then all she would have had to do would be walk back around to the school and get her car and leave. If she'd even had her car at the school. She lived close by. She'd mentioned that the other day. She could walk the few blocks back to her house and be in her car on the way to the coast to establish her alibi.

I stopped rocking. I had to get these papers to Detective Waraday. I checked my watch, automatically calculating whether I had enough time to drop everything off at the sheriff's office, but it was too close to dismissal. I certainly didn't want to be driving around with this stuff in the van when I had the kids with me, and I wasn't going to take the chance of leaving the papers and the ledger at the school with Mrs. Kirk. I didn't think she was involved, but . . . well, Marie had worked for her. Mrs. Kirk should have looked over the school's finances. I suddenly wondered where Marie was right that moment.

With shaking fingers, I sent a text to Abby. **Emergency. Can you get the kids for me? I promised I'd get them out of school early, but can't. I'm still at Klea's house.**

Her text was a quick affirmative reply. I spread some of the pages out and photographed them, then took pictures of the matching pages in the ledger. I attached the images and tapped out a short message to Detective Waraday, saying that I'd found what looked to be some important files at Klea's house.

After a few minutes, he replied. **In your area. I'll come pick them up.**

I texted back that I would wait there. I quickly stacked the pages and the ledger, then returned everything to the envelope. I wound the string around the brad to keep the flap closed and stood up. I hurried across the living room, intending to peek out the blinds so that I could watch for Detective Waraday, but my foot connected with the cardboard box and sent items flying across the room. I'd forgotten that I'd set the box on the floor.

Hand to my heart, I quickly collected the sweater, books, and coffee mugs, tossing them back in the box. I spotted one of the little wooden cubes from the calendar under the rocking chair. I retrieved it and tossed it back in the box, then stopped as a thought struck me.

Slowly, I picked up the second cube of wood with the numbers on each side and looked at it. That elusive fragment of thought that had been teasing at my mind suddenly came to me, blooming into completeness like those time-lapse pictures of flowers that transition from bud to blowsy fullness in seconds. *Marie was at the school the Wednesday morning that Klea died.*

I traced the number cut into the wooden cube with my finger. On the morning of the Muffins with Mom event, I had left Marie a note, saying that idea of a final fundraiser for the school had been shot down at the PTA meeting. I'd put the sticky note with the news on the two wooden cubes that made up her calendar. They had been positioned so that the numbers one and zero formed the date, the tenth of May.

My mind scrolled back through the many times I had arrived at the office at the same time as Marie. The first thing she did was lean over her desk and arrange the numbers on the wooden cubes so that they reflected the correct date. She did it even before putting her purse away, taking off her jacket, or sitting down at her desk. In fact, she'd arrived late that next Monday after Klea's body had found. I'd been in the office signing in at the check-in computer when she'd arrived. She'd hurried over to her desk and plucked the sticky note I'd left her from the calendar, then changed the blocks to reflect the new date, her purse still in her hand.

Marie must have arrived at the school Wednesday morning for some reason and then done what she always did first thing, change the date on her calendar. It was a habit—an unconscious rote behavior. She probably didn't even think about it when she did it.

Marie had been there Wednesday morning, not in Jekyll Island. It wasn't evidence that Detective Waraday could use. He would say anyone could have changed the date on the calendar, but combined with the evidence in the envelope—

At a whisper of sound, I jerked around. Marie stood in the doorway of the dining room.

Chapter Twenty-three

"Hello, Ellie," Marie said. "I let myself in." She jingled a pair of keys, the clatter of metal sounding loud, even against the constant hum of the window cooler. But it wasn't the keys that caught my attention—it was the gun she held loosely in her other hand. "It was so thoughtful of Klea to leave a second set of keys for me so that I didn't have to climb in that window over the sink again."

Her fluffy blond hair haloed her face as it always did, but she wasn't wearing one of her pastel shirts and matching skirt. She had on a loose, flowing black top and pants with a bright, primary-colored pattern. A choker necklace with small rocks spaced along stiff wires encircled her throat, and huge hoop earrings of the same design dangled from her ears.

She waved the barrel of the gun up and down her figure. "I can see you're surprised by my new look. What do you think? This is the real me." She widened her eyes. "You have no idea how sick I am of baby blue, pale pink, and yellow. And twin sets and those bell skirts and sensible pumps. Ugh. I wanted to burn them all—it would have been such fun—

but I simply don't have time. Of course, the clothes served their purpose. Stereotypes are so useful, you know? Harmless, middle-aged woman . . . who would ever think that I would do that?" She jabbed the gun at the envelope on the floor by my knee. I'd put it down when I picked up the items I'd kicked out of the box.

"Marie, I'm not sure what is wrong," I said. "Why don't you put the gun down, and we'll sort this out?" I said, wondering how far away "in the area" was for Detective Waraday. Did that mean he was close, like a few miles, or merely on this side of North Dawkins? If it was the latter, then it could be ten or fifteen minutes before he arrived. I licked my lips and took a steadying breath. A lot could happen in ten minutes, I thought, glancing at the gun, but at least Detective Waraday was on his way. If I could just keep her here, once Detective Waraday was on the scene . . . well, it would probably be chaos, but at least he'd have a gun, too, which would go a long way to even the odds.

"Really, Ellie. I expected more of you," Marie said, her tone heavy with disappointment. "I know you're aware of what's going on."

"I'm not sure what you mean," I hedged, listening for the sound of a car pulling up outside, mentally running through what would happen when Detective Waraday arrived. He would come to the front door, but what would he do when I didn't open it? I knew he had a set of keys because he'd opened the door with them that first time he asked me to look around. How long would he wait before he decided to use the keys? Would he even have the keys with him? I could shout at him that Marie was inside and had a gun, but he might not be able to understand me through the closed door, and I couldn't imagine Marie not firing at the door if she thought a sheriff's detective was on the other side.

My stomach plunged at the thought of Marie firing the gun. School would be out soon . . . all those kids and parents swarming around the school. No, I had to keep her in the house and somehow keep her from firing the gun. Maybe I could distract her somehow or trip her or . . . something. My insides twisted again at the thought of getting any closer to her when she had a gun in her hand.

Marie sighed, then said rapidly, "Don't pretend, Ellie. You know Klea was a snoop. She found those papers and my ledger. She was going to expose me, so I killed her. There. Now you don't have to pretend you don't know." She made two little movements with the gun barrel and my heartbeat kicked. "Move away from that box, please," she said.

I was still kneeling on the floor and made a move to stand up, but she said, "No. Stay there. Just scoot backward." I moved back a few inches. I still held one of the wooden cubes from the calendar in my hand. I curled my fingers around it and held it behind my leg.

"That's right," Marie said. "Sit crisscross applesauce, like a good girl."

While I was so scared I was jittery and my palms were sweaty, her stance was relaxed and her grip on the gun was casual and familiar. I heard a car engine and tensed, but it didn't slow down. "Okay," I said, "if we aren't pretending any more, what about Peg?"

"Did I kill her?" Marie asked. "Yes, of course," she said matter-of-factly. "She was the perfect opportunity to distract everyone. I couldn't pass it up. I knew all about her little blackmail thing," she said, her tone dismissive. "Nothing like what I had going, of course, but she was trying, I give her that. I knew that if Peg appeared to commit suicide, it would wrap everything up so neatly. Because Peg was blackmailing people, the police would assume Klea had discovered her secret. They would think Peg had killed Klea to keep her blackmail quiet. You know how the rest of it played out. With the police closing in, Peg killed herself. Did you like the suicide note?"

"Marie—"

"I went to her house on my lunch hour," Marie said, speaking over me. "It is a relief to talk about this," she said in an aside. "You see, it's rather ingenious, and it's a shame that no one knows. I took a bowl of chicken soup—doctored with the pain pills from my medicine cabinet, you understand—and told Peg we needed her signature for a file at work. Poor dear, she was still feeling awful from that ipecac—from the nurse's office, you know. I put it in her coffee that morning, and she signed the paper without looking at it closely. I had another sheet of paper over the top so she wouldn't see, but she didn't even give it a second glance. Then she tried the soup and"—Marie lifted both shoulders in a shrug and smiled—"that was that. So easy. All I had to do after that was remove a few pills from Peg's medicine cabinet and leave the prescription bottle beside the note, and it was done." Marie gave me a disappointed look. "And you didn't even appreciate the setup I gave you. I made that appointment on Peg's computer so that you'd be the first one on the scene. I know how you fancy yourself a sort of sleuth, but you didn't seem to enjoy it at all."

Marie looked rational, and her tone of voice was completely normal, but the words coming out of her mouth . . . I was stunned. I had been totally fooled. She wasn't who I'd thought she was at all. She was talking about killing a woman—no, two women—without a trace of remorse. "I don't know what to say," I finally said. "You sound as if you think I should say how clever you are."

"I *am* clever," she snapped. "Clever enough to put my life back together after Heath's company went belly-up. Years and years, Heath invested in that company, trusting them when they said their pension plan was terrific, and then suddenly—the money is gone because of some financial accounting scandal? He couldn't take it. I don't care what the doctors said about his heart. He couldn't handle the pressure of the job hunt. He should have been looking forward to his retirement, not filling out job applications. And once he was gone, I should have had the spouse pension, but no, I had to rely on the little job at the school that we'd been using as side income. Instead of a little bonus, suddenly my check had to provide for *everything*."

She pressed her lips together for a second, then said, "Do you know what a level-one admin makes in this school district? Of course you don't. You're just like all the other stay-at-home moms with their comfy income from their husbands. The money rolls in, and you spend it."

As she spoke, her easy stance disappeared, and her face contorted. I'd always thought that Marie was pretty in a faded sort of way, but now she looked ugly.

"You don't have to work for anything in your cushy world," she said. "It only took me a couple of years to realize I didn't have to work quite so hard to get what I deserved." She gave a sharp nod. "I was cheated out of what was rightfully mine, so got it back."

She was quite worked up, speaking more passionately than I had ever seen her. She shifted her shoulders and took a deep breath, then seemed to calm down a bit. She pointed the gun at the envelope. "Where was it?"

"Taped to the bottom of the china cabinet."

She snorted. "And to think I spent hours in this house,

night after night, looking for my ledger. I knew Klea had found it."

Faintly, I heard the school bell ring. It was the last bell of the day, the final bell of the school year, in fact. Outside, the street and the school parking lot, only half a block away, would be flooded with parents, which was hard to believe in the dim cocoon of the living room with its closed blinds and the hum of the window unit.

"Did Klea tell you?" I asked, straining to listen for any movement outside, but I only heard more cars drive by and then the louder rev of a bus engine as it cruised by.

"No. I discovered what the little sneak was doing," Marie said. "She thought I was on vacation, so I'm sure she thought she was in the clear. But I'd forgotten my sunglasses at the school. It's a long drive to Jekyll Island. Directly into the sun. Good thing, too, that I had to go back, or she would have told Mrs. Kirk and ruined everything. Odd, when you think about it, that a pair of sunglasses did her in. I left them on my desk, so I walked over to the school that morning. It's so much easier to walk over during morning drop-off, isn't it? You know how congested the street and parking lot get. Anyway, they were right where I'd left them, but one of my desk drawers was open."

Her eyes narrowed. "I *knew* it was Klea. I'd caught her snooping around the desks in the office before. So I waited in Mrs. Kirk's office, behind the door, watching out the crack between the hinges. It was Klea all right. She came in, bold as you please. She must have been making copies of my files because she returned some papers to my drawer, but kept some others. Then she came in Mrs. Kirk's office, and left the pages she'd copied on Mrs. Kirk's desk with a note."

Marie was getting agitated again, her face flushing pink

as she said, "Klea left Mrs. Kirk's office—walked right by me without knowing I was on the other side of the door. As soon as she left the main office, I slipped over to Mrs. Kirk's desk to read her note. Klea wanted to meet with Mrs. Kirk later that day. She said she had more papers like the ones she'd left, and she had my ledger in a safe place, that she could bring it later."

The flush deepened on Marie's face, and I could see the muscles in her hand flex as she squeezed the handle of the gun. "Klea must have slipped the ledger out of my purse a day or two before. I'd looked for it earlier in the week, but it wasn't there. I'd assumed I'd left it at home, but as soon as I saw her note, I knew what had happened. She'd stolen it," she said, her tone incensed.

The irony of Marie being angry over something being stolen from her was lost on her, and I wasn't about to point it out to her. She was worked up enough.

Marie raised her eyebrows and said emphatically, "There was only one thing to do. It was so simple, really. Klea came back in the office, and was so surprised to see me that she stood stock-still for a moment. That was all I needed. The phone cord was right there. It only took a second to get it around her neck." She rotated her shoulders again as if she were working a kink out of her neck. "And the rest was incredibly simple. I suppose you've worked it out?"

"I think so. You hid her in the storage closet, then moved her after you set off the fire alarm."

"Very good. The only bad bit was when I had to wait in the janitor's office until the last bell of the morning. I knew if I pulled the fire alarm during drop-off, it would be a madhouse. I needed the school to be cleared in an orderly fashion so that I could get out of there without being seen." She eyed me, considering. "Of course, you will be more of a challenge. It's too bad I can't leave you here, but my car is parked out front. With the craziness of the last day of school, no one will probably remember seeing it, but I can't take that chance, if I leave your body here. No, I suppose you'll have to come with me and have a little accident. Nearby, of course—" She cocked her head. "What was that?"

Chapter Twenty-four

Ihad heard it, too. The sound of a car engine idling close by, then the engine shutting off.

"Probably just someone picking up their kids from school," I said quickly, but Marie was already moving across the room to the window, her gun still trained on me.

Before she could twitch the curtain back, I flung the block at her and dived for the dining room. The block must have connected with at least some part of her because I heard a gasp as I sprinted through the dining room to the kitchen. I fumbled with the levers on the dead bolts, my fingers slipping. The floor in the dining room creaked as she came after me. I was glad she'd come after me, away from the window and the kids and the school—but glad in a terrified way.

The locks unfastened. I yanked the door open and sprinted down the two steps to the carport. Klea's street didn't have an alley, so I couldn't leave the back way. I ran past Klea's hatchback in the carport. Parked behind the hatchback in the single drive was a gray four-door sedan, Marie's car, I assumed.

I slowed my pace as I came to the front yard, expecting to see Detective Waraday's unmarked sedan parked on the street and him on the porch, but he wasn't anywhere in sight. A large SUV was in front of the house, and the person who I assumed was the driver, a woman dressed in shorts, a tank top, and flip-flops, was several paces away, moving rapidly toward the school.

I spun back around. Marie was already down the steps and coming out of the shade of the carport. She walked with the gun angled slightly up, the barrel pointed at the limbs of the tree overhead, but as soon as she came out of the carport, she leveled the gun at me, her arm straight and steady. "Ellie, stop," she called, but her words about needing only a few seconds to kill Klea popped into my head, and I kept moving.

I skittered backward around her car, moving away from the school and putting the trunk of the sedan between us. She made an impatient exclamation, and my hyper-aware senses picked up the sound of her sandals slapping on the driveway as she hurried toward the back of her car.

With the car shielding me, I crouched and ran down the side yard that sloped away from Klea's property to a rainwater drainage grid set in a square of concrete. The grass was wet and my ballet slippers had zero traction. I slid down the little slope, but I got my balance back as I hit the concrete surrounding the drain. Marie was right behind me. Her sandals must have had as little traction as my shoes because she slid down and bumped into me before I could even take a step.

She had the gun in her right hand, and I lunged for that arm, grabbing her wrist and twisting it away from me. She grunted and jerked backward, but the gun fell from her hand, clattering onto the metal drainage grid. I cringed, thinking it might go off. But like a coin pushed into a slot, it fell through the space between the metal squares and landed with a faint, watery *plink*.

For half a second, we both stared down the drain, our arms interlinked, then I jerked away and scrambled up the little hill toward the school. Marie wasn't quite so scary without the gun, but I still didn't want to be too close to her. She had strangled a woman, after all.

I heard her coming up the slope behind me, but I didn't stop to look back. I managed a quick glance both ways before I sprinted across the street to the grassy verge that ran along the edge of the chain-link fence. I wanted to get to the school, which was still a mass of cars, parents, and kids. Traffic was always bad at the open and close of the school day, but the first and last days of the year were the worst. Parents who usually had their kids ride the bus picked them up instead as a special treat for the last day, and as a result, the car circle pickup line was always extra long.

I ran down the street, feeling every pebble and uneven clump of grass through the thin soles of my flats. I heard the screech of tires and glanced quickly over my shoulder. Marie, in the gray sedan, had backed out of the driveway, into the street. I slowed my pace, expecting her to turn in the opposite direction from the school and accelerate away, but she spun the wheel and turned the car toward me. Her gaze locked with mine, and she gunned the engine, aiming straight for me.

Great, no gun, but she still had a car. The thought flicked through my mind even as I twisted around and made for the school. The long line of the fence hemmed me in on one side, and the row of stationary cars, waiting for their turn to inch into the car circle line, filled one lane of the street.

I came even with the tail end of the car circle line and felt relieved. I was inside the labyrinth of the pickup zone and would be okay. But then I heard the growl of the engine and looked back. With a shock, I realized Marie was driving on the wrong side of the road, in the lane that was open, the one that cars flowing out of the car circle would take.

The engine roared and the car closed in on me. Mitch was the runner in our family, but I put on a burst of speed that would have made him proud. I sprinted, legs pumping, for the end of the fence. I rounded the metal pole that marked the end of the chain-link and raced into the double car circle lane, palms out, arms waving a warning for the two cars that were waiting while kids climbed into them.

The screech of metal on metal filled the air as Marie careened around the fence post and barreled toward the two minivans that were about to pull away from the school. I darted to the side to the parking area, getting out of the path of the car circle and all the vehicles.

With a squeal of brakes, Marie stopped inches before her bumper made contact with one of the vans.

A cacophony of horns sounded from farther back in the car circle, and both moms in the minivans at the front of the line gestured impatiently at Marie to back up out of their way. I raced over to Mrs. Kirk, who had whirled around, a look of severe displeasure on her face.

"It's Marie," I panted as I wove between the cars toward Mrs. Kirk. "She did it. . . . She killed Klea. And Peg, too," I added.

Mrs. Kirk stared at me for a second, but the sound of an engine growling snapped all our attention back to Marie's car. Marie reversed away from the double minivans that barred her way, backed into a parked car with a crunch, then put her car in drive.

Mrs. Kirk unclipped the walkie-talkie from her waist as she scanned the parking lot. Her gaze fixed on a yellow school bus that had turned into the street at the far end.

Normally, the bus would wait on the street behind the cars as they filtered through the car circle pickup line, then continue on to the bus circle, which was positioned past the car circle. "Bus six, do you have any students on board?" Mrs. Kirk asked.

Static cracked; then a faraway-sounding voice said, "No."

"I need you to turn into the exit lane of the car circle and park there."

"Did you say the exit of the car circle?"

The space where Marie was trying to turn was narrow and she had to inch forward, then put the car in reverse again and move back a few more inches before she could make the turn.

Mrs. Kirk put the walkie-talkie to her mouth. "Yes. I did. Come in the car circle exit and park."

The faint voice came out of the speaker again as the bus lumbered closer to the school. "I can't to that. Mrs. Kirk would kill me."

Marie had finally gotten the car turned around. The horns and shouting continued. Some of the parents had half emerged from their cars to yell, adding to the confusion. "This *is* Mrs. Kirk," she said into the walkie-talkie above the din. "Now go around that line of cars that are stopped and come in the exit. Do it quickly."

"Yes, ma'am."

The bus swung around the cars, taking the lane the wrong way as Marie had. The bus turned its nose into the exit just as Marie accelerated. The front of her car crashed into the front bumper of the bus. Her hood crumbled and the air bags deployed just as Detective Waraday appeared on foot, running along the chain-link fence, his gun drawn but held pointed toward the sky.

He dodged around the bus and, as he circled the car to the driver's side, lowered the gun so that it was aimed at

Marie. He reached out and cautiously opened the door, peered inside, then holstered his gun. Marie's body sagged forward over the air bag. I moved quickly around the two minivans that were still trapped in the double lanes. "Is she . . . ?" I called as I neared him.

Over the melee of angry shouts, car horns, and the kids' excited chatter, he said, "No, but she is out cold. I'll call for an ambulance. . . . I don't know how it will get here, but I'll call for one."

It took over an hour to sort out the mess that was the car circle. Eventually, the students and parents were matched up and the car circle line cleared. The bus driver was unharmed, and the bus itself only had one long scratch on its bumper. Marie came around in the ambulance, and Detective Waraday questioned her there, but she refused to say anything. He called for a deputy, who accompanied Marie to the hospital. She wasn't severely injured. Detective Waraday said she would probably be treated and released from the hospital, and then the deputy would take her into custody.

Detective Waraday tapped the ledger and papers that now sat on Mrs. Kirk's desk. "This will be all we need to hold her until we can charge her with the murders of Mrs. Burris and Ms. Watson." As soon as things had settled down in the parking lot, and a search of Marie's car hadn't turned up the envelope with all the evidence that Klea gathered, I'd told Detective Waraday that it must still be in Klea's house. Detective Waraday dispatched a deputy, who returned with the envelope, saying that it had been on the floor of the living room. In her pursuit of me, Marie had run out without it.

Detective Waraday, Mrs. Kirk, and I were all in Mrs. Kirk's office with the door closed. Abby had taken the kids home with her and told me she wanted a full rundown later. Detective Waraday had asked me to go through what had happened this afternoon. I was glad Mrs. Kirk was sitting down as I recounted what Marie had said.

Mrs. Kirk shook her head. "Marie? I'm so—stunned. I don't even know what to say. I would never have thought she would do anything like steal money from the school. And the thought of what she did to Klea and Peg . . ." Mrs. Kirk's voice faded as she gazed at the papers spread across her desk. "I trusted her. She'd been here longer than me. I never once thought she was anything but honest."

"That's what she counted on," Detective Waraday said. "These all-cash fundraising things are the easiest way to skim money."

"Well, we're going to have some very strict rules around her from now on . . . if I get to keep my job, that is."

"In most cases of this sort," Detective Waraday said, motioning to the ledger, "the organization doesn't press charges. I know the DA will be much more concerned with the murder cases."

Mrs. Kirk nodded, but didn't seem to be too reassured. She looked like she was still stunned at the news, and I felt a little guilty that the thought she could be involved in the murder had even crossed my mind. Since Mrs. Kirk was still processing the details of what had happened, I turned toward Detective Waraday. "Klea's list . . . she must have suspected . . ."

"That either the blackmailer or the person skimming money worked in the office," Detective Waraday said, finishing my sentence. "She seemed to be a collector of secrets."

I agreed, knowing he was referring to Mrs. Harris's pen name.

"Do you think she knew about Ms. McCormick's past?" I asked, avoiding mentioning Mrs. Harris.

"I haven't seen anything that proves she did. We do know that she liked to know things so it's possible she found out."

"But her list," I said. "Those names, every one of those people had a secret, except Mrs. Kirk."

Startled, Mrs. Kirk rejoined the conversation. "Sorry, I was a bit distracted. Did you say Klea had my name on a list?"

Detective Waraday said in a soothing tone, "No need to get upset. Whether or not Mrs. Burris knew about the other . . . illegal things going on in the school, we know she was aware of the skimming." He tapped the envelope. "These pages prove that she was collecting evidence. She probably made that list when she first discovered the skimming and listed the people she thought could be involved . . . for one reason or another."

He didn't say it, but I thought that Mrs. Harris had probably been at the top of the list because Klea had known she'd hidden her pen name. Klea had probably wondered if Mrs. Harris was hiding other activities as well.

"She must have narrowed it down to the office staff as the most likely culprits," Detective Waraday continued. "That's why the list included people who worked here, like you, Mrs. Kirk."

"I promise you, I had no knowledge of what she was doing," Mrs. Kirk said.

"I understand that, and a preliminary look through Marie Ormsby's check register—she was old school and still wrote down everything in her checkbook—matches up with amounts in the ledger. She was an excellent record keeper, I'll give her that. No, she kept everything for herself. I don't see any indication that she gave anyone else a cut."

"Well, thank goodness for that," Mrs. Kirk said faintly.

"Speaking of Ms. McCormick," Detective Waraday said, "you'll be happy to know she came into the sheriff's office of her own accord this morning. Apparently, her boyfriend convinced her to come in, with a lawyer, of course."

"What will happen to her?" I asked.

"That's another matter for the school board. If she had bribed someone to falsify records, it could be a criminal matter, but there's no evidence of that. She's claiming the misspelling of her name on the original application was a mistake and that she never noticed it. She thought that somehow her record hadn't come up in the background search. She decided to keep her head down, do her job well, and hope it never came up again. I'm afraid this will be another of those cases where the district would rather the whole mess go away and it will fade away," he said, his tone regretful.

"Well, I know one thing—she will not teach again after this. I've already had several calls from the media, asking for a comment. The story is out and has been reported. Someone must have spoken to the media about it. She won't be able to pull the same trick again in another state."

"I don't think she has any interest in that," Detective Waraday said.

"She's going to release the computer game?" I asked.

"I believe so. Her lawyer was insistent that they get the flowchart schematics back or, at the very least, copies of them, because they had no direct bearing on the case. I expect to see *Adventure-matics* for sale in a few months."

"It's a shame because she was a good teacher. Livvy did really well with her in math," I said.

"I think she's much more suited to working outside the classroom," Mrs. Kirk said with finality.

Detective Waraday said to Mrs. Kirk, "Moving back to the other incidents here at the school over the last few weeks, the broken pipe and vandalism. It appears they were related."

Mrs. Kirk closed her eyes briefly. "You're saying that Marie was responsible for those things, too? I see what you're thinking, that Marie did those things to make sure no one could discover what she did after she retired. It does explain why we've had such a run . . . of . . . bad luck. Marie moved all her old files into the records room right before the leak, and she handled the destruction of the damaged files," Mrs. Kirk said, her voice getting tighter and tighter. "And I didn't have a second thought about it when she said she would take care of the removal of the damaged files—that gave her a free hand to destroy whatever she wanted."

Detective Waraday said, "And the damage to the office could have been to cover the real reason for the attack, the destruction of her hard drive. I had my suspicions that something was off with the vandalism once I saw the destruction."

Mrs. Kirk said, "What do you mean?"

"Well, in the first place, your janitor described cleaning up some glass from the concrete porch. It could have been tracked there if someone walked through the glass, but it did make me wonder if someone had entered the school with a key, then broken the glass out from the inside to make it appear as if there had been a break-in. She must not have realized that breaking the glass from the inside would give away that it was an inside job."

Mrs. Kirk sighed. "Marie occasionally had access to my keys to the main doors. I keep them with me, but there have been times when I was out of town on vacation when I gave them to her as my backup."

"And then the damage inside the office was uneven. . . . Special attention had been given to the computers. They were pulverized, in particular the hard drives," Detective Waraday added.

"But you didn't say anything at all," Mrs. Kirk said.

"I couldn't," Detective Waraday said, then looked at me. "Just like I couldn't say anything to you to confirm your suspicion that Ms. Watson's death wasn't a suicide."

"So you didn't think she'd killed herself?"

Detective Waraday said, "No, but I couldn't reveal that to you. The less you knew, the better. Several things brought up questions, including the ones you mentioned, the typed suicide note, and the appointment. But there were also other strange things. The autopsy showed Ms. Watson had ingested chicken soup, but we couldn't find a trace of any can or container of chicken soup. If she was as sick as everyone reported her to have been, I couldn't picture her going home and making chicken soup from scratch. If she'd picked up some at a store or restaurant, there should have been something in the trash, but there was nothing."

"Marie must have taken the container away in case it had residue of the drugs in it," I said.

"I was interviewing the employees at the sub shop a few blocks over when I got your initial text, Mrs. Avery," Detective Waraday said. "They serve soup there and the owner recognized a photo of Marie as a customer who came in and purchased a bowl of soup to go on Thursday afternoon."

"If you were so close, why did it take you so long to get here?" I asked, thinking of the long minutes inside Klea's house.

Detective Waraday shook his head. "I came in from the south. I wasn't thinking about the time of day and got caught in the traffic around the school."

"Oh, I see," I said. "No wonder." The traffic, especially the road that Detective Waraday had arrived on, was awful in the afternoon. Parents began lining up in the car circle line twenty to thirty minutes before school let out, causing terrible gridlock.

"It took me fifteen minutes just to get to a place were I could park and come in on foot. I had no idea that Marie was there, or I would have sent a deputy."

A tap sounded on the door, and we all looked up to see Gabrielle poking her head through a crack in the door. "Oh, am I interrupting?"

Detective Waraday gathered the papers from Mrs. Kirk's desk. "No, I think we're done for now. I'll contact you both for formal statements later."

He shook hands with Mrs. Kirk, then turned to me. "Stay safe, Mrs. Avery," he said. I looked at him closely to see if it was a dig, but he seemed to be completely sincere.

He left, and Gabrielle came in the office, then dropped into the chair he'd been in. "Such excitement. I heard all about it. Sweet little Marie! Hard to believe," she said as she put a folder on the desk. "So glad that's all cleared up, and so glad I caught you both. I have a proposal."

I blinked, marveling that this was the woman who had been so freaked out about being associated with a possible murder that she'd dragged me into investigating Klea's death. Her ability to switch tacks was truly amazing. I wasn't in the mood to hear any proposal. I just wanted to get home, hug my kids, and see Mitch. He was due to arrive back from his trip later tonight.

Mrs. Kirk said, "I don't think this is the time—"

"But it is," Gabrielle said. "It's perfect, really. You know I've finished the last of my organizing projects, except for the digital organization class for the teachers proposed for next year." She tapped the folder. "But an opportunity has come up that I just can't say no to. Fitzgerald has asked me to take on a complete overhaul of their systems." She grinned as she looked from me to Mrs. Kirk. Clearly, she expected congratulations.

"That's great," I said.

"Thanks." She wrinkled her nose. "I'm so excited, but the downside is that I can't do any more work for the district. I simply won't have the time. But Ellie will. She can take over the digital organization class. Mrs. Kirk, I'm sure if you recommend her, the district will approve. And, Ellie, you're here at the school all the time anyway. You might as well get paid for it."

"I'm not sure I'll have any pull left at the district after today," Mrs. Kirk said, dampeningly.

Gabrielle flapped her hand at her. "Don't be so pessimistic," she said, then leaned forward and whispered, "Just between you and me, out of all the schools I've worked in here in the district, you are the best principal, hands down. I'll be happy to put in a good word for you, and I'm sure your students and teachers will as well."

"It's true," I said, for once agreeing wholeheartedly with Gabrielle. "I'd be happy to let the district know that I wouldn't want anyone else as principal, and I'm sure the teachers and parents feel the same."

"That is very nice of you both," Mrs. Kirk said. "I'm touched. It makes this day not quite so bad."

"Bad?" Gabrielle said, rearing back in her chair. "What are you talking about? Ellie rooted out a murderer from the school and you," she said, speaking to Mrs. Kirk, "were instrumental in capturing her. I heard about your quick thinking, having the bus block Marie in the parking lot. You've got to frame these things the right way. You're a hero, not a victim."

"You know, I think you're wasted in organizing," I said to Gabrielle. "I think you should be in public relations."

"Oh, no. I have plenty to do with Fitzgerald, which brings us back to the district's contract with me," she said, eyeing first Mrs. Kirk and then me.

Mrs. Kirk said, "If the district is interested in my opinion, I'd certainly be in favor of working with you, Ellie."

"You're giving me the contract you have with the school district?" I asked Gabrielle in what I was sure was an unbelieving tone.

"Yes. Don't you think it's a perfect solution?"

"And you think she won't demand you give it back to her later?" Mitch asked the next morning as we stood in the hallway, waiting for Nathan to find his shoes so we could go to lunch for my delayed Mother's Day celebration. Mitch had arrived last night after the kids were asleep. I'd been glad about his late arrival because it had given us time alone, and I'd been able to tell him everything that had happened. Once we'd rehashed everything, he'd said, "So, next year, private school?"

Livvy appeared in the hallway. "Where are we going to lunch?"

Mitch looked at me with eyebrows raised. "It's your day."

"Portofino's," I said, naming North Dawkins's fanciest Italian restaurant.

"I better get another book," Livvy said and turned away. Portofino's had more leisurely service than the restaurants that we usually frequented. As she went to her room, I said, "Getting back to Gabrielle, I wouldn't put anything past her, but I have a feeling Fitzgerald will keep her too busy to worry about one contract with the North Dawkins School District. Imagine the contacts she'll make! I bet her business will be one hundred percent corporate by this time next year."

"So you don't mind that?"

"Are you kidding? I don't like the corporate stuff. I'll stick with the school and helping individuals. That's my line."

Nathan came around the corner holding a rather crushed gift bag with a picture of Spider-Man on the outside. I recognized it as one of the extra bags I'd saved after his last birthday celebration. He held out the bag. "Happy Mother's Day."

Livvy, who had just returned with books, said, "Oh, I have something for you, too," and darted away.

Mitch sighed. "Glad we don't have reservations."

I shushed him, and Livvy was back in seconds with another package wrapped in newspaper and decorated with hand-drawn flowers.

"This is so nice," I said, reaching for the single sheet of tissue paper stuffed in the gift bag that Nathan had handed to me.

"Hadn't you better wait and open them at the restaurant? You know, during the official Mother's Day lunch celebration," Mitch said with a twinkle in his eye.

"No way. I've waited long enough. Mother's Day celebration starts now." I took out the tissue and removed two potholders. Each one had an imprint of Nathan's hands and the words *Mother's Helper* across the top.

"Oh, I love them," I said, squeezing him close. He wiggled away quickly, but I could tell he was pleased.

I took the paper off the box Livvy gave me. It contained a pair of leather flip-flops decorated with a flower motif. "I need flip-flops," I said, hugging Livvy. "These will be perfect for summer."

She grinned and hugged me back. "Dad and I went shopping before he left on his trip."

"There's a little something else in there, too," Mitch said.

I checked the tissue under the shoes and found a pair of silver earrings. "I love them, too," I said, and gave Mitch a kiss. "What a perfect Mother's Day."

"So you're good?" Mitch asked. "Because there's a game on I'd like to catch. Want to eat here? You could use your new potholders."

"Funny. To the car, everyone."

Livvy and Nathan both charged for the door and bumped shoulders.

"Ouch."

"Hey!"

Arguing about who truly was at fault, they made their way to the van.

Mitch grabbed my hand. "Ah, the return to normalcy. Glad to see nothing has changed."

"It's a pretty good normal. Overall, I mean." I squeezed his hand.

He returned the pressure. "I agree."

Acknowledgments

Ten Ellie books! I am amazed and very happy to get to this point. I would never have reached this milestone without Faith, who enabled me to start this wonderful writing journey. To Michaela, thanks for choosing Ellie and company, and thanks for shepherding me through the publishing process for ten books. To the crew at Kensington, thanks for all your hard work that makes the Ellie books look wonderful. To the Ellie readers, I appreciate so much the kind words you send my way. Thank you for reading and reviewing the books and for spreading the word about the series. You are the best! And, of course, to my family, thanks for your encouragement, your support, and your endless patience while I finish one more sentence.